THE IMMOLATION OF EVE

Helen Fields

First published by Wailing Banshee Ltd in Great Britain in 2011
18 High Street, Overton, Hampshire, RG25 3HA

ISBN 978-0-9571246-1-5

With love to David, for always believing in me.
And thanks to Andrea, Emma and Allison for reading
when they had a thousand other things to do.

One

Gnarled fingers of lightning jabbed the sky, illuminating the trees that lined the train-track. When I left Krakow earlier, the sky was clear but on crossing the Slovakian border the air had become dense with electricity. Thunder rumbled softly in the distance then rolled in, echoing through the valleys and cracking like a giant whip. Eventually every passenger in the sleeper compartment stopped what they were doing to watch the light show.

There was a long silence, as if the storm had burned itself out, when a stray bolt of lightning hit our carriage with a deafening bang. The train remained steadily in motion but the overhead lights flickered out, leaving the carriage black. I remained motionless in my bunk, still excited from the storm and thrilled by the unexpected dark. There was the slightest movement of air above me then insistent lips bore down on my mouth before I could stop them. Not that I wanted to. A taut body lowered itself onto mine and an indecent warmth spread through my body. I wish I could pretend there was some force used but the truth is I didn't want it to stop. The stranger pulled away and moved his mouth to my ear, muttering a single word in a language I didn't understand. In the next heartbeat I was flung violently out of my bunk, landing in a crumpled heap against a luggage rack.

I could hear myself screaming but couldn't stop. Sparks flashing outside the window created a sickening slow-motion effect. The teenage girl in the bunk next to mine jolted through the air in front of me and I heard bones snap as she landed. Metal and glass were ripping and smashing, debris bombarding me from all sides. The train began to tip and I grabbed furiously for anything to hold. There was a moment of darkness then in the light I saw a human leg, boot still on, flying towards my face and blood was dripping into my eyes. There was only white noise and a feeling of being dragged, pushed and shaken. Something flashed past, travelling in the opposite direction and I realised the engine had jack-knifed like the head of a snake turning on its tail. There were ricochets as each carriage crashed into the one in front and then followed the engine's lead. Another tilt had me rolling across the floor towards the window when a tree smashed through the glass showering shards everywhere. The heavy case that had landed on me saved me from the worst of the shrapnel but crushed my arm as it came. We were sent back and forth, the screams of metal and man indistinguishable. Then, as suddenly as it started, everything was still. The sounds of wailing and moaning got louder as I opened my eyes. The train had been ripped open – I was laying half inside and half out. A cloud of dust enveloped my carriage, choking me. I wondered why I could see again then realised that patches of fire were lighting up the night. Fear of burning spurred me into action. I ignored the pain in my arm and head, pushed off the debris covering me and staggered away. The flames were going to surround me if I didn't get well clear.

I climbed over a wall of twisted steel using the mound of rubble at its base to get a step up. I heard groaning beneath my foot and saw that I was treading on a man's torso. He twitched one hand as if asking me to pull him up. As I reached for him I saw that his head was cracked open, blood and matter oozing out. My stomach cramped, forcing its contents into my throat. I managed not to vomit but it was enough to quell any thoughts of heroism. I wanted to survive, to get out of there as fast as possible and that's exactly what I did. The fire was running out of control now and I could hear the cries of people trapped, knowing what was coming and helpless to fight it. Terror overwhelmed me. What was left of my carriage collapsed in on itself, hundreds of tonnes covering the place where my bunk had been. Oily smoke filled the air. Those people I'd deserted in my compartment weren't screaming or crying; they were already lost. I kept moving, stepping over bodies without checking if they were dead or alive, until I was sure I was out of reach of the flames. When I turned to see the wreckage from a distance, there were at least ten carriages broken into pieces and scattered across the valley floor like the junk yard from hell. Human remains in burning piles filled the air with the stench of burning meat. A buzzing grew loud in my ears and my vision dimmed. I fell to my knees. I knew I was losing consciousness and I welcomed it.

When I came to I was on a stretcher, being loaded into a helicopter. In the noise and chaos no-one tried to speak to me. I opened my eyes after we'd taken off to see monitors and drips attached to me and a well-oiled machine took over – medics communicating with each other, the pilot and the hospital. They were much more concerned for another passenger than me and with good reason – my companion didn't make it as far as the hospital. When I tried to speak I was rasping and incoherent. Torches were shone in my eyes and notes made although I couldn't understand anything they were saying. Finally we landed.

Hours later I was alone in a hospital bed, unable to sleep, the sedative no match for the recurring nightmare of my last few hours. A young doctor walked in and muttered a question at me. I looked blank and said simply 'English'. He nodded, left and was replaced almost immediately by an older man who shut the door quietly and sat at my bedside.

'I'm Doctor Radowic. You are in the Hospital Roosevelta in the town of Banska Bystrica. How are you feeling, Miss?'

'MacKenzie. Eve MacKenzie... I'm okay, I think.'

The doctor smiled slightly and glanced at my left arm. 'You have a fracture half way between your wrist and elbow. You will need to be in the cast for six weeks. Other than that Miss MacKenzie you have had a very lucky escape. A small wound to your head that required stitches, a badly sprained ankle and bruising but no internal injuries. The marks on your feet, I take it they are old scars?'

'I was born with them. My parents said it was a birth defect.'

'Really? It appeared to me to be scarring. Do they give you pain?'

'Only after exercise or a day on the beach. It's nothing, doctor. Can you tell me anything about what happened to the train?" He paused, obviously contemplating what to say.

'What do you remember?'

'Fragments. It started with the storm. It knocked the train off the tracks but we just kept on moving. Eventually the carriages broke apart and, well, that was it. I couldn't help anyone else, I was too scared. I'm so sorry.' I was desperate to unload the guilt of my inaction but nothing I said could do justice to the awful weight I was carrying.

'What is it you think you could possibly have done?' he patted my arm. 'You need to get some rest.' I struggled to regain my composure and some manners as he walked to the door.

'Thank you for coming to speak to me, doctor. You must be at breaking point with so many people on the train.'

He turned back towards me, paused a moment. 'Were you travelling with friends or family Miss MacKenzie?'

'No, alone. I was in Krakow on business and decided to take a couple of day's holiday and see Budapest. Why?'

'Because as far as we know, you are the only survivor.' It took a while for that to sink in. I could see the doctor watching for a response.

'How many people died?' I asked and he shrugged awkwardly.

'One hundred and eighty, maybe more. You shouldn't be thinking about that now. Is there anyone we can contact for you? Parents or a partner?' I shook my head. He could see the tears welling in my eyes and was kind enough to look away. 'Call if you need anything at all.' He left and I was glad of the solitude. I cried until I fell asleep.

The next day bureaucracy took over. In the morning a police investigator took a statement from me whilst medical staff bustled in and out of my room. Apparently, I'd become something of a spectacle. As my injuries were minor I was to be transferred that evening to Bratislava and flown home the next day. The hospital had identified me from a business card in my jacket pocket and phoned my chambers' clerk, Tom, to arrange my return home. I suspected Tom would be more concerned about who would cover my court cases for the next couple of weeks than my travel plans.

I studied the view out of my window. From here the town of Banska Bystrica comprised only church spires and industrial rooftops, multi-storey housing with washing hanging from balconies and the haze of distant hilltops. I tried to close my eyes but every time I did my head was flooded with images and sounds from the train wreck. Rest was the one thing that wasn't going to help – I had to get back to England, and to work, as quickly as possible.

I spent that night in the Slovakian capital Bratislava. The journey there by ambulance was long but at least it left me tired enough to finally sleep. When I did, I dreamed that I was in my hospital bed but on board the train. The wheels of the bed caused it to roll around the carriage until I got my bearings enough to jump out. I left my compartment and walked slowly down the passageway, the train exactly as it had been, full of people trying to sleep their way through the long journey. Ahead of me was a man, always half in shadow, never turning round. I walked faster and faster trying to catch up, not really understanding the compulsion I felt to see his face. As I passed between carriages I walked through a doorway into complete darkness and felt strong arms slide around my waist. I knew he would kiss me again just as I knew that when he did the storm would sweep the train off its tracks once more. I thought of all the faces I'd seen as I walked through the train but still I didn't stop him. I wanted to feel his mouth on mine again so desperately that my desire left me powerless. I could feel the heat of his body pressed against me and my own rising excitement and I just let it happen. I let him kiss me. I let the train crash all over again. Even as I screamed and awoke I felt a lust I'd never experienced before. It was only then that I recalled the sound of the word the man had whispered to me – forgotten in the trauma of everything I'd seen: Cakooshkar.

Later that morning I opened my eyes to find a very real man at my bedside reading a newspaper. I took one look at his suit and knew he was English. I checked that I was decently covered and hadn't been dribbling in my sleep, then coughed quietly. He jumped.

'Miss MacKenzie, forgive me, I was trying not to disturb you. My name is Patrick St. John, from the British Embassy here in Bratislava. We were contacted by the hospital to oversee your safe return home.' He must have been in his in his mid-thirties, well-spoken with an air of charm that was bred rather than learned. He was good looking in the floppy haired, public school boy way.

Under any other circumstances I would probably have been tempted to flirt.

'Thank you, Mr St. John. I appreciate your help. I'm afraid I lost everything in the crash. I have no ID at all – I'm not quite sure what I need to do.'

'Very little, actually, we've had the necessary security checks carried out already. Luckily, as a barrister, information about you is easily accessible. If you wouldn't mind just confirming a few details for me, if you feel up to it, that is?'

I poured a glass of water and caught a glimpse of myself in the mirror, suddenly feeling horribly self-conscious. I smoothed down my hair and pinched some colour into my cheeks as he took papers from a briefcase.

'You live in Bratislava?'

'I've been posted here for nearly a year; I have a bit of an advantage as I speak passable Slovakian. My mother is Czech. It's an extraordinary country, living half in the past and half in the future. Have you been here before?'

'No, I'd literally only just crossed the border from Poland when…'

'Goodness, I'm sorry, there's me trying to avoid the subject and putting my foot straight in it.'

'Please don't worry. It's not a subject I'm going to be able to avoid thinking however hard I try.'

'They will fade, you know, the memories. It's no consolation now but give yourself plenty of time. Everyone thinks that life with the British Diplomatic Service is all cocktail parties and luxury yachts. Mostly it's helping out in the most dreadful situations when people are at their lowest. I am constantly surprised by how resilient human beings are.'

I smiled then had to look away before the tears started again; kindness when I'm fragile always makes me cry. He took the hint, changing the subject seamlessly.

'So, just a few bits to go through. Forgive the formalities. Your full name is Eve MacKenzie, date of birth twenty-first of March nineteen eighty-three, living in Kingston, London?' I nodded and he carried on. 'We have a copy of your last passport photo here. It sounds ridiculous but I need you to confirm that this is you? We're issuing an emergency temporary passport and this is standard procedure.' I looked at the copy of the photo he was holding. Taken just six months ago when I'd renewed my documents, it looked like a picture of a stranger. The green eyes were the same; the red hair, my trade mark, shorter and tidier than today. It has always meant trouble, my hair, a deep cherry red that looks almost metallic in bright light. Usually people concluded it was dyed. In childhood it marked me out as facetious, as a teenager a rebel, and as an adult it makes men believe me wanton and women see me as a threat.

'It's me.' I replied.

'It is, isn't it?' He looked at the picture again for a long moment and then handed me my papers. 'You're unmarried and you only hold a British passport, yes?'

'Yes, to both,' he was scribbling on a form and signing multiple copies. I took the opportunity to ask a question of my own.

'I was told there were no other survivors. It doesn't seem right, how one person can walk away when so many others...' I couldn't finish. Patrick reached out and took my hand so gently I thought he was scared I might bite.

'I know it doesn't make any sense but these things are never explainable. The storm that caused the crash was off the charts and hadn't been anticipated by the met office. You'll never know why you instead of all those others. Don't punish yourself for being alive. Fate must have a plan.'

'I don't believe in fate, Mr St. John. The only controlling influences in my life are chaos and my clerks.'

He withdrew his hand and replaced it with a bundle of papers to get me through immigration. He stared at me without speaking for several moments and then remembered himself just as I was wondering if I should break the silence.

'I've ordered a car to take you to the airport at midday. You don't need to worry about anything,' he smiled warmly. 'It's a shame you're here under these circumstances. It would have been a pleasure to have shown you around the city. I don't suppose you'll want to come back after all you've been through.'

'I never say never Mr St John and it would've been lovely to have seen Bratislava with you.'

He picked up his brief case and took my right hand in his.

'Well, goodbye then. Safe onward journey. If you need anything I've left my card inside your passport.' I showered carefully to keep the plaster cast dry then dressed in some clothes provided by the hospital. The ones I'd been wearing on the train were too badly damaged, not that I could bear the thought of putting them on again, anyway. Before long, the car arrived to take me to the airport.

Two

When the plane touched down in London I realised I had no idea who was meeting me. I had no luggage, of course, everything had been lost in the accident. Even so, it felt wonderful having my feet back on home soil and even better when I saw my flatmate, Naomi, peering at me through the crowds in the arrivals area. I ignored my throbbing ankle and broke into a run, throwing my good arm around my friend's neck.

'Oh Eve, thank God you're alright. I didn't know what to do.'

'Just take me home, that's all I want and a proper cup of tea, obviously. Okay?'

'The car's right outside the terminal. Come on, lean on me.'

At home, Naomi had brought me a drink before I'd even sat down. She fussed around until I told her a dozen times I was fine and then left me to my own devices a while. It felt strange in my room. I'd only been away a few days and yet the world had tilted on its axis. As I sank into a burning hot bath, my cure for almost everything, I thought of Krakow.

I'd been visiting a crime scene where the soldier I was defending, Albert Cornish, was charged with raping a female colleague. They'd spent the evening out drinking before their return to England.

My musings were broken by the smell of roasting chicken and I knew that Naomi had done what she always did in a crisis: she had cooked. I dragged myself out of the bath, put on my oldest jeans and sweatshirt, then went to eat. Naomi was already piling food onto plates.

'Here, you need a decent meal. What was the food like at the hospital?'

'I couldn't tell you. I wasn't really hungry, anyway.'

'Sorry, that was idiotic of me. Do you…want to talk about it?'

'I wouldn't know where to begin. Maybe it's easier not to try.'

'I saw it on the news, before we found out you'd been on the train. We didn't think anyone could have come out of that alive. Do you remember much?' I gave Naomi a few sketchy details as we ate, pretending no memory of the carnage I'd seen. We made small talk for a few minutes about chambers and mutual friends. Naomi had finished and was packing dishes. I set down my cutlery and put my head in my hands. I had to talk to someone about this or I'd go crazy.

'There was one thing,' I said.

'What?'

'It's going to sound awful in the circumstances but there was a man, on the train. Before we crashed.' I felt sick for even talking about this after the lives that were lost but the memory was on a loop in my head. 'We were kissing.'

'I don't understand, what man? Where did you meet him?'

'You're going to think I've got post-traumatic stress disorder or something. I don't know who he was, I can't describe him to you, it was dark and I was falling asleep and then, well, that's pretty much it. Only he said something to me and I want to find out what it means. It was in a foreign language, it was something like 'Cakooshkar'. You're better at languages than me. Any ideas?'

'I don't know what it means but it sounds Slavic, presumably he was eastern European. What was the context?'

'No context at all. Just that one word. It's all I remember.' Naomi stared at me.

'Are you sure you're alright, really? You've been through a dreadful trauma. Was this man, well, did he make it? We were told that you were the only…'

'I have no idea what happened to him, I just need to know what it meant, if anything. Please help, Naomi, I just can't get it out of my head. It felt like he was giving me a message.'

'Tell you what, promise you'll get some sleep and I'll find the answer for you. Would you please put those plates down? You can't open the dishwasher with one arm in a sling and the other hand full of crockery.'

I smiled. Naomi's the sort of friend who makes life better in a thousand tiny ways.

'Go!' she said. I went to bed. No dreams that night. I awoke once thinking there was someone in the room, not a scary feeling, just a presence. I turned on my lamp on but there was nothing, just me dishevelled in the mirror. I slept again until past seven.

Naomi knocked gently and came in carrying a mug of steaming coffee.

'Sorry, I've got to run. Southampton Crown Court, gang of drug dealers being sentenced, should be finished by lunchtime though. I'll come straight back and we'll do each other's nails or something equally mindless. Sound good?'

'Sounds perfect.' I gave her an impromptu kiss on the cheek. 'And thank you.'

'Take it easy this morning.' She walked to the door, brushing toast crumbs off the black suit that was our usual work wear. 'Oh, I meant to tell you last night, a box of papers arrived from your mother's solicitor while you were away. And that other thing you asked about – I did an internet search. The word you heard must have been Kukushka. It means cuckoo. Make sense now?'

'No, not at all, but thanks anyway.'

I sipped the coffee lying back against my pillows. Cuckoo. Perhaps I had misheard after all. I was so certain it would make sense to me. Maybe I was more traumatised than I thought. I pushed the bedcovers aside and determined to get on with my day. First job was to phone the clerks and get my work diary in order. I arranged a conference in chambers for the Krakow case the following day whilst it was all fresh in my mind. I'm right handed so the sling wouldn't stop me scribbling notes. I grabbed some breakfast and contemplated my day. All my briefs were in chambers so work wasn't an option and I decided not to watch the news in case they were still showing footage of the crash. Unable to face the well-intended emails I turned to the only thing left on my 'to do' list: the box of papers from my mother's solicitor.

I took a kitchen knife and slit open the parcel tape. Everything inside was immaculately filed except a letter on the top.

'Dear Miss MacKenzie, I enclose for your safe keeping some papers that your mother wanted you to have in the event of her death. Now that matters of probate are concluded I hope you will have some time to go through these. Before she died so unexpectedly in February, Susan had intended to talk to you about the contents personally. I know she would regret not having had the opportunity to do so. Please contact me if I can assist in any way. Yours sincerely, Jacob Slade.'

I had no idea what the letter meant. My mother died three months ago when she slipped in the shower. The autopsy concluded that she'd died instantly and thankfully didn't suffer. My father died four years before from cancer that he'd fought for half a decade, taking not just his strength but every shred of dignity. Of the two deaths I knew which I would choose. I had no brothers or sisters so sorting out the estate was simple once the paper work was complete. My parents had used the same solicitors for years and were sticklers for organisation. Their obsession with having everything in its place that I'd rebelled against as a teenager was at last something I appreciated. Now this bizarre reference to whatever my mother had wanted to talk to me about. My parents never struck me as the sort of people to have skeletons in their closets. I was reaching for first file when the doorbell rang. Grateful for any distraction, I went to answer. A young woman stood at the door asking me to sign for a delivery.

It was a day for surprises, apparently. The parcel was very light and rustled gently. Under several layers of tissue paper was a posy of wild flowers wrapped in silk – red campion, watermint, sowbread, burdock and giant horsetail. It was exquisite and could only have been sent by someone who understood my tastes perfectly. I looked for a card but found none so I set about finding a vase. When the phone rang I was so startled that I jolted back from the tap and got a complete soaking. I grabbed a handset and said my name.

A man's voice replied, 'You got home safely, I'm so glad. Forgive me, Miss MacKenzie, it's Patrick St John here, from the British Embassy in Slovakia.'

'Oh, hello Patrick, yes everything was fine. No trouble getting through immigration, I'm so grateful for all your help.'

'It's what we're here for. I'm sorry to bother you so soon after your arrival home but we've had contact from the Slovakian authorities. Their incident investigator would like the opportunity to speak with you to piece together more details about the accident.'

'Of course, I'll help in any way I can.'

'I was wondering if your chambers or home would be the best place for them to call. Perhaps we could arrange something in a couple of days?'

'That should be fine. Why don't you pass on my home number?'

'I shall. It was a pleasure to meet you and I'm glad you're sounding so much better.'

There was a moment of silence and then Patrick coughed gently.

'I was, um, just wondering if you'd received the flowers we sent. As a welcome home gesture.'

I grinned at his obvious embarrassment and tried to keep the amusement out of my voice. 'They've just arrived. I would have thanked you but there was no card. They're so beautiful. How clever of you to send wild flowers. I just got a complete soaking putting them in water and I'm standing here dripping wet.'

'Miss MacKenzie, anything I say in reply is going to come out wrong so I won't even try.' I laughed. 'The choice of flowers just seemed to suit you. Well, back to more routine matters here, unfortunately. Do keep in touch.'

As I put the phone down my clerks rang to let me know that the prosecution had sent over more documents in the rape case which I needed to read before my conference. Well, I had said I wanted to stay busy. The courier from chambers arrived as I was putting on dry clothes and considering Patrick's very sweet gesture. Somehow I didn't think that everyone the British Embassy helped was treated to the same thoughtfulness. As much of a catch as he was, I wasn't likely to find myself in Slovakia or his company again. I went into my study with the files and there I remained until Naomi got home that evening.

Three

The following day I was in chambers for my conference with Albert Cornish and his commanding officer. Courts Martials are the armed forces' criminal courts with penalties which are not for the faint hearted. Albert was having a run of bad luck. Last year I'd successfully defended him in another case so I guess I was the natural choice second time around. The earlier allegation had been more straightforward. Albert was charged with insubordination to a superior officer, refusing to follow a direct order. It turned out that the officer in question had been repeatedly bullying a young Private. When ordered to hold the lad so that the officer could beat him with his boots after he'd failed to finish a training run, Cornish had refused. The trial turned into a media frenzy. The victimised soldier, obviously fearing reprisals, had a sudden memory lapse in Court but at the end of the day Albert's impeccable army record and attitude won the Court over. He was likeable, straightforward and patently honest. The publicity from the trial had been devastating for his career but he'd stood his ground which is why I found it so unbelievable that he was back in my care on an altogether more serious charge. He was escorted in by his commanding officer, Captain George Mallard.

'Albert,' I said. 'I wish I could say it's a pleasure to see you again, but I'm sure you'd prefer not to be here at all.'

'Hello Miss MacKenzie. It's good of you to take the case at all, thought you'd be sick of the sight of me by now.'

I poured coffee as we settled down to go through the prosecution papers and plan Albert's defence.

'Let's start from the top,' I said as I looked at the prosecution charge. 'The allegation is that you raped Angela Smyth at Smocza Jama, if I've pronounced that right, in Krakow on 4 March 2011. You've read Angela's statement?' He nodded. 'And seen the medical evidence?'

Captain Mallard spoke before Albert could answer. 'There's no DNA evidence connecting Lieutenant Cornish with Angela Smyth. As I read it no bodily fluids were found at all. Isn't that right?'

'Absolutely, but her witness statement does say that the assault stopped prior to ejaculation.'

'It rather sounds as if you're arguing her side of this. Albert has clearly stated that they did not engage in intercourse at all.'

'Captain, you need to understand what we're trying to achieve here. Albert knows I will do everything in my power to make sure he is not convicted, but I have to find the weaknesses in our defence. It won't help for me to sit here and nod without testing Albert's version of events. I need to examine the evidence the way the Court Martial will see it. You're right, of course, Albert's DNA has not been identified inside her body. However, Albert accepted in interview that he'd been socialising with her, they'd had several drinks at the bar and left together at around eleven-thirty.'

'That's right,' Albert joined in. 'But there was another man, someone we met at the bar. He left with us. I can't understand why she doesn't mention him at all.'

'You don't have a name, any more details?' Albert shook his head and put his face in his hands.

'I know you've gone through this all before but take me through that evening, step by step. Remember every detail you can, however insignificant it may seem,' I encouraged.

'Okay, we'd finished training operations, been given a pass for the night and told to be back at the base by 4am. Angela had been my partner for the training, we got on really well.'

'Had anything happened between you during the operations? Was there anything more than just a working relationship?'

'No, to be honest she's not my type. I've got, sorry, I had a girlfriend back in Colchester. She's a teaching assistant at a primary school. I was planning to ask Beth to marry me this summer, been saving up for a ring. What are my chances, Miss MacKenzie? I don't want to lose her.'

'One thing at a time, Albert. Let's try to get to the bottom of this allegation first. How long were you at the bar before you met this other man?'

'About two hours, although we'd noticed him in there before he joined us. He came into the bar just after us.'

'How do you know that?'

'You couldn't really miss him. He was well over six foot tall, slim build, looked pretty fit. You know the type, big shoulders, all cheek bones and smouldering eyes.'

'Smouldering? Not the sort of word I imagine you use very often.'

'Not my word: Angela's. She'd noticed him before we'd ordered our first round of drinks, couldn't stop staring at him. Eventually he just got up and came to sit at our table.'

'Did he introduce himself? He must have said something. Think about his accent, clothing, tattoos. We need to see if we can get any witnesses to confirm his presence.'

'It's all been covered,' said the Captain. 'The local military police interviewed the bar staff. Apparently the place was packed, quite normal for a Friday night. No-one seems to remember anything at all.'

'He was definitely not English. He spoke with a strong accent – a bit like the Polish soldiers at our training camp only not exactly the same.'

'But he spoke English?'

'Yes, he must have done. I don't speak anything except English and schoolboy French. We were talking for a good hour before we left, I just can't remember what we were talking about. From the moment he joined us everything's a bit vague.'

'How much had you drunk by then?'

'Several beers, maybe six.'

'Nothing else, no spirits, no drugs?'

'Absolutely not.'

Captain Mallard again. 'How can he be expected to put together a defence if he was drunk? Most of my men out on a Friday night would be in the same state.'

'I understand that, Captain, but drunkenness isn't a defence and just because someone can't remember doing something doesn't mean they didn't do it.'

'But I didn't.'

'I believe you Albert, but we need more than just my faith in you. Do you remember walking through the city after leaving the bar?'

'I remember seeing faces at windows on the way. No-one spoke to us. It was like watching a film with the sound off. I remember feeling….' He paused.

'You remember feeling what? Albert?' I prompted.

'Like I was watching my own dream. One minute we were walking through the City. The next we were going down these stone steps, flickering lights. A real steep passage with a chain to hold on to and I know it sounds stupid but I could swear there was music playing, I couldn't see where it came from, but deep inside the cave. That's the last thing I remember until I was arrested.'

'Still in the, sorry, how do you say the name of this place?'

Captain Mallard helped, 'It's pronounced Smocha Yama. Literally 'Dragon's cave'. According to a local legend Prince Krak saved the city by slaying the dragon that lived there.'

'I went to see it when I was on the site visit last week. It's eerie down there; I still can't understand why it was unlocked at night.'

'Neither can anyone else. Our liaison at the Polish camp asked the Wawel Castle security officers. It was their night guard who called the police when he heard a disturbance in the cave. As far as they were concerned it had been locked up in the usual way but there was no sign of damage to the lock.' Captain Mallard picked up his cold coffee, changed his mind and put it down again. 'Lieutenant, what I don't understand is how no other man was present when the police arrived. No one mentions him but you.'

'Looks grim, doesn't it, Sir? I don't know what else to say.'

The phone rang and my clerk told me that the military police transport had arrived for my visitors. We agreed to leave it there and continue the conversation at the preliminary hearing in Colchester next week. As Albert walked out he shook my hand.

'Is it true that you were in the train wreck in Slovakia last week?' he asked.

'Yes, but I'm absolutely fine. It won't affect my handling of your case.'

'I know that already Miss MacKenzie. I'm just so grateful to you for helping. I feel responsible – if it weren't for this mess you'd never have been over there in the first place.'

'Now, Albert, don't start thinking like that. We'll see about the engagement ring by the time this is all over, okay?'

'I hope so, Ma'am. See you next week.'

Captain Mallard had hung back as Albert was escorted out.

'I apologise for my outburst earlier. I know you're just doing your job. The army is keen to avoid the sort of publicity that rape charges attract, you understand. And for what it's worth, no-one who knows Lieutenant Cornish believes he's capable of such a thing.'

'I'll do all I can, Captain. Thank you for coming today.' Defending in rape cases is always a heavy responsibility. Albert was facing years and years in prison if convicted. There was a victim who had no obvious reason to lie and medical evidence of internal injuries caused by very rough sex. Then there was this mystery man not even mentioned by the victim who could apparently disappear at will. This wasn't going to be easy.

I rolled my head around my shoulders to release some tension. I knew I had to go home and rest before I reread the case. Still, Naomi was cooking dinner which always made me feel better. As I said goodbye to my clerks I could see through the grimy London windows that the weather had turned bad.

'Best take an umbrella, Miss MacKenzie. There a storm brewing,' said Tom.

I took his advice and when lightning flashed across the ancient buildings of Middle Temple I quickened my step and refused to think back to the last storm I'd witnessed.

Four

As I walked through the door of our flat I could hear Naomi clattering pans in the kitchen. The aroma of curry reached me before I'd put down my umbrella.

'Wine's on the table. You've got fifteen minutes if you want a shower before dinner. God, I sound like your wife!' I laughed and walked through to greet her.

'I should be so lucky. Thanks for cooking.' I showed my appreciation with a kiss on the cheek.

'You know I love it. You get to wash up afterwards so it's perfectly fair. How did the conference go?'

I gave her a potted version of my afternoon and headed for the shower. As I reached for the shampoo my back brushed the metal door handle leaving a stinging graze. It triggered a nagging feeling as if I'd missed something important but by then Naomi was calling me to eat and I was too hungry to care about anything else.

It wasn't just a curry. Naomi had made chicken jalfrezi, pilau rice, naan bread and my favourite, aloo gobi. There was a glass of wine already poured and candles lit, a sure sign that Naomi was in a particularly good mood.

'Out with it,' I said. 'What's up?'

'Eat. It's getting cold. I'll tell you when I'm full.' She started cramming herself full of naan dipped in jalfrezi sauce and I knew when to give in. She was smiling like the cat that got the cream and I thought again how lucky I was to have her as a flatmate. When we were both so full we couldn't eat another mouthful, I leaned towards her.

'Oh come on, tell me,' I said. 'I've waited fifteen minutes and eaten a week's allowance of calories. What's happened?'

'Well, you know that Tim and I went for a hiking weekend in Dorset whilst you were in Krakow? We were tucking into fish and chips, watching the fishermen in Bridport harbour, when he proposed. Said he hadn't planned it, just looked at me and knew it was the right time and here we are.' She raised her left hand, opened her palm and in it was the most beautiful sapphire ring I have ever seen. I threw myself into her arms, not a bit embarrassed by the fact that I was already crying.

'I can't believe you waited this long to tell me. How could you! Oh congratulations, I think that a proposal over fish and chips is the loveliest thing I ever heard. Put the ring on, I have to see.'

'It's too big at the moment. I'm going to get it properly sized tomorrow. He chose it all by himself. Isn't he a clever boy?'

'He's a very lucky boy, landing you. You guys were made for each other.'

'Sorry I didn't tell you sooner, we've been doing the rounds announcing it to family before telling anyone else. I've had to avoid you for days so that I didn't blurt it out.'

'So…go on. Tell me about dates and venues and dresses and honeymoons.' I was ready to go out that minute and start buying mountains of those ridiculous bridal magazines that tell you what sort of lingerie you should wear on your wedding night. As ever, Naomi was much more practical.

'Oh, I haven't even thought about the details yet. Christmas, we think, or maybe just after New Year. You know you have to be my bridesmaid, don't you? No question about it. I promise not to make you wear pink. Please say yes?'

'As if I'd miss it. And I don't care if you do make me wear pink. Okay, that's not strictly true, but I can compromise on a sort of dusky tea-rose shade.'

We laughed and ranted about weddings for the next two hours until the bottle of wine was long since finished and the remains of the curry had congealed on our plates. We walked into the kitchen together and I caught sight of the box of my mother's papers.

'I suppose I'd better get on with that some time.' I poked at it.

'How about right now? No time like the present. We can go through it together.'

'Oh, Naomi…'

'No more excuses. Neither of us has to get up early tomorrow. You never know, there might be some precious family heirlooms waiting to be discovered.' She walked over to the box and began pulling papers out, setting them in two piles. 'There, some for you, some for me. You get started while I make tea.' I sighed and gave in. Naomi was unstoppable once she decided on something and I preferred the idea of not doing this alone. It was fairly predictable; old photos, the odd postcard from a favourite holiday and a lace christening gown carefully wrapped in brown paper.

'I've got all the birth and death certificates. Your parents certainly were organised. They're even filed in date order.'

'You have no idea. They used to make me do that with my homework.'

'Wow, your house must have been a bundle of joy. Oh sorry, I didn't mean…'

'Don't be. It was like growing up in a giant filing cabinet.'

'Who was Emily MacKenzie? You never mentioned her.'

'I have no idea. Long lost cousin? Let's see.' I flicked through the papers.

'She was born just a year before you – her birth certificate's in here. Oh.' Naomi stopped abruptly and I knew that something was wrong.

'What is it?'

'Her parents...' Naomi motioned towards the document in front of her. I peered at the file. The birth certificate was for Emily Joanne MacKenzie, born 4 January 1982, parents Susan and Peter Mackenzie. I had a sister. The world tilted beneath my feet.

'Eve. Are you okay? Sorry, I had no idea what I was looking at.'

'This must be what the solicitor meant. He said there were things in the papers Mum had wanted to talk to me about in person. I had no idea. How can they have had another daughter and never mentioned her?'

By the time I said it Naomi had turned to the next page.

'This must be why. It's a death certificate for Emily. June 1982. She was just five months old. Looks like it was pneumonia. Maybe it was just too painful for them to bear talking about.'

'But still, something this important? I never saw them visit a grave, they never spoke her name. It's so sad. It feels like there was a whole part of them I never knew.'

'Shall we put this away for the night?' Naomi asked.

'No, let's keep looking. Perhaps I can find out where she's buried, lay some flowers or something.'

We carried on turning pages, doctors' notes about Emily, letters of condolence from friends. My mother had kept everything. I thought I had found the surprise in the papers but I was wrong. At the very back of the file was a sealed envelope. On it was the single word 'Confidential'. I recognised the Court seal immediately. Perhaps I should have stopped looking right then, there were enough warning signals going off in my brain. I didn't, of course. Curiosity wins over common sense every time.

I opened the envelope and pulled out a sheath of papers, typewritten and formal. My name and date of birth were listed together with my parents' full names. There were a variety of signatures, I recognised both my parents', one from a County Court Judge and another in a distinctly feminine hand I didn't know. The papers were for the adoption of a three month old baby girl. The address of the birth parents was foreign, a place I didn't know. The address for the adoptive parents, however, was the house I'd grown up in. The meaning of the papers finally sank in. I couldn't say a word. I turned to look at Naomi who must have seen the blood draining from my face but before she could reach me I fell. By the time I came round she had me propped against the table leg, covered in a blanket with a cushion behind my head. Naomi was holding a cold flannel to my forehead and taking my pulse.

'I'm okay,' I muttered.

'You're not okay. I should call a doctor. You're hands are like ice.'

'There's nothing medically wrong, Naomi. I just had a shock.'

'What on earth gave you such a shock that you reacted like that?'

'Look at the papers,' I said.

'Whatever it is can wait, I'm more worried about you.'

'You need to look at the papers.' Naomi sighed but did as I asked. I could hear her slow intake of breath as she stood at the table above me. Twice I thought she tried to speak and then stopped. When she crouched back down next to me her face was composed but full of a pity that was hard to look at.

'Oh Eve, I can't believe they never told you. Come on; let's get you to the sofa.'

We sat for a long time saying nothing. I felt like I'd woken up in the middle of the night when the duvet has fallen on the floor: Exposed, cold and vulnerable.

'I think I just want to go to sleep,' I whispered.

'Of course, let me help you to bed.' As she walked through to my room with her arms around me, Naomi said, 'It makes sense, though, doesn't it? They lost a baby girl and were obviously desperate to fill the void, so they adopted. It's just sad they didn't ever tell you.' The rational part of me understood why they hadn't. I just wasn't sure how I'd be able to forgive them for it.

'Will you be okay?' my friend asked softly as she turned off the lamp.

'I need to find out who I really am,' I replied. She nodded and silently closed my door.

Five

The next morning when I awoke the flat was quiet. Naomi must already have gone to chambers. I showered and made coffee although the thought of breakfast was a step too far so I sat back down at the table where the papers remained in disarray.

Contained in the adoption documents were the usual statements from my parents, social workers and legal forms. At last I found a single tattered piece of paper entitled 'Rodny List'. Whilst I was unsure of the language, the information on the paper could only mean one thing: I'd found a birth certificate. In the top box was 21.3.1983, my date of birth. I took a deep breath and read on. In the boxes below it said first 'Eve' and then 'Karas'. My mother and father were named as Adela and Branimir Karas. My place of birth was a town called Brezno. I closed my eyes and imagined I had never opened the file. For me, though, ignorance is torture and Pandora's Box was well and truly open. When my father, my adoptive father as it turns out, was diagnosed with cancer I made it my mission to arm myself with every bit of information about the disease. It did no good in the end, of course, but the process of learning helped occupy my mind. So I took out my laptop and as the internet got ready to work its magic, the phone rang. It was Naomi.

'How you doing? I've been so worried. Sorry I had to go out this morning but the clerks booked me in for an emergency domestic violence injunction.'

'I'm better than I thought I would be, considering. You are speaking to the person originally named Eve Karas. At least my birthday is on the same day I've been celebrating it for the last twenty-seven years. I was born in a town called Brezno.'

'Where's that?'

'I'm waiting for my computer to tell me but our wi-fi is hit and miss, as usual.'

'Hey, I'm on my way home. Why don't you wait for me and we can do this together? You shouldn't be on your own.'

'I'll be fine. You don't need to rush back. Can you bring any papers that have come in on the Court Martial?'

'No problem. I'll be about an hour. Try to stay conscious until then!'

I laughed and hung up, taking a break to think rationally about what I'd learned. I lay on my bed, looking at the photo of mum and dad at my graduation, proud and happy. I wondered how often they'd thought about the secret of my adoption. My mother had obviously decided that the time had come to tell me. I tried to imagine the words she would have used, where we'd have been. How do you tell your daughter that everything she believed about her family was a lie? The warmth of the duvet lulled me and my last thought as I fell asleep was that Brezno sounded familiar. Then I was back on that train again.

I was staring out of the window from my bunk but in spite of the dark I could see every detail of the mountains outside. We passed through a clearing and I could make out the reflection of the moon in a black lake. I raised my eyes to the sky but the moon wasn't visible up there. We passed into a tunnel and I knew what was going to happen before I felt anything. Fingertips slid smoothly from my wrist and up the back of my hand to push, interlaced between my own. I didn't pull my hand away, enjoying the toned muscles pressing down on me, the dark lustfulness I couldn't control making me cry out in the dark. I waited for him to kiss me. I knew that when he did the train would face its horrible and inevitable end but no consequences were enough to dampen my carnality. A vicelike hand wrapped itself around my chin and cheek. In the dark I could see the orange rim of light around his irises. I was all but gasping with anticipation and still he did not kiss me.

'Kukushka,' he whispered 'Come home.' I couldn't stand it any longer. I thrust my face upwards and pushed my lips roughly onto his. The crashing and rolling sensation of the train was no surprise but the pain I felt was appalling. I opened my eyes to find myself surrounded by flames. My clothing was alight, the fabric was melting into my flesh and I could smell the burning meat of my own body in the choking smoke. The hand that had been holding mine so gently gripped me in place as I screamed and flailed my arms. Finally I opened my mouth and screamed.

'Eve, wake up. It's okay. It's Naomi.'

As my bedroom swam into focus I felt Naomi's hand on my forehead and sank back down onto the pillow shaking uncontrollably.

'It was just a dream. You're safe now.'

'No, not safe, losing my mind.'

'You're traumatised. You haven't stopped for a single day since you got off the plane. Honey, I don't know what you saw that night and I can't even start to imagine how bad it was, but no-one walks away from that unscathed. You need time to rest.'

She held her arms out and I let myself be held. I cried again feeling weak and pathetic. When the tears dried up Naomi ran me a bath. As I undressed I caught a glimpse of my back in the bathroom mirror. A large pink graze had been left by my brief contact with the shower handle yesterday. I instinctively reached my hand round to touch it and found it still sore. As I did so, I realised what had been eluding me about the alleged rape in the Dragon's Cave. Angela Smyth said that all her clothing had been pulled off her and that she had been thrown onto the ground and roughly assaulted for around fifteen minutes. I'd been concentrating on the medical evidence relating to her internal injuries and yet there was not one scratch on her anywhere else. Nothing, not one single mark. The floor in those caverns was stone and gravel. They would have lacerated her and the marks should have been obvious for days afterwards. Either she was lying or she was deluded. I thought about Albert Cornish's loss of memory and wondered how clearly Angela Smyth really recalled events.

I'd taken photographs of the crime scene on my camera but it had been lost in my luggage on the train. We would need evidence about the state of the cave floor. Before I could lose my train of thought I wrote a note to email my solicitors and then climbed into the bath. After a few minutes of relaxation the doorbell rang. Naomi answered and from her squeal of delight I knew that her fiancé had arrived. I got dressed so that I could go and congratulate him on pulling off such an impromptu proposal.

'Timothy Bussey-Hughes. How dare you ask my best friend to marry you without first asking my permission?'

'Ms MacKenzie, you're quite right. How improper of me. Let's see...could I please have permission to spend every day of the rest of my life making Naomi insanely happy? How was that?'

'Now I wish I hadn't asked. I'm not sure if I'm jealous or nauseous. Come here and kiss me.' I hugged and kissed the very lovely Tim and wished them both well. Just occasionally fate does its job properly and pushes two ideally matched people together. I couldn't help but feel a twinge of sadness at the thought of losing my closest friend to her man on a full time basis.

'Eve?'

'Sorry Tim, in a world of my own.'

'I said how's the arm mending? You look fairly mobile.'

'It looks more impressive than it really is! Haven't thought about it too much, actually.'

'No, you haven't had time to. You just keep running around non-stop.' Naomi chided.

'I hope you know what you're getting yourself into Tim. She hates to be disobeyed.'

'That's what I love most about her. That and her cooking!'

'Oh stop it you two, I'll put the kettle on while you compare how much you've missed each other.' I walked into the kitchen to make coffee while they said proper hellos. Tim is a head-hunter in the grimy world of international finance. As a result he spends a huge amount of time at airports, hotels and hushed breakfast meetings. He seems too grounded to do something so covert. I've always thought that his laid back approach to life must be what worked for him, unassuming and likeable. He's the ideal foil for Naomi, a perfectionist who worries too much about what everyone thinks. I spied on them through the kitchen doorway, holding hands like teenagers at a school disco, her long dark hair in its usual topknot, petite and pretty, him with his strawberry blonde messy look, dwarfing her at six foot three. I sighed, not unhappily.

'So,' I said, as I put coffee mugs in front of them. 'Now that you've made this official it seems only right that you take the plunge and move in together. And no, you're not pushing me out, I don't want an argument. It's about time I did the grown up thing and got a mortgage.'

'Oh Eve, we hadn't even discussed it. Tim's away so much of the time that I'll just end up buying dozens of cats if you move out.' I looked at Tim's face. As well as he and I got on, I could see that the idea appealed to him, whether he wanted to admit it or not.

'I don't mean right this minute, but I am going to start looking.'

Tim cut in. 'I have to give three months' notice on my place anyway, so there's no rush.'

'That's perfect. Now I'm going to be bossy for once. I don't want to discuss it anymore tonight and I mean it!'

Before Naomi could protest Tim said, 'Nate's still asking after you. He was really concerned when we heard about the train crash. He emailed you but Naomi said you haven't had time to do much since you got home. Why don't we all go out for dinner this week?'

'I don't think I'd be good company for Nate at the moment. As lovely as he is, getting involved with my flatmate's fiancé's best friend is a recipe for disaster.'

'You're such a pessimist, Eve. I think it's a wonderful idea.' Naomi was clearly having visions of double weddings.

'I know you do Naomi, but that's because you're a hopeless romantic imagining the four of us sipping champagne and eating strawberries on tartan rugs. The truth is that I'd mess it up, like I do every relationship and then we'd never be able to go out in a group again. Please don't say it's not true, you know my track record better than anyone.'

'You've always chosen the wrong men before. Nate's different. He won't feel threatened by you or as if he has to prove he's an alpha male.' Naomi said.

Tim added, 'Plus, I've told him about every detail of your relationship disasters and he still hasn't run away screaming, so that's got to be a good sign, right?' I threw a cushion at his head as I laughed.

'You two are incorrigible. The most I'm prepared to say is that I'll think about it. Now who fancies Chinese takeaway? I'm buying.'

We argued over menus for a while and then Tim phoned in the order. The mention of emails made me feel guilty so I went into the kitchen and switched on my laptop. For a change the wi-fi kicked in first time and I scrolled through my mail as I fiddled with plates and cutlery. Tim was right about the one from Nate. I read it as I opened a bottle of wine.

'Hi Eve, Just wanted to say how sorry I am about what you went through in Slovakia. Wish there was something I could do to help. If you need a driver whilst the plaster's on then I'm only a phone call away. We ought to go out and help the lovebirds celebrate (if they promise not to snog in public). Best wishes, Nate.'

Nate was the kind of guy most women would throw themselves at. If I'd met him any other way, through work or less important friends, I would certainly have given in to temptation, but the thought of jeopardising my closeness to Naomi and Tim was too much. I've never been able to maintain a relationship for more than six months. Something always went wrong and if I'm completely honest it was usually boredom or irritation. I recognise that the problem lies with me, not them. I don't compromise well, don't share space easily (except with Naomi) and I don't suffer fools. Apparently that means that I'm destined to grow old alone! I laughed out loud at such self-indulgent musings and then started to type.

'Hi Nate, Thanks for the message. Recovering quickly and already back at work, arm not a problem although I haven't tried driving! Will call if I need help and appreciate the offer. Lovebirds here as I write so have escaped into kitchen in case it's contagious. I agree – must do drinks soon. Guess the champagne is on us. Tim and Naomi can sort out time and place. Regards, Eve.'

The doorbell had still not rung to signify delivery of food so I opened an internet search for the town of Brezno. The result made me cough out a mouthful of wine. It turns out that Brezno is in Slovakia and, as the crow flies, not a hundred miles from where the train crashed. It felt as if someone were playing a sick joke on me. I double checked my spelling against the documents in my mother's file. The coincidence was bizarre. I decided not to tell Naomi and Tim, they deserved to enjoy one another uninterrupted. I took a long shot and typed 'Adela and Branimir Karas, Brezno' into the search engine but got nothing back. It wasn't going to be that easy.

Around midnight I awoke to the sound of Naomi being violently sick in her bathroom. I put on a robe and fetched a jug of water, an extra toilet roll and a cold flannel. She looked dreadful. I held the flannel to her forehead and opened the window above her.

'Prawns. They get me every time. Should've known better.'

'Don't try to talk. Here, have sip of water.' I handed her the glass and felt her forehead. 'You're burning up. You sure it's just the prawns? Feels more like a virus to me.'

She went to answer and threw up again. We gave up conversation and I sat holding her hair back until her stomach was completely empty. I was concerned. Naomi's temperature was continuing to rise; she was weak, had terrible stomach pains and was starting to shake. Her face was grey and her speech slurred and difficult to understand. When her stomach was empty I got her back to bed. Too worried to leave her alone, I climbed in, put an arm around her and she relaxed. A little colour came back into her face.

'Thank you,' she said. 'How do you do that?'

'Do what?'

'You always make me feel better when you hug me.' She managed a weak smile in spite of the last hour.

'Go to sleep, you're exhausted. The fever's just burned itself out, that's all. I'll phone the clerks first thing in the morning and tell them you can't make it in to chambers.'

'Thank you. You know you can't move out – Tim doesn't do the hair holding thing.'

'I promise I'll train him before I go.' She fell asleep in my arms and, in spite of my best efforts to stay awake, I followed her.

The next morning I was awoken with the customary cup of tea and a fully fit Naomi bustling around in her court suit. She was humming as she did her hair and put on lipstick.

'You've got to be kidding,' I said. 'At once point I was considering calling an ambulance.'

'Right as rain today,' Naomi countered. 'It was you, I swear it was. As soon as you put your arm across me I felt better. You should hire yourself out.' My friend giggled and I was relieved to see she wasn't just putting on a brave face to make it in to court. 'Honestly, it's like you have healing hands. Has that happened to you before?'

'Naomi, you're starting to freak me out.'

'I'm serious. I absolutely believe that some people have healing powers. When I was a child we had a cat that knew which part of your body was hurting. It would come and curl up on just the right area and minutes later the pain would vanish.'

'So not great for toothache, then.'

'Your problem is that you have no faith in anything you can't see or touch. Whatever happened to exploring the great unknown; keeping an open mind?'

'I left it in my dressing up box with my Cinderella outfit and glow in the dark wand. Now go to work you before you give me your virus.'

'Be nice or I'll have to rethink the colour of your bridesmaid dress. I'm starting to think candy-floss pink with lacy frills might be the way to go after all.'

I shoved my head under a pillow but could still hear her laughing as she left the flat. Shame I couldn't try Naomi's imagined healing out on myself and mend my arm faster. I was bored of the cast. In a moment of silliness I took hold of the cast with my good hand and imagined healing the break in my arm. Luckily my idiocy was interrupted by a text alert. Nate and Tim had arranged to take myself and Naomi out to dinner that night. Slightly unkindly, I thought it might have been better if Naomi hadn't recovered quite so quickly. I had more than enough going on in my life without encouraging further trouble.

Eager to stay busy, I opened my mother's papers again, pulling Patrick St. John's card from my wallet. I wrote him an email giving as much detail as I could about the adoption. I needed him to find the Slovakian agency that had arranged it. If the regulations were as strict there as they are in Britain they should still have all the files. My email was met by an out of office message telling me that Patrick wouldn't be back until tomorrow so I settled down to do some more work on the Albert Cornish case.

I emailed my solicitors asking them to obtain photographs showing the cave floor then contacted the prosecution to request the original medical notes on Angela Smyth's injuries. Satisfied that I could do no more until the hearing next week I phoned chambers to collect my messages.

'Tom, it's me. Just thought I'd check in.'

'Hello, Miss MacKenzie. How are you feeling?'

'Oh, much better. Itching to get back into the full swing of it. What's on next week?'

'Only the preliminary Court Martial hearing. Miss Anthony threatened to have me hung drawn and quartered if I booked you for too much work, especially with your arm the way it is.' Naomi was organising my life again. I couldn't blame her. It was exactly what I'd have done if our positions had been reversed.

'Fine, but after next week I'm back full time, okay?'

'Understood, Miss.'

'Is Miss Anthony there?'

'Still at court. She did leave a message though. Hang on. Here it is – reservations have been made at The Restaurant on the Hill for 8pm. Wear something fabulous, she said.' Heaven help me.

Six

A horn beeped outside the front window and I ran down the steps to see that Nate had driven Tim's car to pick me up. I was wearing a shorter skirt than normal and a wraparound woollen top which went easily over my cast. Nate opened the door for me. I did my best to enter with dignity, not easy with only one arm, a mini skirt and a sports car. Nate was sweet enough to look away. He bent over to kiss me on the cheek once he was back in the driver's side.

'Sorry for the confusion. Naomi was running late at court so she went straight to Tim's and my car's in the garage so I borrowed this to get to a meeting in Oxford today.'

'Don't apologise, it's lovely being chauffeured around. I'd have got a cab if I'd known. How are you?'

'Really well, thank you. Struck lucky and been promoted, hence the celebration dinner tonight. I'm glad you agreed to come out. I thought you might have wanted to rest.'

'No rest required. It's wonderful to get out and wear something other than a black suit. Congratulations on the promotion. I hadn't realised.'

'I kept it quiet until it was certain. Nothing worse than having your mates commiserating with you. I'd rather be miserable on my own.'

'Couldn't agree more,' I murmured, thinking about how much information I was keeping from Naomi at the moment. 'So what does the promotion mean in practical terms?'

'A bit more money, better benefits, the usual extra responsibilities. I get to travel more which is what I wanted. I've been stuck driving between London, Oxford and Manchester for three years now so I'm ready for a change of scenery.' Nate was a senior editor at an international publishing house. I knew that they had connections worldwide but I wasn't sure where. I asked him.

'It'll mainly be the States. We only operate in English speaking territories. It's mainly for book releases that launch here and get published later in the US. You know, making sure all the publicity's in place, liaising with agents, that sort of thing.' Compared to my trips to various prisons and courts this sounded incredibly glamorous. I was jealous for a moment until I thought how my last trip abroad had ended. We made small talk until we arrived at The Restaurant on the Hill. It's an old favourite of mine and the sort of eatery that Notting Hill does so well: that combination of shabby chic and extraordinary cuisine that makes it impossible to get last minute reservations. Unless you know the owner, of course. Nate did, an old school chum from what I gathered when they greeted one another. Tim and Naomi were well into their first glass of wine and looking excitedly at menus.

Naomi whispered in my ear. 'You look gorgeous! You can't tell me you're not interested in a man when you put on clothes like that.'

'You are in so much trouble with me; I dare you to make it any worse!'

'What? Tim arranged all this with Nate, nothing to do with me. You did email Nate yesterday to say we'd all go out.'

'Is my life so dull that you could be certain I had nothing else booked already?'

'Well,' Naomi stuttered over a reply.

'Don't answer that. Just get me a drink and don't do any more matchmaking.'

'Gin and tonic?' She ordered for me without an answer. I can't drink wine. About half way through a glass I get the sort of headache that doesn't leave for two days. On the other hand a couple of measures of spirits and I'm under the table. Cheap date, I guess. Getting drunk tonight was out of the question. I'd decided to avoid any mention of the bizarre turn my life was taking whilst my friends were celebrating. Tonight meant two things and two things only: Sobriety and good cheer. So when a double gin appeared in my glass in the first five minutes I knew I should have asked for an extra bottle of tonic and made it last. Best intentions, and all that. I finished it in about three minutes.

By the time we moved from main course to dessert I was finishing my third double and losing my constraint. Naomi was equally giggly and the men seemed to be enjoying themselves so I decided the sobriety rule could stand to be broken. Everything was fine until Nate recounted a story about his mother having yet another round of plastic surgery and using up his inheritance. He stopped mid-laugh and looked at me, aghast.

'Damn, I'm such an idiot. I shouldn't have said that, I'd completely forgotten that you just lost your mother. How insensitive. Sorry Eve.'

'Not to worry, turns out she wasn't my mother anyway. Let's have a toast; to squandered inheritances and lying mothers!' I raised my glass, spilling quite a lot on the way.

'What are you talking about? What's going on?' Tim looked genuinely confused.

'Oh hell. You hadn't told him? Wow Naomi, you are the most discreet person I've met in my entire life. Let me explain. I was going through the papers left to me by the person formerly known as Mum when I discovered that I am, in fact, Eve Karas, born in Slovakia and adopted in England. I think I need another drink.'

Tim looked mortified. He stared at Naomi. 'This isn't a joke?' She shook her head and fiddled with her napkin as she gently reached out and held my hand under the table. My brain finally caught up with my mouth. I smiled softly at Naomi. At least I know when it's time to go home.

'Nate, would you mind cutting your evening short and dropping me home? I think I just overstepped my alcohol limit. Tim, I'm so sorry.'

'Are you kidding? I can't believe you got though the first two courses without screaming or throwing anything.' He hugged me as I stood, slightly wobbly, and I willed myself not to cry. 'Why doesn't Naomi go home with you? You shouldn't be alone.'

'Yes, because I really need to feel even guiltier about ruining your evening by depriving you of your fiancée for the night. I think not. Anyway, I'll be fine; the gin and tonic should keep me numb until midmorning tomorrow.'

'I'll take care of her. Come on Eve.' Nate put a protective arm around me and I certainly wasn't going to shrug it off.

Walking in a straight line might prove challenging. 'You guys finish dinner. We'll get coffee at the flat. Call you tomorrow, Tim.'

I stumbled my way over to the car which thankfully was parked only a little way up the road. Nate managed to manoeuvre me in without any additional embarrassment although it was a bit late to be worried about that now, having already done such a good job. Before turning on the engine he surprised me by taking my hand in his and kissing my cheek.

'I know you're going to spend the rest of the journey saying sorry for what just happened, so listen: Don't apologise and don't worry about it. I'm not sure why you're not hiding in your room with the duvet over your head. Family is family, good or bad, so finding out that none of it was exactly as you thought, well, you must feel lost. Close your eyes and let me get you home. Okay?'

'Okay.' Nate let go of my hand and started the engine. I had seriously underestimated him. I didn't close my eyes during the journey, partly because the alcohol was making everything spin but more so that I could take a look at Nate. He was the definition of laid back, little smile lines at the corner of his mouth, broad shoulders and the sort of body you want to wrap yourself up in on a cold night. He's the kind of man you want to take home to your parents because he'll charm them instantly. He was the complete package; warm, funny with an interesting job and friends you don't mind spending the weekend with. He made women smile and men want to drink with him. Away from the heat of the restaurant I started to sober up and contemplate why I hadn't responded to Nate's previous invitations. Perhaps I was just scared of meeting the right guy. Making a mess of relationships with the wrong kind of man was easy to explain. Messing up a relationship with Nate would require a lot more self-analysis. I knew I'd been on a self-destruct mission for years as far as my private life was concerned. So much was changing right now that maybe it was a good time to take a leap of faith.

Nate pulled into a parking space some distance away from my flat. It was always impossible to park nearby and we'd have to walk for a couple of minutes to get inside. Already feeling guilty about the scene at the restaurant, I didn't want Nate to think he had to walk me to the door.

'Nate, I'll be fine, you go on home.'

'You've got to be kidding; Naomi'll kill me if I don't see you safely indoors.'

He was right, she would. I gave in and we walked without talking to my front door. Nate took the key from me and opened up.

'At least let me get you coffee.'

'Only if I make it.' Nate flicked the switch on the kettle. I took mugs out of the cupboard and opened chocolate biscuits. There's something reassuring about a man who's happy to tuck into biscuits without pretending he doesn't eat that sort of thing. Fitness is wonderful, but eating the odd chocolate biscuit is good for the soul. We took everything through to the lounge and settled on the sofa. Nate pointed at a photo of Tim and Naomi on the mantelpiece.

'They really do make a great couple, don't they?'

'Made for each other, I'd say. Lucky things.' I must have sounded wistful as I said it.

'You've never felt like that?' he asked.

'No. I don't think I have enough faith in the human race to let myself feel like that. What about you?'

'A couple of near misses, but at the last minute I found I couldn't compromise on someone who just ticked most of my boxes. I don't mean I'm looking for the perfect woman, just the woman who fits perfectly with me.'

'That being?'

'I don't have a list; just the stuff that matters to me has to matter to them. I don't care if someone can't cook if they are interested in what's going on in the world. I'd rather spend a weekend in a grotty cottage in the middle of nowhere with people I like than lounging on a yacht in Monaco with 'the right set'. I can't stand women who have to put on makeup to come down for breakfast. I adore women who say what they mean without worrying what everyone else will think. I do have a bit of a thing about slim ankles, but that's just cosmetic.' I giggled.

'That doesn't sound like too much to ask.' I put down my coffee cup.

'It shouldn't be so complicated, but the sort of women I meet at parties and work all seem to be scoring points and stepping up the social ladder.'

'You're either very complex or very simple. I'm not sure which yet.' I smiled at him.

'Do you want to find out?' The atmosphere changed. He was looking me straight in the eyes waiting for an answer.

'I want not to mess things up with Tim and Naomi and all our friendships.' I said, completely honest for once.

'Then don't.' He put his coffee cup on the table and moved to my end of the sofa. My stomach flipped as he slid his hand around my neck and I felt his fingers stroke my nape. A tingling sensation ran down my back to the base of my spine. I couldn't help but breathe a little faster, even if I was trying to hide it. My lips parted as he pulled my head gently forward to his. When he kissed me I felt as if I had slipped into a warm bath. My whole body heated up and when he slowly probed my mouth with his tongue I let out an involuntary gasp and grabbed at his shirt. I pressed myself into his mouth and returned the kiss. He slid his free arm around my waist and I let myself be crushed into his chest. His fingers scratched my skin and I ran my hand up his chest to undo his shirt. One of his hands came to meet mine and stopped me undressing him.

'What is it?' I asked. 'Is something wrong?'

'No, nothing's wrong. I just don't want to do this when you've been drinking. I don't mean you're drunk, I just know what a dreadful time you've had and I feel like I'm taking advantage.'

'You're not and I know you wouldn't.'

'This matters to me. I want you more than you could possibly know but I don't want you to spend tomorrow figuring out how to let me down gently.' I couldn't speak. My body was in that post-adrenalin moment between pleasure and pain. I knew he was right and that I should let him go but I didn't want to. I really, really didn't want to. He stood up, closing the buttons I'd already opened at the top of his shirt as I regained my senses.

He picked up the coffee cups and took them into the kitchen. I smiled at his thoughtfulness and stood as he came back into the lounge.

'I'd better go.'

'Thank you for a wonderful evening,' I said as we walked to the front door. 'Thank you for driving and for being so sweet.'

'Don't call me sweet,' he whispered. 'That's not how I want you to think of me.'

'I guess I'll have to find that out some other time,' I said. Determined not to let him leave without a farewell kiss I pushed my body against his and raised my face. I was being wanton and he felt it. I let my head back as he kissed me and felt him harden when he pushed towards me. I finally pulled away and he swore under his breath. I smiled. I knew I was behaving badly but for the first time in a long time I felt the exhilaration of being out of control. He tucked a strand of hair behind my ear, drew his thumb along my lower lip, then left. I pushed the door closed behind him, turned and let my back fall against it, my legs shaking. In trying to show him what he was missing I'd only succeeded in frustrating myself. I decided to remedy things with a cold shower, not least to help dissipate the remnant of the gin. He was an exceptional man. There weren't many who would leave in the midst of so obvious an opportunity. I didn't doubt that his motives were genuine. I ran my hand through my hair and breathed out hard. Shower and sleep would be an excellent idea.

I started the shower on a cold setting, found it more painful than bracing, resorted to my usual temperature and scrubbed off the evening's makeup. As I was beginning to feel normal again the doorbell rang. It was after midnight; Naomi must have decided to come home and look after me, probably leaving her key at Tim's. I wrapped a towel around myself, hair dripping down my back.

'Okay, I'm coming. Hold on.' I pulled the door open without looking through the security peephole.

'Do you always open the door wearing so few clothes?' Nate looked amused.

'I assumed it was Naomi.'

'I tried to leave. I sat in the car for fifteen minutes. I told myself that doing this tonight was a huge mistake. Tell me go home.' I giggled, as I always do when I have no idea of what I ought to say. That was all the response he needed.

He walked through the door, slamming it shut behind him with his heel. I took a step backwards, ending up with my back against the wall and Nate pinning me to it in a way I wasn't a bit sorry about. When his lips ground down on mine I reached straight for his shirt and continued where I'd left off. Doing it one handed was clumsy but I'd still undone all the buttons before he carried me into the bedroom. As Nate laid me on the bed the towel, more hindrance than help, fell loose and slipped away. I didn't pull it back; things were too far gone to pretend coyness. Nate stared down at my body in the glow of the streetlight. He trailed his hand slowly down from my shoulder, so lightly brushing my breast that I could barely feel his touch, then tracing a line from my belly button to the tops of my legs. He looked me straight in the eyes and purposefully lowered his face to kiss me again as his fingers dipped between my legs. I raised my hips to meet his fingers and he shifted his body to the side of me so that he could slide the flat of his thumb onto my clitoris, making little circles that made my whole body buzz.

I ran my tongue across his chest, grazing my teeth against his nipple. He groaned and I enjoyed the thrill of making another person lose control. I undid his jeans and he kicked them on off without losing a beat. When he moved on top of me I opened my legs for him without hesitating.

'You're sure?' he breathed heavily.

'Do you need me to convince you?' I replied and wrapped my legs around him so that he had only to lower himself inside me. When he did our bodies went into a rhythm of push and pull. I knew he was holding back, willing me to come and whilst I knew I wouldn't be able to I didn't want to ruin the moment for him. Rather than act out a lie, I thrust my hips harder at him, pushing my nails into his shoulders and grinding my body into his. He bit my neck as he came, shuddering, his face buried in my hair. As he relaxed, he raised his head and looked a little sheepish.

'I'm sorry, I just couldn't hold on any longer.'

'I thought we had a ban on apologies tonight,' I said and kissed him again, more gently.

He kept his arms wrapped around me and I appreciated the warmth. He showed no sign of leaving and I didn't want him to. In so many ways he was perfect for me. With a whisper of goodnight we slept. The next morning there were none of the awkward silences I always dread. He was up and showered before I woke and brought me coffee. I wondered what sort of sight I must have been but the smile on his face said he didn't care. I sat up and yawned, it was only ten o'clock.

'I'm playing rugby today. Wish I didn't have to go.'

'Well, I can't keep you to myself forever, can I?'

'Now there's a thought.' He pulled his clothes on and sat on the edge of the bed next to me. 'So, no regrets?' He stroked my shoulder and I thought how easy it would be to fall in love with him.

'Only that you have to go. Then again, Naomi will be home in about two hours and I think it best we don't let this slip yet.'

'You're worried they'll have us paired off and married before you can run away screaming in the opposite direction?'

I appreciated both his insight and the sense of humour with which he delivered it. 'Something like that. I need to manage expectations a little. Could we…'

'Keep this quiet for a while? It's okay, I understand.' He checked his watch. 'I should already be gone. Can I persuade you to sneak out for dinner one night this week? I promise not to tell anyone.'

'Sounds ideal. I would offer to cook but you really wouldn't enjoy the experience. I'll call you tomorrow and let you know when's good.'

I went to kiss him goodbye on the cheek. 'Don't you dare,' he said and pulled my mouth towards his. 'Now I really am leaving and this time I'm determined to start the car engine. Bye Eve.'

The day passed in a haze. I had to actively avoid Naomi so I didn't give anything away. She checked that I wasn't too hung over and then went into chambers to catch up on some paper work. I finally got around to some domestic chores; washing, ironing, and vacuuming. It gave me time to consider how I felt about the adoption. I could see it from my parents' perspective. How do you tell a child they're adopted? They had already lost one daughter. Why would they want to risk another? I thought about the right age to do it – too soon and you undermine a child's stability, too late and you shatter trust with the revelation of a lie.

I wondered if some part of me, deep down, had known something was wrong and wilfully ignored the signs. There was my hair of course, unlike either of my parents', but that's not uncommon. They were obsessed with order and routine when I would flit from here to there with no thought of consequences. Isn't that the same with every child? I hadn't had the sort of relationship with my mother that some of my friends had and I'd felt jealous listening to stories of girly shopping trips with 'mum'. I phoned her regularly after my father passed away but she wasn't the sort to linger making small talk. The truth is that, as much as I'd like to be able to claim some sixth sense about the situation, I had none. Perhaps that's what made it all the more of a shock.

I tried to picture my biological parents. I had some romantic notion that my mother had the same long red hair as me and that my father was tall and strapping. Perhaps they owned a little farm up in the mountains although I knew the reality of families who had to give up their children for adoption was often a lot less picturesque. I scanned the documents from my mother's file so I could email them to Patrick. My head clearer, I took a walk along the river for some fresh air until Naomi got back. It was easier than I thought not to tell her about Nate. Happily, it was more to do with enjoying the secret than because I didn't want her to find out. I contemplated dinner with him that week and found I was already counting down the days. Perhaps things were going to get better, after all.

Seven

Monday morning I was at the Court Martial in Colchester. Albert and I were discussing what would happen at the preliminary hearing. He would enter his 'not guilty' plea and the Judge would make directions for the trial, fix a date for it and order any outstanding documents we wanted from the prosecution. As I walked through the building to find the court clerk I glanced into the prosecutor's room and was disappointed to see Marcus Brandt straightening his wig in the mirror. He caught my eye so I opened the door to say good morning.

'Marcus. Which case are you here for?'

'The rapist. Is Cornish one of yours then?'

'Alleged rapist, thank you. If you'd read the correspondence you would already know that he's one of mine. Can we agree trial directions?'

'Oh, darling, you have to be joking! You don't seriously think you can win this one. Anyone with half a brain would persuade their client to plead and get some time off their sentence for admitting it early.'

'Don't lecture me on sentencing and don't call me darling. The point about pleading is that you only do it if you've committed the offence. Albert Cornish is not guilty and he will plead not guilty. At least my only having half a brain will make it easier for you to win, won't it?' I stalked out of the room, furious for letting him get to me. Marcus and I were old adversaries. We were a fair match for each other as far as our advocacy skills were concerned but in every other way we were poles apart. He's one of those people who believe the class system should dictate who can enter blue chip professions. He certainly thinks females should be at home having babies instead of working as barristers. He's also convinced that he's irresistible to women so when I turned down his offer of dinner a couple of years ago I made a bad enemy. He is short for a man at only five foot five inches which makes him overcompensate with the size of his ego. The truth is that he needed not just one lesson but an entire schooling in humility. I hoped our on-going war wouldn't make things even worse for Albert and knew that I'd need to play it exactly right with the Judge. I put on my wig and prepared for battle.

'Miss MacKenzie. Is your client ready to enter his plea?'

'Yes, Your Honour.' Albert heard the charge read out and replied with 'Not Guilty.' We settled to the task of agreeing directions. The only witnesses I required were Angela Smyth, the doctor who saw her on arrival at the hospital and the security guard at the Dragon's Cave.

Marcus stood up to make his usual over the top fuss. 'Really, Your Honour. I don't see how the security guard is going to be able to help; Miss MacKenzie has his statement. It will mean flying him out from Slovakia. At least both the victim and the doctor are members of the armed forces serving in the UK.'

'Your Honour, I have the right to question any witness relied upon by the prosecution.'

'Yes, but it might be helpful Miss MacKenzie to know exactly what areas of his statement are in dispute. I can understand why Mr Brandt doesn't want to go to the expense of flying a witness out from Slovakia.' I hesitated. I hadn't wanted to give my line of questioning away, knowing that Marcus would take advantage of anything I let slip. Still, I had to answer the Judge; there was no point in alienating him.

'Your Honour, there are issues about how the entrance to the cave came to be open at night…' Marcus was on his feet to chip in before I could finish my sentence.

'…Which cannot possibly be relevant to whether or not the offence was committed.'

'Shall we allow Miss MacKenzie to finish and then perhaps you'd like to add your comments afterwards?' the Judge said kindly.

'I'm obliged,' I murmured. 'There are also issues about the existence of CCTV cameras in the vicinity. Finally there is the physical state of the cave; there will be some important questions about the interior which the security guard will be able to answer impartially.'

Marcus may be vicious and egotistical but he's nobody's fool. He went in with a line of attack that I simply didn't see coming.

'If there are issues about the interior of the cave that are vital to the defence then perhaps we all ought to have an opportunity to visit the location together.' Marcus smiled as if he'd won a prize. He'd obviously heard what I'd been through on my last trip to Poland and was banking on me feeling unable to go back. I would either have to change my line of questioning or drop out of the case. I was caught between the devil and the deep blue sea and I knew which one Marcus Brandt reminded me of. It was a dirty trick.

'Your Honour,' I spoke slowly, having to think on my feet. 'I've just been on a site visit. If it assists the Court, I have asked my instructing solicitors to obtain photographic evidence as to the layout and interior of the cave. I'm not sure I need to go back or that Your Honour needs to be troubled with a site visit for this case.'

The Judge paused for a moment while he thought it over. 'Do the issues relating to the cave have a serious bearing on your defence?'

I couldn't evade that one. 'They do.'

'Then I'm afraid that Mr Brandt is right, Miss MacKenzie. I will need to have both of you in attendance. The photographer can visit at the same time and we can use the photos for the hearing when we return. It's too serious a case not to visit the scene if it's relevant. I shall adjourn the Court for a few minutes whilst the clerk telephones both your chambers to see what the earliest available date is for us to visit Krakow.' We bowed as the Judge left the courtroom. Albert was escorted out for a restroom break while I pretended to busy myself with my papers.

'Eve, I should have said how sorry I am to have heard about that dreadful train crash. I saw the footage on the news. Bodies ripped limb from limb, I gather some of the passengers are having to be identified from dental records. You can't relish the thought of going back out there. I'm sorry I had to ask but we each have our duty to our client, don't we?'

'Of course we do, Marcus and I wouldn't have expected anything less from you.' My tone was sugary but the meaning was clear.

'Never mind, I'm sure plenty of your colleagues in chambers will be willing to take the case over from you. Frankly, I'm surprised to see you back on your feet after such a trauma. One might have expected your judgment to be clouded having witnessed so much horror.'

I knew he was trying, in rather a crass way, to put me off. As ever with him, it had quite the opposite effect. Even without my desire to see Albert Cornish's reputation restored, I would never be bullied by a piece of work like Brandt.

'You don't need to worry about me, Marcus. The crash happened in Slovakia, not Poland and I won't need to go back on a train. In many ways it's better to get straight back on the horse, isn't it? This will probably be the best thing for me. And you're absolutely right, it is extremely important to my case – I'm glad the Judge will have the chance to see the alleged crime scene in person.' I smiled and walked out leaving Marcus' sneer fading on his pompous face.

Sadly I didn't feel half as confident as I sounded. The thought of going back to Krakow made me feel sick. I went to the bathroom and splashed cold water on my face, phoning my clerks to let them know what had happened. When I turned my phone on it beeped to tell me I had voicemail. It was Patrick, back in his office and responding to my email about the adoption agency. He had news but didn't want to leave a message. As anxious as I was to call him back, this wasn't the time or place. Before I could even think about getting a cup of tea the court clerk was calling us back in.

'Miss MacKenzie, Mr Brandt, good news. The clerk has liaised with both your chambers and we've identified a date when we can all be available. In fact, it is this Friday.'

I lost my composure. 'Your Honour, that's just four days, we'll never get flights.'

'Already been checked. There are plenty of flights either Thursday afternoon or early Friday morning. We'll make the site visit at 2pm to give everyone plenty of time to get there and as the next day is a Saturday no-one will have to rush back for Court. It has the benefit for your client, Miss MacKenzie, that we can proceed to trial sooner rather than later. Agreed?'

'Your Honour is most thoughtful.' I muttered.

'Bail is extended on the same conditions as before. Unless there is anything else I look forward to seeing you both in Krakow. Good day.' The Judge bowed briefly and left the courtroom.

'Know any good hotels in Krakow, Eve? Perhaps I could ask my clerks to book for you as well?' I wanted to slap him but that doesn't go down well in Court. I settled for bitchiness to make myself feel better.

'I think you and I have different standards, Marcus. I can't imagine we'll end up at the same type of hotel.' He just laughed. I picked up my papers and walked out, keeping my head up. Back to Krakow, this Friday. It didn't bear thinking about. I couldn't let Marcus see the effect it had on me. More important, I couldn't let my client see how shaken up I was.

Albert was simply pleased that matters were moving fast. He didn't have time to pick up on my emotional state before his transport arrived to escort him back to quarters. I phoned for a taxi to the station. This wasn't part of the plan. Everything was spiralling out of control. By the time I spoke to my clerks they had were already in the process of booking my flights.

'You sure you're ready for this, Miss? I can ask someone else to take over the case.'

'Not fair on the client Tom. Anyway, I need the money! Book me a flight Thursday night would you, please? I don't want to be worrying about delays Friday morning.'

'Will do. I gather you're being prosecuted by Mr Brandt? Rumour has it he's applying for a judicial position this year. He'll be after some good publicity from this one. Make sure you show him up for the idiot he is, for all our sakes.'

'Tom, if I were in chambers now I'd kiss you.' I set off for home, grinning.

Eight

I arrived at the Hotel Copernicus, nestled just below Wawel Castle in the centre of Krakow, at six o'clock Thursday evening. It's a boutique hotel that makes you feel like a movie star when you walk through the door, quiet and discreet with wonderful food and architecture. There was no way the legal aid fund was going to pay for me to stay here so I had to foot most of the bill myself. It seemed a small price to pay to avoid the local chain hotels and threat of food poisoning. I hung up my suit for the next day and checked emails in case Patrick had been in touch. We'd had a long conversation yesterday and I'd sent him the scanned documents. He was doing his best to find the original adoption papers and had promised to call if he found anything. We already knew that the agency who'd handled it were in Bratislava. Patrick still had to persuade them to hand over what we needed. I'd sent him copies of both my parents' death certificates and a written letter of authorisation; fingers crossed that would be enough. Although there was no new email from Patrick I did find one waiting from Nate.

We'd been unable to have the planned dinner that week as a result of my sudden departure but were in the habit of sending texts morning and evening. He was busy himself and I recognised someone whose career is a compulsion, even if he hid it well. I respected him. That seems to be about the best start a relationship can get. The fact that he's also fun and gorgeous helps.

I decided to visit the one place I'd missed last time I'd been in Krakow; the bar where Albert and Angela met the mystery man that no-one else remembers. I wanted to see the layout of the bar and time the walk from there to the Dragon's Cave. The New

World Bar is in Krakow's Old Town, just ten minutes from my hotel. I took a map with me in case I wandered down the wrong street and then went out to do a little detective work of my own.

I missed the entrance to the bar twice before finding it amidst the hub of drinking establishments in Old Town. It was still early when I went in but there were already several seats taken and a steady queue of people waiting for drinks. I perched on a stool and didn't have to wait too long before being handed a beer. There was loud music playing from multiple speakers hanging from the ceiling and everyone seemed to be shouting. In the evening the Old Town area is packed with twenty-somethings enjoying life before consequences. I felt a moment of jealousy then reminded myself why I was there. Albert Cornish was all too aware of the consequences of his night out drinking in Krakow's hot spot.

There were inconsistencies about the case evidence that went beyond the lack of injuries to Angela's body. Albert's own version of what happened that night was disjointed, and the alleged victim had notable memory lapses although there were no drugs found in either of their systems. And why go to the Dragon's Cave at all if they had no way of knowing it would be unlocked? Unless, of course, the man accompanying them was much more influential than Albert had realised.

'Fancy seeing you here.' I jumped in my seat and whirled round to see Marcus overdressed and standing out from the crowd for all the wrong reasons.

'Marcus. You startled me. I didn't recognise you in your party clothes!'

'You're catty tonight. Not enjoying being back here so soon after all?'

'If you were trying to push me out of the case it hasn't worked, so why don't you settle down and do your job. Prosecuting isn't supposed to be about shifting the goal posts to make innocent men look guilty.'

'Seriously, you have to get over that pious streak of yours, Eve. It's dull. You used to be much more fun as I remember. Let me buy you a drink. You do still drink don't you or are you too saintly even for that these days?'

'I'm still half way through this one and I've never regarded myself as saintly, thank you. I gather you're thinking about becoming a judge this year. I would have thought that might restrict your social life too much.'

'I'm bored. Same old same old. Drug dealing, credit card fraud, sex offences. Different names but the cases don't change. I thought I could do with some new scenery. At least life as a Judge will give me paid holidays and a pension.'

'Doesn't something about this case seem disjointed to you?'

'Don't even think about trying to charm me into dropping this one. Just because we're sitting in a bar rather than a courtroom doesn't mean I've lost my senses.'

'You know what, Marcus, put the tough guy aside would you and give me some credit. Albert Cornish has an impeccable service record, there's no tension between he and the victim and they'd both been drinking. Why walk all the way down to the Dragon's Cave for this?'

'You're assuming he was drunk.'

'I believe he can't remember the evening clearly and there were no drugs in his body.'

'Just an opportunistic rape. We've seen hundreds like this before.'

'If it's opportunistic why not just pull her into a side alley on the way back to the army base? Why struggle down all those steps into the cave? She doesn't even say she was unwilling to go into the cave. Come on Marcus, this is far from opportunistic, quite the opposite.'

'Rapes never make sense, planned or unplanned. You have too much faith in your client. It'll be your downfall. Now, I've had quite enough of the noise in here. I'm off to my hotel for supper. I would invite you but I know your policies on sleeping with the enemy. I don't know what you're looking for but I doubt you'll find the answers here. See you tomorrow.'

I watched him as he stuck his nose in the air and made his way through the revellers to the door. By the time I turned round a man had taken Marcus's place on the empty bar stool beside me and was ordering a drink in a language I couldn't understand. I picked up my beer, drained my glass and stood to go.

‘Do you know where you are?’ the man said. I didn’t even look up. His voice made me stop exactly where I was, trying to place him.

‘Centuries ago Krakow was a city in the land of the Bohemians. The King kept a little town house for his mistress so that he could stroll down from his castle on the pretence of visiting his people and see her without the Queen’s knowledge. This was that house. For years it was known as The King’s Folly.’

‘How could they know that, with certainty, so many hundreds of years later?’

‘Stories passed down from generation to generation are the building blocks of history.’

‘Or myths concocted to intrigue tourists.’ I replied, not sure why I was even carrying on the conversation.

‘A myth is the truth to the person who believes it and a lie to anyone who doesn’t.'

'Myths are stories told to entertain children and influence the superstitious. I'm neither.' The man looked up from his drink and met my eyes.

'Of course you are. You are afraid of fire even though you have no idea why and you make a wish when you look at the stars the way you did as a child. You close your eyes when you are scared as if not seeing something means you cannot be harmed by it. Am I wrong?'

I said nothing in reply. I found I’d lost my voice. The man in front of me was perfect. I don’t mean that as a compliment in this context. He looked like the picture of a man you’d see on the illustrated cover of a romance novel. His skin tone was so even that it was difficult to read the expression on his face; he was unlined to the extent that he appeared ageless. His eyes were almost black but the irises caught and held the reflections of the coloured lights of the bar. His teeth were white and even, lacking the tiniest flaw. He was like an image of a human being drawn by someone who had heard descriptions but never met one. He spoke English fluently but with an accent that marked him only as foreign rather than of any particular origin. He gave me chills and at the same time I couldn’t take my eyes off him.

‘Who are you?’ I asked.

‘Who are you looking for?’ he countered.

'Don't play games with me, I don't like it. Why did you come over here and sit next to me?'

'The seat was empty and you did not seem to be enjoying the company of the last man you were with. I was only seeking to make conversation. Do you not like to have your views challenged?' He smiled.

'I asked who you were.'

'And I could give you my name but what good would it be? Would my name tell you something about me? Would it give you a better reason to go or stay? Let me tell you a story about Wawel Castle.' I sank back down onto my bar stool, more certain by the minute that his arrival was no accident. I would bide my time. If there was one thing I'd learned as a barrister it was that if you listen long enough people usually tell you what you want to know.

'When King Casimir IV died in 1492 he had held the Polish throne for fifty-five years. He had six sons and seven daughters, a dynasty that would dominate Europe for centuries. He and his wife were interred in a chapel in Wawel Castle like so many Kings and Queens before them. Years later, with the consent of the Archbishop, Casimir's tomb was opened for research. What did they expect to find, do you think? He was, after all, just a man, just another dead body rotting away. And yet his legend was so powerful that someone wanted to probe the dust of his remains and for what? The secret to the power he had accumulated so successfully? It was a Friday when they opened the tomb. The thirteenth day of the month. There were those who said the tomb should have remained untouched, that opening it was unholy and disrespectful. Some people questioned the judgment of the Archbishop who had authorised the request. There were whispers that no good would come of it.'

I couldn't help myself. He paused long enough to force me to ask him to continue. 'Fine, I'll play. What happened?'

'They opened the tomb. They disturbed the King's peace and that of his beloved Queen. Within days four of the twelve people present at the opening of the tomb were dead. A few weeks later another six had also perished. Only two men survived. Myth or truth?'

'If the historical records are accurate, and these sorts of stories are always embellished over time, then it must have been bacteria or fungus that caused the problem. These days that sort of thing simply wouldn't happen. And the whole Friday the thirteenth hocus pocus is exactly the sort of embellishment to add some mystery to an otherwise unremarkable event.' I motioned to the bartender for another drink.

'You seem so certain and yet everything you have said is coloured by your assumptions about when this took place. Let me enlighten you. The man who authorised the opening of the coffin was the then Archbishop of Krakow, who later became better known as Pope John Paul II. The year was 1973 and the day really was Friday 13th. One would have thought that even in 1973 scientists knew enough about microbes to wear face masks. It doesn't take centuries to create a myth, Eve, just a cautionary tale.'

'I didn't tell you my name.' I stared hard at my companion. The game was not fun anymore.

'It is the name your previous companion called you. Was I wrong?' I didn't bother to answer. By now I was feeling angry and tense.

'You are presumptuous, if nothing else.'

'Then let me level the playing field. My name is Perun.'

'The fact that you are here with me now is no coincidence, Perun. Be straight with me or I will leave and I suspect that if I do neither of us will have found what we came out looking for tonight.'

He rose to his feet in one fluid motion, taller than I'd expected and stooped to whisper in my ear, his lips brushing my cheek as he did so and sending a shiver through me like an electric shock. He took hold of the cast on my arm and his voice echoed through me, low and deep.

'You are right, Kukushka. But you have no idea how to run away, it is the one thing you have never been able to do. If you want answers you will not find them in Krakow. When you decide to take control of your fate, come and find me.' He let go of my arm, took hold of my chin and kissed my forehead. I sat rigid as he kissed me but before I could get control enough to push him away, he'd gone.

I spun round to follow him but the crowd in the bar had already filled the space he'd walked through and there was no chance of finding him in the unfamiliar streets. I wasn't at all sure it would be safe to look.

I waited until I'd stopped shaking, desperate to get back to my hotel. Outside the bar I looked around cautiously but felt no sense of danger, just mild vertigo. Back in my room I saw a face I wasn't even sure I recognised. My eyes had taken on a hollow, haunted look. The world I'd inhabited a month ago was an illusion. I couldn't pretend that everything was normal anymore. Something extraordinary was happening, creating a forward motion I was unable to stop and try as I might to pretend it was all my imagination, I knew better.

Kukushka. Cuckoo. Was he the man on the train or had that all been a dream? He was like no other person I had met and yet his presence was familiar. I admitted to myself that I'd felt a thrill just being next to him, but it was a like a ride on a ghost train, dark and unsettling, exciting only because it's laced with fear.

I felt icy cold inside and knew it was the shock of a dawning realisation, something far beyond the events of that evening. I poured a drink, flexing the muscles of my right arm as I turned the bottle cap and realised the fracture in my arm felt different. There was no sensation of movement, no discomfort at all, in fact. Perun had held his hand over the fracture site as he held me. At the time I felt nothing unusual, focused only on what he was saying. I thought back to what Naomi had said about me making her better and it seemed that a veil had been lifted. Whatever the cost, I had to find him again. I picked up my mobile, dialled Patrick's and let it ring.

When the answer message kicked in I left a voice mail to tell him where I was and that I wanted to talk to him the next morning. I didn't need to say that it was urgent, I felt sure he would tell just from my tone. Unable to sleep I settled down to the task of dismantling my cast. I requested a pair of kitchen scissors from room service and it took me three hours to cut, saw and snap my way through to an arm that felt and looked absolutely perfect. It would be difficult to answer questions the next day about the disappearance of the cast and I knew I'd have to keep my arm covered. When I glanced at my watch it was nearly four in the morning. I had no idea where the night had gone.

Nine

My phone rang a few hours later and I wasn't sure how much I could say without Patrick thinking I needed to be committed. In the end I didn't have to do much of the talking. Patrick had been doing some detective work of his own and he had enough to say for both of us.

'Miss MacKenzie, how are you? I hope the flight to Krakow wasn't too tiresome?'

'Patrick, given how much of a nuisance I'm being, I'd feel a lot better if you'd call me Eve from now on.'

'Of course, but it's no bother at all. I'm only sorry you've had such a shock since your return to England.'

'What were the odds? The train crashing so close to the town where I was born.'

'My mother used to say there are no coincidences, only accidents waiting to happen. That may have been a little too prophetic in your case, of course. I do have news for you but I'm afraid not all of it is good.'

'I'm only expecting bad news to be honest, the more I think about this the fewer scenarios occur to me where my birth parents had me adopted for a good reason. So go ahead, pretend you're ripping a plaster off a child's knee, best do it fast and in one go.'

I don't know what I was expecting but at least I hadn't gone into this imagining a happily ever after. I wasn't wrong.

'Well, your birth father, Branimir Karas, is dead. He died in April, 1985. I'm afraid the circumstances are rather upsetting. He committed suicide whilst he was a patient at what they then called an insane asylum. Do you want to know any more or shall I move on?'

'I think I need to know everything.'

'It seems as if he got hold of a lighter from a staff member's bag. He locked himself in a caretaker's cupboard, doused himself with cleaning fluids and set his clothing on fire.'

'How long had he been institutionalised?'

'I don't have the exact date but it seems he was committed about the same time you were adopted. I'm sorry Eve. It's not the news I'd hoped to give you.'

'It is what it is. Can we get hold of any more information, medical records?'

'I'm afraid not. The files were destroyed when the asylum was closed down in the early nineties. They would have contained all the committal papers. It's a dead end.' I couldn't help but wonder what had driven my father insane. If it were an inherited condition maybe it explained what was happening to me now. Or was it the adoption? Perhaps he couldn't live with the decision he and my mother had taken. It prompted me to ask about her.

'And my mother, Patrick. Any news about her?'

'I've drawn a blank, really. There's no death certificate lodged in this country but there are no tax returns filed in the name you gave me for as long as the computer records go back. What I do know is this. She was a nurse at the hospital in Brezno where you were born; it gives her occupation and place of work in the adoption files.'

'Nothing else? No way to trace her? I have to find out what happened, I'm falling apart Patrick. Any other details, however tiny, might help.' I could hear the sound of papers being shuffled and Patrick sighing with frustration.

'Nothing that I can see. The adoption file gives the name of the midwife who delivered you. The only other thing is a medical examination record from when you were taken out of Slovakia and transferred to the UK. There's nothing remarkable except some injuries to your feet.'

'My feet. What about them?'

'Burns, it says here. Third degree burns to both your feet. No explanation on the papers. Is it relevant?' I didn't speak. I was kicking off my shoes and running my hands over the scarring that had never faded. I couldn't wear the strappy sandals favoured by my friends, didn't bother with shoe shopping. I wore sensible boots for work and trainers at the weekend. My parents had told me it was a birth defect. If it had been an accident, why the lie? 'Eve, are you still there?'

'Sorry, still here.'

'Hold on, just checking one last thing.' I could hear keys tapping on his computer, pausing, tapping again. 'The midwife's name is Olga Hornik, again no death certificate on record. Local council records give an address in Brezno but no telephone number. She's in her late eighties though; it might be a wild goose chase.'

'It's better than nothing. Could you email me the address, please?'

'Eve, are you serious? You're can't just turn up at her door. Think about it, it's nearly thirty years ago, she probably won't remember and if she does what is it you think she'll be able to tell you? Chances are she doesn't speak English and you'll have a wasted journey. And that's another thing, how are you going to get to Brezno?'

'My flight out isn't until Sunday night. I'm looking online now. I can get from Krakow to Brezno by train. If I go out on the first one tomorrow morning I can be there by lunch time. It's no good trying to stop me Patrick; I really don't have a choice. If this is my only lead then I'll take it. I'll just have to figure out what to do when I get there. If you're right that my mother worked as a nurse in the same hospital then there just might be a chance that Olga will remember her. Believe me, at this stage the slimmest conceivable chance is better than none at all.'

'You can stand to get on a train again, after last time? Then I understand how much you want to find answers. I'll meet you in Brezno. The least I can do is translate for you. Consider it my consulate duty.'

'Patrick, I would never have asked you to go so far out of your way. You don't have to, you know. I've imposed so much already...'

'You don't strike me as someone foolish enough to turn down an offer of help when you need it.'

'I'm not and I won't. As long as you know how grateful I am and that if you change your mind over night, I'll understand.'

'Keep your mobile with you and switched on. Text me the time of the train you're getting and I'll meet you at Brezno station. Don't take any risks or go off on your own, okay? Slovakia is a wonderful country but off the beaten track people can be mistrustful of strangers.'

'I hear you.'

'See you tomorrow. Just don't get your hopes up too high.'

Even I couldn't believe that I was getting on a train that would take me back through the Tatra Mountains after my last experience. The only way I can explain it is that I felt as if I were being driven by something I couldn't control. If I were advising a friend in my position I'd have been on a plane to drag them home. For precisely that reason I avoided phoning Naomi or Nate to let them know what was going on. This was a task best undertaken without pause. The thought made me look at my watch. As distracted as I was, I had other duties in Krakow requiring my attention.

I slipped on my suit jacket and ran a brush through my hair. This time tomorrow I would be in Brezno. One step closer to resolution. Whether that was the same thing as finding peace of mind I didn't know. Then I did the thing I've always been able to do so effectively. I closed the door on one set of thoughts and opened another. This afternoon had to be about Albert Cornish, not me. I picked up my brief, a pen and started the short walk to the Dragon's Cave.

As I approached I could see that Marcus had already arrived and was stood with the photographer. As I joined the group two security guards introduced themselves.

Marcus was deep in conversation. The photographer was snapping away at the entrance to the cave by which Albert and Angela had entered. I could see a door with large padlocks, so prominent that it would have been near impossible to have neglected to secure it. One of the security guards had been on duty that night and remained on the scene with the police. The other was his superior, keen to ensure that no blame was laid at their door. We were told that the cave was closed to the public for the afternoon so that we could visit uninterrupted, but left in no doubt that our visit wasn't particularly welcomed. They could obviously do without this sort of publicity. The Judge turned up with a court clerk in tow to make notes and we ventured down the steep slope into the body of the cave.

I'd been here before but was interested to see the reactions of the others. Marcus made a great play of how easy it was to get down the stone pathway by scarcely touching the guide rope next to him then slipped and landed on his backside. I leaned over to help him up but he saw the smile on my face before I could hide it and brushed my hand away.

'Steep isn't it?' I said.

'It's fine. I just missed my footing, that's all.' He disappeared off ahead. From a little way behind I was pleased to hear the Judge muttering that he couldn't believe no-one had broken their neck coming down here late at night, especially whilst drunk. What can have been going through Angela Smyth's mind? Even with people I knew and trusted, I wouldn't have done anything so foolhardy in a foreign country at night. When I'd asked the guard if music was played in the cave he'd looked at me as if I were an idiot. Perhaps that had been part of Albert's drunken imaginings, but if the music hadn't been real then maybe he'd been wrong about other parts of his story, too.

The photographer covered every inch of the caverns including ground shots of exactly where the rape was said to have happened. The floor was rough and sharp in places. I commented on it mildly to the Judge whilst Marcus was busy telling the photographer what a perfect place it was to commit an assault without witnesses. I couldn't argue with that although I thought it was a fairly inconvenient place if you were blind drunk in the dark. I was managing to keep my temper with Marcus until he stepped over a line and started suggesting alternative ways the attack might have happened.

'Of course, the victim may have been hit on the head which would explain why she was so compliant. Quite often head injuries and concussion aren't diagnosed, in my experience.'

'Marcus, this isn't the trial and you're not here to make up stories to suit your case. Stop trying to influence the Judge when we're not even in the Courtroom.' I snapped.

'I'm simply considering all the possibilities. You can close your eyes to the fact that a rape happened at all, if that's what helps you believe your client is innocent.'

'We're on a site visit. This isn't the time or place for your speeches.' I was suddenly furious. I wanted out of that claustrophobic cave and some natural light. More than that, I wanted to be out of the loathsome company of Marcus Brandt who was much too close for my liking. The Judge walked between us.

'Miss MacKenzie, if you don't mind the 'Judge' is standing right here so you can address me in person. And Mr Brandt, she is quite right. You are not here to make speeches, just to look around and point out anything specific you will refer to at the trial. Now, if you've both quite finished I think I've seen enough. Does anyone want to add anything to the points already raised? No? Then I'm going back to my hotel to write up my notes. Let security know when you've finished.' He was obviously feeling as uncomfortable as me. The Judge made his way back to the exit and I saw him taking one last look around before starting the climb to the outside.

Marcus and I were both quiet for a few moments, soaking up our reprimand. In the silence I thought I could hear sounds coming from the very furthest corner of the cave. Without speaking to Marcus I began to make my way deeper into the gloom. As I stepped beyond the reach of the lighting and into a tiny nook in the rock I heard noises again. It sounded like drumming, rhythmic and soft. I put my hands on the stone to see if I could feel any vibrations. The music seemed to getting louder, as if it were approaching through the walls.

'Looking for divine inspiration?' Marcus was directly behind me and I had nowhere to go but to shrink into the wall face first.

'Get away from me Marcus, group visit is over.'

'I don't think so, not just yet. I want to look at whatever you're looking at. See what little gems you think you're going to come up with a trial. Romantic, isn't it? You can just imagine the two of them down here fooling around.'

'I'm not sure who was fooling around down here but it wasn't my client. You've read his interview. He says there was another man. Did you even try to investigate that or would it make things a little too complex for you to deal with?'

'Angela doesn't mention the other man and I think she'd remember, don't you? Or maybe you're right. Perhaps it started out as a threesome and she was too embarrassed to admit it. Maybe your client got jealous about having to share, sent this other man packing and decided to show her who was boss.'

'I think you need to get some air, you seem to be getting a bit over excited.' I tried to push past but I was in a corner with a wall behind me and Marcus in front. 'Marcus, get out of my way.'

'Now, that's not very polite is it? Although it's probably exactly what the victim was saying to your client just before he pushed her to the floor.' He took another step towards me and I instinctively shrank closer against the wall.

'Marcus, whatever game you're playing it needs to stop right now. This is beneath even you. One last chance, get out of my way or I'll start shouting for security.'

'I think Angela Smyth found out that the sound of screaming doesn't reach the surface when you're all the way at the back of the cave here.' As he said it he put one foot between my two and pushed his knee against the wall so that I couldn't move left or right. 'I never know why women barristers defend rapists. I have a theory it's because they find it secretly exciting, the thought of what the man next to them is capable of. Is that it, Eve? Does the thought of man forcing himself inside you get you off?'

I did the only thing I could think of and kneed him in the groin. Unfortunately, because of the way my feet were spread, it didn't do as much damage as I wanted and he was able to grab my ankle as I tried to run. He was stronger than he looked for his height and easily a match for me. He launched himself on top of me where I was scrabbling to get up, put one forearm across my throat and with his other hand ripped at the front of my shirt. I struggled to breathe and started seeing stars. His whole body weight was bearing down on me and I couldn't move.

'Marcus, please, this isn't you. Don't do it, you'll hate yourself.' I started sobbing. 'Please stop, Marcus, please stop.' His hands were inside my bra now, hurting me and laughing, pressing his face into mine. He was grinding his crutch into mine and his pathetic grunting and thrusting at me was repulsive. He moved his hand down to his trousers and pulled desperately at his zip. I forgot trying to plead with him and did the one thing I knew he wouldn't be able to stand and spat in his face. I didn't care about consequences. He wasn't going to stop. He pulled his lips back from his teeth in anger and snarled like a rabid animal, opening his jaws as if preparing to bite. Then a voice shouted from the entrance of the cave. A torch was flashing in the distance. Marcus had already rolled off me and my eyes began to focus again as I got some oxygen. Footsteps were coming closer and Marcus was on his feet desperately trying to pull himself together. As the security guard rounded the bend into the cavern he saw me on the floor and ran to help. I pulled my shirt together, winded and unable to speak.

'She fell over,' panted Marcus. 'I was about to come and get help. I couldn't move her.'

'You need an ambulance?' the guard said.

'No, I just need to get out of here,' I whispered and gratefully accepted the offer of his arm. Marcus came along behind us, repeating over and over that there was nothing he could do. When we were up and out of the cave I collapsed onto the grass. The guard had run to get some water and a first aid kit.

'Eve, I don't know what happened. I'm sorry. That just wasn't me. You have to believe me. What are you going to do? Eve, listen to reason…'

'I'm not going to do anything Marcus. It's your word against mine and I know how manipulative you are. But come near me again, touch me, walk into a room with me unless there are other people present and I will end your career. You hear me? Now get away from me. I don't want to see or hear from you until we're next in court.' He acknowledged the warning and half walked, half ran away.

The guard sat down with me as I drank some water and dabbed antiseptic wipes on the scratches to my face, hands and chest.

'You ripped your shirt like that just falling down?' he asked. I didn't feel a need to be too convincing.

'I'll be ok.' I said. 'You don't need to worry.' He waited while I had a drink before speaking again.

'There is a story that the cave is cursed, you know?' I stared at him.

'Tell me.' I said.

'The story goes that after Prince Krak killed the dragon, his daughter was pursued by a knight trying to win her hand in marriage. He proposed to her down there in the Dragon's Cave. The Princess did not accept and the knight was enraged. He is said to have forced himself upon her so that she could not marry anyone else but left open the offer of marriage as he wanted to acquire the wealth of her father's lands. Rather than marry him she ran from the cave and threw herself into the Vistula River where she drowned. You are not the first woman I have seen come out of that cave shaken and injured, followed by a man looking as ashamed as your companion did.' He poured me some more water. 'Are you sure I cannot call someone for you?'

'Have there been other reports of assaults down there?' I asked.

'No case ever went to court, not since I've been working here.' He looked as if he regretted starting to speak with me.

'No, but what about complaints or incidents. Have the police ever been called?'

'We're not supposed to talk about it. We rely on the tourist trade, here.'

'I don't want to bring you any bad publicity and I certainly couldn't use it in court but it might just help me reason with the prosecutor. That's the man in the cave with me, you understand?'

'There are security logs. After my shift I may be able to copy some of the papers but it will not be until late tonight.'

'That's fine. I don't want you to do anything that could get you into trouble, though. Can I meet you somewhere to get the files?'

'I can drop them at your hotel. It's better no-one sees you here again today or they might think something is wrong.'

'I understand. I'm staying at the Copernicus. You know where that is?' he nodded. 'My name is Eve Mackenzie. Here's my card.' I slipped my details out of my wallet. 'If you don't mind my asking, why are you helping me?'

'The soldier, your client, I was with the police when they went down into the cave. He had no idea what was happening. I could see it in his face. I don't go down into that cave alone with women, Miss MacKenzie, none of us guards do. You don't play with fire. I feel sorry for him. He seemed like a good enough man.'

'He is. Thank you. I'll be alright now. I can get back to my hotel.' He dipped his hat at me and went off about his duties. I did my best to look normal and started back to my room to get cleaned up.

When I got in I locked and bolted my door, pushing a heavy chair under the handle. It wasn't that I thought anyone was actually going to try to get in, it just made me feel better so that I could go and scrub away the feeling of Marcus's hands on my flesh. There were no injuries except for the abrasions where I'd scraped the stone floor. At least I knew first hand that my concern about the lack of marks on Angela's body were well founded. It seemed like a high price to pay to be proved right. I thought about Marcus's reaction when he'd come out of the cave; there was genuine horror on his face. If I'd thought any differently I wouldn't have hesitated to call the police. He might be odious but I never had him pegged as the sort of man who'd behave like that. It was as if he'd been possessed. I hated even to think something so superstitious, but possessed was the only word for it. I'm not prone to hysteria or paranoia but the face and voice of the monster who had me pinned to the floor in no way resembled the man I'd known for the last five years. I believed it when he said that it just wasn't him.

As tempting as it was, I wasn't going to sit around feeling sorry for myself. I had no sense of continuing threat and suspected the person suffering real anguish tonight was Marcus. Reception would hold the files from the security guard when he turned up.

There was no doubt that Perun was the person I needed to find to answer my questions so when I'd caught up with my emails, I went back out into the city. I made my way to the New World Bar where Perun had found me last night. It was virtually empty and remained that way for the hour I sat drinking. In the end, after sipping another beer until I had no excuse to stay any longer, I rose to leave. A bar tender caught my eye as I stood and came over.

'You Eve?' I was taken aback by the Australian accent, then nodded. 'A man left something for you.' He reached below the counter from where he pulled a large envelope. It was light and had no writing or markings on the outside. I made no attempt to open it.

'I've been sitting there an hour and a half. Why didn't you give it to me earlier?' I couldn't hide the irritation in my voice.

'He asked me to wait until you were leaving, said you wouldn't be in a rush. We're a bar, not a post office, lady.' He tutted at me, understandably given my failure to say thanks, and went off to serve someone else. Feeling guilty, I left a larger tip than usual and left. I walked slowly, checking to see if I was being followed, but that was wishful thinking. It was my night for envelopes; the security guard had dropped off the papers as promised. I took them both up to my room with a nightcap of Lagavulin whisky from the hotel bar.

I unlocked my room, threw the envelopes onto the coffee table and kicked off my shoes. Lagavulin is my thinking drink. I keep a secret bottle stashed in my flat. Whilst I don't touch it often, when I do I consider it a sin to toss it back without appreciating the art that went into distilling it. I swirled the whisky round in the tumbler and stared at the envelope. What was I doing, collecting furtive evidence from a story about a haunted cave and sitting alone in bars trying to catch a glimpse of a man I didn't know? My sensible voice (it always sounded vaguely like my first teacher) was telling me not to open the envelopes. It even suggested I should just rip them up, put them in the bin and go back to life as I knew it a month ago. Fight Albert's case on the evidence presented by the prosecution, no more wild goose chases and ghost stories. Perun is just an exotic man in a foreign bar playing games. Coincidences are just that, stop reading too much into everything. Go to bed. Go back to England. Go home.

And so, of course, I did what any self-respecting woman would do. I picked up the first envelope, a letter opener from the drawer and slowly sliced it open. It was the file copies of incidents from the Dragon's Cave. There were more than I'd expected. Mainly made up from the security officers' incident logs, but also some letters from the police, I could see that the guard had highlighted at least fifteen different names and dates over the last three years. I needed to get the file translated for it to be any use in negotiating with Marcus.

I held the second envelope for some time as I sipped the remaining whisky. Perun had been so sure I'd turn up. What if I hadn't? I suspected he'd have found some other way of finding me.

Whatever was in the envelope, it was something he had his own reasons for wanting me to see. If it were just to help me, he'd have asked the bartender to give it to me when I first walked in. It was all part of a much larger game and I had no idea what the rules of engagement were. Having tortured myself enough with anticipation I opened it.

Inside were two documents. There was a note, handwritten in English. It said simply, 'A gift to help you on your way to Brezno.' The gift was a photograph. It was A4 size and looked as if it had been taken without the subject knowing she was being filmed. The shot was a close-up of a woman's head and shoulders in black and white. She was turning profile, I imagined her looking round at someone next to her as her face was animated, her mouth open in mid-speech. She was in her early forties, with dark shoulder length hair, dressed in a simple shirt, no hat, glasses or jewellery. I couldn't even use the surroundings to guess the place or the year of the photo. Whilst I had no way of being sure, it was a fair bet that this was Adela Karas, my birth mother. Why else would I need it for Brezno? Perun knew where I was going and why. It had been one hell of a day. I left the debris from the envelopes where it had fallen, took the photograph without even realising it was still in my hand, and went to bed.

Ten

Saturday morning I was up before daylight. I packed what papers I had together with the photo and a change of clothes. It was going to be a very long day indeed.

Aboard the train to Brezno I panicked before I'd even taken my seat, got off the train again and stood on the platform staring at the carriages. Having first thought that I could overcome my fear it was apparent I may have overestimated my own courage. I felt sick. All I wanted to do was turn round, go back to my hotel and get into bed. People were jostling past me to get on board and the guard strode down the platform slamming doors as he came. I took a step back. As he reached to shut the door in front of me I felt the relief of resignation and started to walk back up the platform towards the exit when my empty hands reminded me I'd left my bag on the train. I didn't care what else I lost, nothing mattered but the photo. It was all I had in the world that might lead me to Adela Karas. I wrenched open the nearest door as the whistle blew and the train's engine fired up. The guard was shouting at me at the top of his voice as I ran with the train, jumping on as it picked up speed. I slammed the door and collapsed against the wall. In a few moments I rose and walked, shaking with adrenalin, to where I'd stowed my bag, found it untouched and sank gratefully into the seat.

The journey was unpleasant because of the memories it brought but uneventful in every other way. No one spoke to me or asked to see my ticket. No one sat next to me or glanced at the photo in front of me that I stared at for almost two hours. The trees outside were calm and motionless, without so much as the wind rustling the leaves. Apparently, this time, Slovakia had decided that I was welcome to visit. When the train pulled into Brezno I tried to get to my feet, only to realise that my hands were still gripping the arm rests. I don't think I'd moved them for the entire journey. I relaxed my fingers and willed myself to let go. Even so, I never wanted to board another train as long as I lived. My courage was spent.

Seeing Patrick's smiling face as I walked through the concourse was the most welcome thing imaginable. For someone I'd only met once he'd certainly gained an extraordinary importance in my life. My steps quickened and by the time I reached him I was all but running. I put my arms around his neck and held on for dear life.

'Patrick, thank heaven you're here. Sorry, I'm just a bit unnerved.'

'Don't apologise. I wasn't expecting you to enjoy the journey. Come on, my car's out front. We'll stop and get you coffee on the way.' Patrick kissed me on the cheek and took the bag from my hands. 'Even under these circumstances, I'm very pleased to see you again. It's about a twenty minute drive. You're sure you want to do this? It might be a terrible disappointment.'

'I'm here now, and I have to do something to make that journey worthwhile, even if it's only finding a dead end. I appreciate this more than you know. You must think I'm crazy.'

'Not at all. I think you're very brave and I believe that being slightly crazy is tremendously helpful in life. Let's get on with this then, shall we?' We pulled away at a speed I wasn't expecting. He might be as mild mannered as a puppy but behind the wheel he was a tearaway teenager. It didn't take us long to reach the outer suburbs of the town. We found the block of apartments easily enough but it took some time to figure out the system of numbering of the flats. I gave a hard knock and stepped back waiting for it to be answered. Patrick said nothing but gave my hand a reassuring squeeze. There was no movement for some time until at last the door opened a crack.

'Olga Hornik?' I asked.

The woman behind the door said something I couldn't understand and then pulled the door open further. My heart sank. The face I saw was no more than 50 years old, clearly not Olga. Of course it couldn't be that easy. Patrick stepped forward and began speaking rapidly in Slovakian, showing his identity papers from the embassy. The two of them continued to speak, the woman glancing at me occasionally. Eventually she walked away but left the door ajar and another voice could be heard in the far rooms of the apartment. When she returned there was a much older lady holding her arm for support. We were ushered in.

'Patrick, what was all that about?' I asked.

'That was Olga's daughter. She just wanted to make sure who we are. I told her you're after some information about an old work colleague of her mother's. How much detail you want to give is up to you. From here on in I'm just the translator.' Olga's daughter settled the older woman in a chair and moved cushions around to get her comfortable. Whilst she was frail, the alertness in her eyes showed she hadn't succumbed to any sort of dementia. Patrick translated as we talked. It was difficult at first until I got into the pattern of speaking in short sentences and waiting for Patrick to do his bit.

'Miss Hornik, my name is MacKenzie. I'm sorry that we couldn't let you know we were coming but there was no telephone number. I'm trying to find information about someone who used to work at the hospital in Brezno where you were a midwife. Is that right?'

'That's right, thirty-two years in the same ward at the same hospital. I've lost count of the number of babies I delivered.' Her voice was raspy and quiet but her eyes never left mine, even when it was Patrick speaking to her. 'You look pale, child. My daughter will make us some tea.' Her daughter, obviously concerned not to leave her mother alone with strangers, hovered for a few more moments until her mother shooed her from the room. 'Now tell me, what is so important that you have come all this way?'

'Adela Karas. She was a nurse at the hospital at the same time you worked there. We found documents naming you as the midwife who delivered her baby. I know it's a long time ago but I just wondered if by any chance you remembered her?'

She stared out of the window and I wondered if she would recall much at all from so long ago. I felt foolish suddenly, bothering this elderly woman with no real reason to believe she could help.

'Why do you want to know? Is it because of the adoption? It was very hard for Adela, you know, but we all understood why she did it.'

The room span for a second. 'So you did know her. Can you remember much about what happened?'

'I am old, not senile, dear. I remember everything. Adela was forty when she got pregnant. She had been working at the hospital for about ten years. I knew her well enough to say hello and talk about the weather. We were not close friends but then we worked in different disciplines. She was a specialist nurse working with Parkinson's disease patients.' If nothing else, I had learned something about my mother from this visit. It felt like a gift from the Gods, just that tiny bit of information.

'Did you ever meet her husband, Branimir?' I was curious about my father if only because of the way things had ended.

'I saw him sometimes; he would drive to pick her up after late shifts. If we were finishing at the same time we would sometimes walk out together. I knew that they were desperate to have children. Adela was so happy when she got pregnant, they had been trying for many years. She was much older than most of the mothers I looked after back then. These days it's more common to have older women pregnant for the first time. I got to know her much better during her term. I suppose you could say we became friends.'

'What happened at the birth?' I felt a growing sense of excitement. This was more than I had hoped for. Not just a vague memory of my mother but someone who really knew her. My face must have been flushed because Patrick raised his eyebrows at me enquiringly. I smiled at him reassuringly. Olga's daughter came back with a tray of strong black tea. Patrick paused while he sipped his politely and Olga took a drink to soothe her throat. I could hardly bear to wait for the rest of the story and only touched the tea to my lips before setting it down and leaning forward to encourage Olga to continue.

'Don't you know that from the adoption papers? I assumed that you would have known the rest.' Olga looked ill at ease suddenly and put her tea down.

'I just wondered what happened to Adela after she had the baby. We know that she had a little girl, named Eve, on 21 March

1983 and that the baby was adopted a few months later. There are no records other than that.' I kept my voice soft, afraid that Olga was changing her mind about talking to me. I had still not told her that the baby was me. I didn't want to stop her from telling me the story exactly as it had happened in case she tried to spare me any of the details. I fully intended to tell her the whole truth at the end.

'Eve? Well, it was a baby girl and I'm sure the date you have must be right. But in the week Adela was there recuperating she only ever called the child Zora. Such a beautiful name! It means sunrise. That's the only time I spoke to Branimir, when he was visiting her and the baby. They had chosen the name months in advance, if it was a girl. Back then there was no way of finding out in advance, no scans until a couple of years later. They must have changed their minds about the name later. Adela was physically well after the birth but she was worried about Branimir. He reacted badly, you see. They had both been so excited all the way through the pregnancy and then Branimir didn't cope at all well after the birth. She left the hospital with the baby and I never saw her in person again. We knew she wanted to stop working and look after the baby, they were sure it would be their only one. Then we heard about the adoption and there were rumours that Branimir had taken the whole thing very badly.'

'He ended up in an asylum and died there soon afterwards, I know about that already.' I said. 'But we can't find any records for Adela. Do you know what happened to her?'

'It was all anyone talked about at the hospital for a long time. We heard nothing, you understand, for several months. I knew about the adoption but only because I was her midwife. After Branimir's death she must have wanted to get as far away as possible. Adela had been treating a patient on a regular basis and developed a very close relationship with her. The patient was a woman, about ten years younger than Adela, diagnosed with Parkinson's just as her career was taking off. Adela talked about her often when she was pregnant; she was an actress you see, Sabina Roman. She had just been discovered by an agent who saw her in a play in Budapest whilst he was on holiday. The Parkinson's was the only thing in Sabina's way and Adela was an excellent nurse who understood how to minimise the symptoms. When Sabina moved to America she asked Adela to go with her as her private nurse. I can only guess that with both the baby and Branimir gone she had no reason to stay here. As far as I know Adela never set foot in Slovakia again.'

'She's in America.' I breathed out. 'Oh thank you, thank you so much. You've been more help than you could ever know. I should have told you when I came in, but I'm looking for Adela Karas because I was the baby you delivered to her twenty-seven years ago.' I smiled into her eyes at the revelation but there was no reaction, only garbled Slovakian and Patrick repeating the same thing over and over.

'Patrick, what is it? What's wrong?'

'She's saying something I can't understand. It's a term I'm not familiar with. Just hold on, I need to make sure I'm getting this right.'

Patrick asked a few more questions and there was much gesticulation and raised voices. Eventually Patrick turned to me and for the first time Olga did not meet my eyes.

'She says you can't be the baby Adela gave birth to. She believes the reason Adela gave the baby up for adoption was because Branimir rejected her when she was diagnosed with Down's syndrome. Back then around here people still thought that babies born with disabilities were cursed and her life expectancy was low. Olga thinks that Branimir couldn't cope and forced Adela to give the baby up for adoption. I'm sorry.'

I stood up. 'Patrick, tell her she's wrong. I have all the papers. It doesn't make any sense. Adela Karas was my mother.' I suddenly remembered the photo left for me by Perun. I grabbed it out of my bag and thrust it towards Olga.

'This is her, isn't it? This is Adela?' Patrick looked at me, confused. Olga spoke to him again.

'She says that is a picture of Sabina Roman, the actress Adela went to the States with. Where did you get it Eve? How did you know?'

'A man gave it to me. He knows a lot more than I do, apparently. I don't know what's going on Patrick. Someone somewhere has made a terrible mistake. I'm never going to find out who my mother is, am I?' Patrick put his arms around me.

'We'll find out. I promise I'll do all I can to help. We'd better go.' He thanked Olga and her daughter. Olga patted my hand as I said goodbye but she looked like she'd seen a ghost. Patrick put an arm round my waist and led me back down to the car.

He didn't bother asking me what I wanted to do; he just started to drive as I stared out of the window. I could feel absolutely nothing. No grief, no anger, just a great black void. In some respects it was the most calm I had felt since the death of the woman I had always thought of as my mother. I held onto the emptiness as long as I could until finally Patrick had to ask where I wanted to go.

'Somewhere peaceful,' I said. 'Somewhere with space, alcohol and telephones I can take off the hook.' He took the next turn and soon we were headed up into the Tatra Mountains. We were driving north of Brezno and mile by mile the buildings slipped away leaving nothing but forest and rock. After a couple of hours I saw signs of a ski resort and Patrick pulled up in front of a large hotel called the Tri Studnicky. He came round to my side and opened my door, picking up my bag for me. I appreciated the small gesture and went to thank him but he held one finger to my lips.

'Don't. You don't need to say anything. You can have all the space you need here.' We walked into reception and I let Patrick sort everything out. After a few minutes a porter arrived and showed us to the top floor. I'd never arrived at a hotel with a man I barely knew, with no reservation and no luggage and I wondered what the staff must be thinking. Then I realised I really didn't care. Today, that was the very least of my concerns.

We were in a large suite and a roaring fire was already glowing in the hearth. The vaulted ceilings and wooden beams made it the most romantic getaway you could imagine. I felt as if I were wasting it, here only to hide and lick my wounds. Patrick was opening the bar and held an empty glass up to me.

'Whisky, please. No water, no ice.' He rummaged amongst the bottles, put a drink on the table in front of the hearth and pulled a chair up for me, close enough to feel the heat of the flames. I stretched out, comforted by the warmth and closed my eyes as I sipped my single malt. Patrick had a gin and tonic in hand, sat himself down and kicked off his shoes. The little gesture of familiarity made me relax. I was surprised that for the first time I could sit and watch the burning wood without feeling anxious.

'I've always been terrified of fire. An irrational childhood phobia, I was told. Funny, but I feel much less afraid now that I know it wasn't irrational at all.' Patrick took one of my feet in his hands and started to unzip the ankle boots I was wearing. At first I pulled my foot away but when I looked into Patrick's face and saw nothing but a desire to help, I leaned forward and slipped my boots off myself. He took my right foot in his hands and ran his fingers over the scarring, more red than usual in the flickering light.

'You remember nothing at all?'

'I would only have been a few months old. I've always felt a sense of panic near fire but I never knew why. Patrick, it doesn't make any sense. I must be the baby that Adela handed over. We've seen the adoption papers and my burns match the medical notes. She only had one baby and yet I can't be the child that Olga delivered at the hospital. What am I missing?'

'I don't know, Eve, it's not making any sense. The photo of Sabina Roman, where did that come from? You hadn't mentioned her before.'

'Something happened, when I was in Krakow, I didn't say anything because I had no idea who the man was.' I leaned against Patrick and told him everything, from the kiss on the train to finding the envelope at the bar. He said nothing as I spoke and I wondered if he was thinking the same thing as me; that maybe I was following my father's footsteps into insanity. Eventually we finished our drinks and I finished my story. Patrick stood up and glanced at the clock on the wall.

'It's getting late. You need to eat and rest. Let's get dinner. We can stay here tonight. I'll get a separate room so please don't think I'm going to try and take advantage of the situation.' He'd picked up the telephone to call reception before he'd even finished speaking. I walked behind him and put the receiver back down.

'Stay with me tonight, please? I could use the company. I need to know I'm not going crazy and I feel safe with you. There's plenty of space for us both.'

'Alright, but there's something I want to say first. I think you're beautiful. From the second I laid eyes on you I haven't been able to get you out of my mind. If I could take away the pain you're in and bear it myself, I would. Now, that's quite enough from me. Let's go down for dinner before I make even more of a fool of myself.'

I smiled and put my shoes back on. We ate at the hotel restaurant, making small talk about my legal practice and his life at the British Embassy. I thought how lonely he seemed as he talked about life here, parties and dinners with no plus one and no real friends. It made me aware how lucky I was having Naomi around for laughter, gossip or just quiet companionship. Not for very much longer, I realised. What would I have to go home to then?

We finished our meal and went back upstairs, feeling better after a hot meal and having told someone the story from start to finish. I had a long bath while Patrick made some calls to his office, then dressed in a robe and crashed out on the bed with my laptop. When Patrick had finished his own emails he came over.

'What are you looking at?' he asked.

'Sabina Roman. Now I feel like an idiot for not recognising the woman in the photo. I've seen her face loads of times, background roles in films, not many leads though. I never knew her name. She's sixty now and I can't find any new films she's made for years.'

'What about Adela Karas? Anything come up there?' We found nothing and I couldn't even be sure that Adela had stayed in the States. I'd had enough for one night, closed my laptop and settled down in the bed. Patrick did the same. We turned out all the lights and laid there just watching the flames fade into red-eyed embers.

I turned onto my side facing Patrick, one arm reached out to hold his hand. We whispered together in the dark like that, drifting into sleep.

'Perun called me Kukushka. Naomi says it translates as cuckoo. At least now I know what he really meant. I'm an impostor, moved from one home to the next.'

Patrick was half asleep. He spoke drowsily into my hair. 'Literally speaking it means cuckoo, but it's used in folklore here, children's stories. It means changeling. I'm sure it was just a reference to the colour of your hair and eyes. You do look a little, well, other-worldly. I don't know who Perun really is but you should stay away from him, he's playing games. Try to get some sleep.' He drifted off into his own dreams as I lay with my hand still in his, a chill seeping through my veins as if all my blood were draining from my body.

I waited as still as I could for about quarter of an hour so that I didn't disturb him then slipped out from under the covers to sit in front of the dying fire. I turned my laptop back on and half hid under a blanket to dim the light.

I recalled what Patrick had said about Slovakia being steeped in superstition and wondered if a mix up between babies at the hospital had sent Branimir Karas into madness. I'd loved to read fairy tales as a child and could recall plenty about human babies being swapped with fairies. What surprised me more was that my internet search brought up a real life account of a so-called changeling child.

Michael Cleary, an Irishman had been so convinced that his wife had been changed for a fairy that in 1895 he burned her to death. He was tried, convicted of manslaughter and served fifteen years in prison. Records suggested that twenty-five year old Bridget had become ill, probably with pneumonia, and Michael had refused to give her the medicine prescribed by a doctor he didn't trust. As Bridget failed to recover the priest had given communion and various family and friends helped care for her. On the night of Bridget's death at least nine people had been in their house. It was likely that fever had made her incoherent and Michael became increasingly insistent that she was a changeling and not his true wife. She'd had urine thrown over her and was laid before the fire to drive the spirit out. Eventually Michael threatened her with burning wood from the fireplace and her gown caught alight. He threw lamp oil over her and the burns she suffered led to her death that night. Her body was hidden in a shallow grave until its discovery some days later. Michael Cleary had always stuck to his story that immolating the changeling was a genuine attempt to get his wife back. Bridget Cleary was burned to death as part of some horrific folklore remedy.

I carried on my search for information and found that in mythology burning a changeling will make it fly away up the chimney and return the original child. I felt my feet prickle as I read on and had no doubt that Branimir Karas had believed the same thing as Michael Cleary. Two things were sure: One was that the sudden appearance of a baby without Down's syndrome had put Branimir into an asylum where he had ended his own life by setting fire to himself; the other was that Adela had put me up for adoption knowing I was not the same baby she had given birth to. At some point I knew that Branimir Karas had held my feet over a fire to immolate the changeling he believed had replaced his baby. It was the most dreadful thought, that a man could be so filled with fear or hatred that he would do such a thing and yet without the immolation, without the scars on my feet, I might never have known any of this. Adela must have known I wasn't her baby. If it had been a mistake at the hospital she would have simply taken me back. Finding Adela was my only chance of getting to the truth and Sabina Roman was the only way to Adela.

Perun knew more than he had told me but had his own reasons for wanting me to find out the rest myself. Olga had looked at me with something close to fear in her eyes as I left. I ran my hand along the healed arm where Perun had touched me. Folklore it might be but it was powerful enough for Branimir Karas to believe that burning a baby's feet could bring back a lost human soul. I believed that one person could heal another through touch. A week ago I'd have laughed at such stories. So what am I? A changeling? I bleed when I'm cut, cry when I'm sad. Yet I survived a train crash that killed everyone else on board and I heard music in the Dragon's Cave that brought a centuries old curse, if that's what it was, back to remind me that I could be hurt. Since my mother's death, fate had conspired to bring me to Slovakia. Whatever else I believed, I certainly no longer trusted coincidence. I also knew that running away from this wasn't an option. My trip home to England the next day would be brief. I had to find Sabina Roman.

The next morning Patrick drove me back to Krakow. Our stop at the hotel had taken us part way and he was happier to drive me than put me on another train. Without Patrick's help I'd have had no hope of resolution. As he dropped me to my hotel I asked him for just one further favour; to translate the file from the security guard at the Dragon's Cave and email it to me. He could see that something had changed but was dignified enough not to ask. He came to my room to collect the papers. As he went to leave I realised how little, nothing in fact, he had asked of me in return.

I walked to him and slid my arms around his neck. He didn't move, didn't speak. I pulled his head down to mine and I kissed him, long and hard on the mouth.

'Call me when you get back to England. I only wish I could have done more.'

'I promise to call you. You've done more than you could possibly know. I'm not sure why you did it but I can't tell you how grateful I am,' I said.

'I did it because I've never been able to resist helping a damsel in distress and you seem to be on a bit of a collision course at the moment. Try to keep on dodging the bullets won't you?' He picked up the envelope and left me to my packing.

Eleven

I got home late last night to find a note from Naomi. She and Tim had gone away for the weekend so she'd see me in chambers Monday afternoon. There was also a phone message from Nate welcoming me back. He was in Edinburgh on business but would be back Tuesday evening and wanted to catch up then. I could have pretended to myself that I felt guilty about kissing Patrick but my world was moving too fast to punish myself for one kiss. I sent Patrick an email to say I'd arrived home without incident then grabbed a couple of hours sleep before going in to work.

By the time I arrived in chambers Patrick had emailed me the translated security logs. I printed them out in the clerks room, put them in a sealed envelope marked 'Private - By Hand' and asked my junior clerk to run them round to Marcus Brandt a couple of lanes away in Middle Temple. I knew from Marcus' clerks that he was in chambers this morning and guessed that he'd read anything from me straight away after the events of the previous week. The files showed a number of incidents of odd behaviour from visitors leaving the Dragon's Cave. It was usually last thing in the afternoon, the final visitors to leave, a man and woman who'd stayed down there longer than expected. Often it was just the security guards noticing women looking distressed as they came out. Twice women had been seen fleeing with clothing ripped or out of place. Only once had a woman asked for the police to be called but there was no note of what happened after that. Even so, it would be hard for Marcus to ignore. I knew I wouldn't be able to use anything so vague in Court but I had no intention of letting it go that far. I was, however, about to do something which would probably end my career at the Bar if anyone found out. I wish I could say I was doing it for Albert's sake, but I wasn't. I was doing it for myself, so that I could leave without feeling guilty about handing the trial over to another barrister.

I left it a good hour and then sent Marcus a text telling him to meet me in The Devereux, a pub at the edge of the Temple busy enough to be safe and noisy enough for a whispered conversation not to be overheard. He replied almost immediately to confirm he'd be there. I walked across the courtyard and through the cobbled streets, ordered an orange juice and waited for Marcus to arrive. When he walked through the door I could tell he was back on his usual cocky form and hoped I wasn't making a very serious error of judgment.

'Marcus, can I get you a drink?' There was no harm in being polite and I needed him to stay around long enough to hear me out. This wasn't a conversation I could have on the phone just in case Marcus was feeling paranoid enough to record it.

'I thought you never wanted to see me again, or words to that effect, so no, I don't want a drink, thank you.'

'I think I said I never wanted to be alone with you again and we're hardly alone here, are we?' The pub was bustling with solicitors and barristers all celebrating victories or complaining about injustices. 'Sit down Marcus, this shouldn't take long. You received the documents?'

'Are you recording this?' he asked. Marcus obviously thought I was about to exact revenge for his assault. I suppose I was, but not in the way he was expecting.

'No, I'm not, and you don't need to say a word so even if I were recording it you wouldn't incriminate yourself. Now sit down and listen before I lose my patience.' He did sit down at that and I saw just how scared he was; Marcus doing as he was told was a very rare event indeed.

'I don't know what you think you're going to prove with those papers but it's all speculation and hearsay. You're wasting my time and your own. The fact that other women have come out of that cave looking dishevelled is irrelevant to this case.'

'How do you think I come to have those papers, Marcus?'

'I suppose they came from the security guard. Why?'

'Absolutely. From the security guard who came into the cave and found you leaning over me with my shirt ripped.'

'And how, exactly, is that relevant to the facts of this case?' I could see a vein pulsing below his left eye, beads of sweat appearing on his forehead.

'It's relevant because he and I had a long conversation when I came out of that cave. The fact that he produced those records for me proves what he thought you were doing to me. Why else would he have gone to so much trouble?' I sat back in my chair to put little distance between us. Marcus was silent for a moment as he considered his position.

'What exactly is it you want? Do you want to ruin my reputation out of spite? Or is it money? That's usually what it boils down to with women.' His fists were clenched and I wanted to get out of there as quickly as possible.

'I'm going to put this very simply and it’s non-negotiable. You're going to persuade the prosecution to drop the case against Albert Cornish. You're going to tell them that the victim's account doesn't make sense because she went willingly into the cave and has no external injuries on her body, which can't be right given the state of the ground. Basically, you're going to do whatever it takes to get this thing stopped straight away.'

‘You have no proof that I did anything to you in that bloody cave.'

'You're right, I don't, but whether anyone believes me or not the scandal alone would be enough to end any chance of you becoming a judge.'

'What else do you want?' I shrugged and held out my hands to show that I was finished. 'That's it? Are you stupid enough to believe you can get away with blackmailing someone in my position just to win a case? You must be getting more out of it than that.'

'You know what Marcus? You may not be able to see this but Cornish didn't rape Angela Smyth. I didn't just show you those files to get you to drop this case, I showed them to you so you could understand that something’s wrong down there. Or perhaps you were fully aware of what you were doing and had it planned all along?'

'You know that’s not true.' He hung his head and I saw remorse for the first time.

'Then drop the case. You have forty-eight hours. Phone my clerks when it's done and don't make the mistake of underestimating me, at the moment I have nothing to lose.' I walked out, my face burning red with anger. As I walked out it started to hail. The icy stones were big and they stung. The freezing cold helped me get my emotions under control before I got back to chambers. I shouldn't have let Marcus get to me like that; I was supposed to be the one holding all the cards. It was still a gamble. In his position I'd simply hand the case over to someone else to prosecute and hope my accuser didn’t have the nerve to go public. The truth is I would never tell anyone what happened, unable to face the media circus that would ensue. I could only hope that Marcus's ego was bigger than his brain. Time would tell.

A shriek from down the corridor broke my introspection as Naomi ran towards me full pelt and enveloped me in one of her hugs. It was more than welcome and I hugged her back as hard as I could.

'Careful, your arm,' she said, but I held up the castless limb and silenced her.

'All better, got it taken off early. Now, before you start asking questions, I'm starving. Come on, lunch, I'm buying.' I threw her coat off the stand and led her out of the door. We went to our favourite cafe on Fleet Street and talked wedding venues and bridesmaid dresses (she'd been terrifyingly busy in the last few days) until the food arrived. I tucked into my caesar salad and then Naomi couldn't hold it in any more.

'I know about Nate. I can't believe you didn't tell me! What sort of best friend are you? Okay, I do understand why, but I'm so excited!'

'You're hiding it well.'

'Oh, shut up. Tell me everything. I want all the gory details. Well, not all of them but most of them. Wow, my best friend and my fiancé's best friend, it's like...'

'A really, really bad romantic comedy?'

'Yes, exactly, I love those!' I couldn't help but giggle with her. Naomi's good moods are infectious; the last thing I wanted was to burst her bubble. We gossiped away the next hour talking about Nate and Tim. I knew I had to tell her something of what happened in Brezno. She'd never forgive me if I kept it from her for long. I explained that I'd been with Patrick to see Olga and that my mother had gone to the States with Sabina Roman. I didn't say anything about Perun, Marcus or the baby with Down's syndrome whose whereabouts was a complete mystery. I had a long road ahead of me and I didn't want Naomi fretting.

'The last press release I can find about Sabina says she does a lot of charity work in San Francisco. It's all I have. I can't find her agent, if she still has one, so I have no way of contacting her. I'm going out there, Naomi, I have to find out what happened to Adela Karas.'

'Maybe we could hire an investigator? Surely you don't need to go all that way.'

'I guess with some persistence I could probably get a message to her, but this is a conversation I want to have in person. It's something I just have to do, please say you understand.'

'Of course I understand, I'm just worried about you. It's not like you'll be gone for that long, is it?'

'Six months.' Naomi looked up from her coffee with an expression of disbelief. 'I know, but I've really thought about it. I'm taking some time out of chambers. I've lost my faith in what we do and the people we work with. Since mum died I've been feeling like I'm drifting and this has been the final nail in the coffin.'

'What will you do for six months though?'

'Travel around the States a bit, get some sun. I've got enough money from my inheritance to finance myself. We've already talked about me moving out so that you and Tim can get on with your life together. It makes sense.'

'Have you told Nate yet?'

'No, I'm seeing him tonight. I'm sorry Naomi but the time will go by in a flash. You've got a wedding to plan and I'm starting a whole new adventure.'

'You sure you're not just running away? You've had a dreadful time, I know that, but things will get better, they always do.' Naomi held my hand. She had tears running down her cheeks. I smiled and wiped them away with a napkin.

'There's nothing here for me to run away from. I don't know where I'll end up but I do know that I need to move on with my life instead of sitting around waiting for it to happen. You can come and visit me; you're due some time off. Promise you will.'

'Well, I suppose there are worse places to visit than San Francisco. Of course I'll come.' Naomi has always known when I've made up my mind and she quickly stopped trying to persuade me otherwise. We spent the remainder of the afternoon in chambers where I sorted out plans with my clerks and made a list of the things I needed to get in order.

When I got back to the flat there was a package waiting. Naomi and I opened it together as we always do when an unexpected surprise parcel arrives. Beneath the brown paper was a metal box. At first glance it looked unmarked but when I went into the bright light of the kitchen I could see tiny shallow engravings across the surface like waves. When I couldn't open it Naomi took a hold and slid the top off with her palm like you would an old fashioned wooden pencil box. Inside was the most beautiful locket I’ve ever seen.

Naomi whistled admiringly. 'Whoever sent you that means business, it’s stunning! Do you think it's from Nate?'

I knew it wasn't; it felt like another piece of a puzzle, designed to keep me guessing without giving away any information.

'I think it's from someone I met in Krakow. It looks Slavic.' The locket was old gold with a single, oval emerald in the middle and I slipped it over my head without thinking about it. It was obviously valuable, much heavier than it looked and in the mirror I could see the tiniest catch on one side. I pushed my thumbnail into it and the front of the locket sprang open. Inside, behind glass, was a lock of hair. It was deep cherry red, like mine. I closed it again before Naomi could start asking questions. I took it off to shower before Nate arrived, pushing the locket beneath my pillow for safe keeping. Perun was making sure I didn't lose my desire to follow the trail.

Tim and Nate arrived at the same time and we had a lovely evening chatting and eating the tapas Naomi had put together. I told them the legends of the dragon's cave in Krakow (leaving out the part about how I came by the information), Tim and Naomi talked wedding plans and we all managed to stay off any touchy subjects until Tim asked for honeymoon destination ideas. It obviously made Naomi think of San Francisco so she pretended tiredness and excused herself and Tim for the night. Nate wasn't fooled at all.

'Why do I get the feeling that Naomi was trying to get away as fast as possible?'

'Because she is the nicest person and therefore the worst liar I've ever met.' Nate laughed and we went through to the kitchen to put the kettle on.

'I missed you. You seem to have been gone for ages.' Nate pulled me into his arms. I returned his kiss but he knew I was holding back. 'So why don't I feel as if you've really come back yet?' he said.

'Because I've got to go away again and this time it's for much longer. If we pick up where we left off it'll be that much harder to leave. I'm sorry.'

'I don't want you to be sorry. I do want to understand, though. It's not anything to do with us?'

'God, no, please don't think that. I’ve found information about my birth mother and I can’t get it out of my head. I've decided to follow it up, see where it leads, clear my head if nothing else.'

'Will you come back?'

'I'm sure I will. My place in chambers will be waiting; I'm not burning any bridges. And I can't let Naomi choose her wedding dress on her own, can I? I hope you don't regret what happened between us. I know I don't.'

'Not for a second, I just wish the timing had been better. I'm a bit pissed off that the only interesting woman I've met this year has decided to go half way round the world after one date with me but in some ways I'm glad it's happened before things went any further.' He took his arms from around me and put his hands in his pockets. 'I don't know where I'll be when you're ready to come back.'

'I'm not asking you to wait.'

'I know that. But if you need me, if I can help, then I'll be here. And if in the mean time I meet the woman of my dreams then obviously it's your loss.' He said it with a smile and a wink. I knew he was letting me off lightly. 'It's late. I'd better go.' I didn't try to persuade him to stay, it would have made it worse. He kissed me on the cheek at the door. I had a fleeting sense that I was doing something incredibly ill-judged. Then he was gone and I was alone in the dark wondering if it would all be worth it. I was starting to think it may not be. I crept to bed, half hoping Naomi's door would open and she would sneak out to see what happened but there was no sign of her.

I'd forgotten the locket during the evening. When I climbed into bed and slid my hand under the pillow the metal was still warm. I put it around my neck and ran my fingers over the symbols engraved on the outside, shutting the clasp as my eyes grew heavy; it had been a day of ups and downs.

I knew I was dreaming. I could turn my head to look around but I couldn't feel my bare feet walking over the forest floor. My feet had no scars, they were pale and perfect. It can only have been a dream because in the real world I was too self-conscious to go barefoot anywhere. All at once there were other people running past me, laughing and shouting to one another. No-one noticed me. Either they couldn't see me at all or I wasn't strange enough for them to stop and stare.

I couldn't see Perun but his presence was all around me. Trees seemed to shift out of my way and were replaced by a moonlit lake. I drifted behind the backs of people sitting in small groups, painting each other's hands and weaving carved wooden beads into hair. They were preparing for some sort of festival and the atmosphere was charged with anticipation. Motionless at the edge of the lake was a woman on her own, staring into the still water. Her long hair, unbound, fell to her waist the colour of deeply polished cherry wood. I wanted to call out, make her turn round so I could see her face but I was scared of breaking the spell and losing the only sight of my mother that I might ever get.

'She misses you,' a voice, intimate and deep, spoke from behind me. I didn't need to turn to see who it was.

'Perun. Is she real?'

'Of course she's real. She's waiting for you to find her, she's been waiting forever. She feels the same pain you feel.'

'But this isn't real. This isn't the world I live in. Who are these people?'

'They are your people and they inhabit the same space as you. They are hidden from view most of the time because humans have closed their minds to anything different, anything wild, out of fear I suppose.'

'What about you? Why can I see you already?'

'You're not the same as the people around you. You felt me before you saw me, remember? You were already searching for something more than the little life you're living. You can see me because you were looking for me.'

I could hear ringing and tried desperately to ignore it; I didn't want to interrupt the dream. Perun had much more to tell me but he was already fading into the woodland. I spun round to catch one last glimpse of my mother and froze in place when I saw she was looking directly at me. She pressed one finger to her lips and held her other hand up to me, palm forwards. There was no mistaking the message: stay away, she was telling me, keep quiet and stay away. Finally the ringing of my mobile dragged me back to reality. With one hand still clutching my locket as it had when I fell asleep, I answered the phone.

'Miss MacKenzie, Tom here. I don't know how you did it but Mr Brandt has just called about the Cornish case. It seems the prosecution have decided to drop the charges. I've let your solicitors know.' I felt almost deflated, having expected more of a fight from Marcus. It shouldn't have been so easy. I felt sick at the thought that perhaps I'd been played in exactly the same way I'd played Marcus.

The dream had shaken me. I got the feeling that San Francisco was the last place in the world I ought to be going. I looked at the locket and thought of Naomi, Nate and the life I had here. It was an awful lot to throw away but here I was. Goodbyes had been said and I'd resorted to blackmail to free myself for the journey. Now, too late, it wasn't what I wanted at all. My courage was failing fast.

Twelve

I arrived at San Francisco International Airport in the middle of June to sunshine and balmy temperatures. I climbed into a cab and made my way to a hotel in the South of Market district, close enough to be able to walk to China Town or the waterfront and it wouldn't break the bank. The streets were clean and the buildings were beautifully kept. London looked shabby by comparison. I was struck by how friendly people were and the slower pace of life. I spent the first few days acclimatising and wandering the streets in tourist bliss, from the Golden Gate Bridge and Alcatraz Island to the Museum of Modern Art and Fisherman's Wharf. It was easy to see why so many people named this their favourite city.

On the fifth day it started to rain which I took as a sign to start what I came here for. Armed only with the photo of Sabina Roman, I made my way over to the New Main Library on Grove Street. It took me half a day to find my way around and scroll through press releases but finally I came across some useful information. The last agent on record for Sabina was Solomon's in Geary Street. The rain was still pouring down and it was hard to find the building number. Eventually I found the address although there was no sign for Solomon's outside. I did my best to smooth down my dripping hair as I walked up and down the stairs looking for help and finally found the Pinnacle Talent Consultancy. It was hardly a surprise to find two theatrical agencies in the same building. Geary Street is the theatre district and every agent in town with a big enough budget to pay the rent has set up shop here. I walked in and tried to sound professional to the perfectly made-up receptionist.

'Sorry to bother you, I'm looking for an agency called Solomon's. It's supposed to be in this building. Can you help?'

'This is the Pinnacle Consultancy. Not Solomon's. You've come in the wrong door.'

'Yes, I know,' I smiled and tried again. 'I can't find Solomon's and wondered if you knew which floor it's on.'

'It's not on this floor. Hold please.' She answered a call as I waited. She was the first less than helpful person I'd encountered here. Perhaps it was the pressure of rubbing shoulders with all those stars, but it certainly didn't bode well for getting anything out of Sabina. She typed for a few moments after finishing the call. 'Is there something else I can help you with?' She raised her eyebrows at me. I'd have one last try.

'Yes, I was saying that Solomon's is supposed to be in this building. If I'm in the wrong place perhaps there's a directory where I could find the right address.'

'I've never heard of an agency called Solomon's anywhere around here so I don't think the directory will help.'

'A current one certainly won't. If you've got this address then your information is out of date, young lady.' I turned round to find an older gentleman, cane in hand and sporting a well-trimmed white beard looking me up and down. 'Solomon's didn't take on any new talent for years before they closed down, so you'd have been out of luck trying to find an agent anyway.'

'Oh no, I'm not trying to find an agent.' I remembered my manners and offered my hand to him. 'I'm Eve MacKenzie. Nice to meet you.'

'Daniel Fortune. What a pleasure to see a young woman who has mastered the art of a good firm handshake. Come into my office, Ms MacKenzie. You look like you need to dry off and I'm a sucker for an English accent. Paris, bring some strong, hot coffee would you please? None of that trash from the machine.'

Paris managed to smile obligingly and look completely pissed off at the same time. I bustled after the man striding ahead of me through the heavy glass doors separating the important from lesser mortals. Daniel stood aside and ushered me into his office. He reminded me of the archetypal southern gentleman from the old black and white movies I watched as a child. I put down my coat and settled into the oversized sofa he motioned towards. Paris was just a couple of minutes behind us with the coffee and I sipped mine gratefully whilst Daniel got himself settled.

'So,' he said as he sat himself across a table from me. 'It's been a long time since I heard anyone looking for Solomon's. What's your story?'

'I'm looking for Sabina Roman. From what I can find, Solomon's was the last agent representing her.'

'Are you a journalist? Only I'd best warn you now that people in this business are mighty protective of their privacy.'

'No, no, nothing like that. She was a friend of my mother's, I think. I'm trying to put together a bit of history. Do you know where I can find her?'

'Well, Solomon's shut up shop some four years ago. Talent changes faster than fashion and all the names on the books at the time slowly fell out of the public eye. New agencies spring up all the time, younger people, throwing ever more elaborate parties. Three of us partners from Solomon's held onto the scraps, joined forces with some up and coming agents and started again.'

'You were part of Solomon's?' he nodded. 'So is Sabina still on the books here?'

'I'm afraid not. She stopped doing any film or television work more than a decade ago. You know about her illness?'

'The Parkinson's, yes.'

'She kept it a great secret for years, exercised, took every medication or therapy going and never went out in public if she was having a bad day. Eventually she knew that she was shaking visibly on camera and couldn't handle the close-ups. She withdrew from any type of work where her condition was obvious. It was a damned shame if you ask me, she was a great actress.'

'I don't suppose you have any idea where I can find her now do you?'

'I don't have an address for her, if that's what you want and I couldn't give it to you even if I did.'

'I understand and you've been more than helpful already Mr Fortune.' I stood to leave. 'Thank you for the coffee, I'll let you get on with your work.' I held out my hand again to wish him well and he took mine in his own but didn't let go.

'You sure you're not looking for an agent? You have the looks and the voice to get you into any audition you want. Take it from someone who's been around long enough to know.'

'I've never tried to act; I suspect it's harder than it looks. I'd better stick to what I know I'm good at.'

'It's the people who have to try hard who are no good at acting, the real art is in not trying at all. I haven't seen Sabina for years but rumour has it she lives down Carmel way. Last I heard she was working with the Pacific Repertory company down there. I hope you find what you're looking for, Eve MacKenzie. Here's my card if you change your mind.' He finally dropped my hand and replaced his grip with a small business card. I put it in my pocket and gave him a grateful grin.

'Thank you so much. I wish I could repay the favour although I doubt I'll be in San Francisco long enough for that.'

'Oh, don't be too sure, this place gets into the blood. You take care now and if you find Sabina tell her I haven't given up hope she'll go out on that date with me. I must have asked her out about a hundred times; she always said it was bad timing!' He opened the door for me and inclined his head in a farewell gesture.

'Well, I'll pass that on, Mr Fortune and I'll tell her I think she was a fool for missing out on a man like you.' I could hear him laughing as he closed his door. The rain had stopped although fog had descended on the city. I went back to my hotel to change for dinner and decided to celebrate this small step forward with dinner in Chinatown.

I put on a cotton wrap dress, tied at the hip, and walked out into the dusk air. With the fog across the bay the air was a hazy pink colour, almost aglow. Rather than waste such a beautiful night by walking north straight through the city I chose to go eastwards to the seafront and wander up the Embarcadero around the edge of the bay. It has stunning architecture on one side and an expanse of water the other, rippling with the colours of the melting sun. As I walked further north around the bay I felt the uncomfortable sensation of being watched but saw no-one and heard no footsteps behind me. When I finally decided on a restaurant, I took a seat in the window to watch the world go by.

This time when Perun took his seat beside me it was hardly surprising at all and even the shiver that ran down my spine was familiar. He didn't bother with an explanation, just sat and watched me pick up my glass to drain the contents. He was looking devastating in a white shirt and black jeans. When he walked between the tables to reach mine I could see women openly staring at him. He didn't bother returning their admiring glances; I think he just took the attention as read. Yet I still couldn't call him good-looking. He had none of those dimensions of a face that tells stories or shows humour, no laughter lines, no battle scars. Just endless perfection and it made him close to bland.

'I wasn't expecting to bump into you in San Francisco.'

'Of course you were. I was following you before, I know you felt it. Why didn't you wait?'

'Because in my experience you show yourself when you want to and not when I want you to. I can take care of myself without a bodyguard, thank you, if that's what you were doing.' I raised my hand to the waiter to request a refill. Perun was already pouring himself ice-water. 'Thank you for the photo, I guess the fact that you're here means that you know what I found in Brezno. I'm a bit tired of the games, Perun. I don't want to play anymore. Why didn't you just tell me what you knew?'

'You wouldn't have believed it from me. You needed to make the journey yourself.'

'I don't need a life coach, thank you. Why are you here?' Perun held my face with his hand and pulled my head slightly towards him so that we were staring directly at one another. 'What colour are my eyes?' he whispered.

'They're...' I faltered, tried to answer, blinked and looked again. 'I don't know,' I said. They were no colour I'd ever seen and I couldn't answer him. 'Stop it Perun, I'm in no mood for trickery.'

'Just because you cannot comprehend something does not make it trickery. The only limit to what I can tell you is what you are prepared to hear. The truth is that you already know a lot more about me than you're admitting to yourself.'

'I know nothing about you, except that you've followed me halfway around the world and I can only assume you have good a reason for it. I think now might be a good time to start sharing.' Perun came around to my side of the table and sat next to me in the booth.

'Don't scream,' he murmured. I had no time to react as he grabbed my hand and pulled it forward over the tea-light candle in the centre of the table. He pushed my wrist down over the naked flame and the burning pierced like a knife. His other hand had snaked round my back and covered my mouth so I didn't scream out loud. He pulled my wrist back out of the flame and turned it over so that I could see the crumpled skin and blackened edges of the wound. Tears coursed down my cheeks, the pain was dreadful. I was shaking all over and I felt certain I was going to pass out.

He put his fingertips over the wound and slowly pressed them into the burn. It took a few seconds but the terrible stinging started to lessen. The raw flesh began to go cloudy and then whitened. As he pressed his fingers down harder, the shrivelled skin turned to dust and the flesh knitted at the edges so I could barely see a scar. When he took his hand away only the palest of pink circles remained. 'That will fade over the next few hours. The new skin needs to get used to your body.' I pulled my hand from his.

'What the hell are you?' I hissed.

'I am the same as you. You can do what I just did. You've lived your life trying to blend in and conform to the rules that desiccate human potential. Eve, have a little faith in the things you feel even if you can't see or touch them. There's a whole other world waiting for you. Pretending this isn't happening is no longer an option. You're needed.'

I grabbed my bag from under the seat, threw some cash onto the table and stood to leave. He put his arms round my waist and tried to pull me back into my seat. I pushed my hands out instinctively and knocked a glass flying, silencing the restaurant. The chatter returned in an instant but I saw that Perun had caught the gaze of a man sat in a large group a couple of tables away and had been distracted by him. I used the opportunity to push past and run out of the restaurant. A waiter immediately stood between Perun and the exit to ensure that the bill was settled. I hailed a cab and jumped in without looking back. Back in my room, I poured myself a large gin and stared out of the window at the world below.

Maybe I'd made a mistake; perhaps it would have been better to have found out everything tonight. I threw myself onto my bed without bothering to do more than take off my shoes. From under my dress I pulled out the locket I'd been sent. The hair belonged to the woman in my dream. If she were my mother, why did it feel as if she had been telling me to keep away? I clutched the locket in my hand hoping that I would dream of her again but the combination of alcohol and exhaustion amounted to a night of nothing but blackness.

Thirteen

The previous day's storms had cleared the skies so that they were a brilliant blue. Whilst trying to quell my hangover with coffee and pastries I found a phone number for the Pacific Repertory theatre from the web. It looked fantastic. I've always loved the theatre; those few hours of losing yourself completely in the writer's fantasy and the energy that buzzes from the actors. The Pac Rep, as it was abbreviated, could be found at the Golden Bough Playhouse in downtown Carmel. I took a large swallow of caffeine and picked up my mobile.

'Good morning, Golden Bough Theatre, how may I help you?' The voice was cheery and professional.

'Yes, morning. I'm trying to get hold of Sabina Roman and I understand she does some work with you.'

'I'm afraid Miss Roman doesn't take calls and she isn't here at the moment. If you're coming for the auditions this afternoon you'll have to wait to see her then.'

'Well, does she have a contact number or email address?'

'We can't give that sort of information out, I'm afraid. The auditions start at 2pm. You'll need to bring your CV and head shots. It's first come first served so get here early if you want to be seen. We close the list at 4pm. Goodbye ma'am.' The line went dead. I sat staring at the floor for a couple of minutes and then realised that, far from having no way of contacting Sabina, I knew exactly where she would be this afternoon. Carmel-by-the-in-Sea was about 90 miles from the city. I jumped up, threw on my tightest jeans, a black t-shirt and some ankle boots then ran for the door. There was no time to lose.

Just where the Embarcadero sweeps under Bay Bridge I'd seen a motorcycle rental company. I'd taken my test a few years ago when I was stuck in the middle of a drugs trial that went on for months. Every day after court I did an hour of training. By the time the trial ended I'd passed my test and bought myself a small bike. The novelty didn't last long, it just wasn't practical enough to get me to court every day in the British weather and I resorted to using my car. Now, finally, it came into its own. I hired a mid-range Honda that was light enough for me to handle safely, some leathers and a helmet. I persuaded them to throw in a satellite navigation unit with headphones free of charge. I filled up with fuel and started the journey south to Carmel.

I found the theatre at three in the afternoon. By then the reception area was full of people nervously walking up and down, doing warm-ups and talking to themselves. A woman thrust a clip board at me with a form to fill in and gave me a number. I was supposed to wait until called and then go through to the stage. I figured that at some point I'd be able to slip quietly into the auditorium and wait until the auditions were over to speak with Sabina. After about quarter of an hour I saw an opportunity and tried to sidle in through an upper level door when one of the theatre staff spotted me.

'I need your form before you can go in there,' he said.

'I just wanted to watch...'

'No exceptions, fill in the form, we're too busy not to get everything done properly. It causes chaos.' He looked apologetic but serious. I dashed my details into the boxes on the form. The man was holding his hand out for it before I got within ten yards of him.

'Thank you sweetie,' he called after me. 'Love the leathers!' I laughed and went through the door to sit in the back row of the theatre. I realised I should have taken off the biking clothes and slunk into a corner to peel them off but as I bent to unzip my boots a voice shouted my name. I really hadn't thought this through.

'Oh bollocks, bollocks, bollocks!' I whispered as I tried to look confident climbing the steps down to the stage.

'Stand on the mark, please. Lights!' A man shouted into the now darkened auditorium. 'This is Eve MacKenzie, reference 24K.'

'Miss MacKenzie, I don't have your headshots or CV, they should have been handed in with your form,' a female voice from the dark replied.

'I'm sorry,' I said, although I couldn't quite make out who I was speaking to. 'I wasn't prepared for this, I just rang this morning and they told me about the auditions. You see, I need to speak to...' I was cut off mid-sentence and the voice was not going to listen to argument.

'Who's your agent, Miss MacKenzie? Jake can phone them and verify who you are.' I thought I'd try one last plea.

'I only arrived on the plane from England this week and I didn't know how to contact you, so I suspect there's been a misunderstanding.'

'We just need the name of your agent and we can talk about the details later, otherwise I'm afraid you'll have to leave. We have another thirty people waiting to be seen.'

'Daniel Fortune. My agent is Daniel Fortune, at Pinnacle. Do you know him?' I stepped over the line separating bending the truth from lying with no hesitation at all. I crossed my fingers behind my back and hoped I could get through the next few minutes without being thrown out.

The female voice was markedly softer when it replied this time. 'Yes, I know Daniel very well. Alright, Jake can contact him to sort out the paperwork. Let's see what you can do, my dear. Your monologue, if you please.' I was sure by now that the woman I was speaking to was Sabina Roman. She had a well-rounded American accent but I could still hear the faintest trace of eastern European.

'I haven't prepared anything actually, I didn't know what to expect. I'm so sorry. If I could just have a moment of your time to talk in private, Miss Roman?'

'Not today, far too busy, but if Daniel sent you I'll give you another chance. I like the leathers and the hair; it's perfect for the role of Kate so at least you've come looking the part. Jake, hand Miss MacKenzie the fifth act soliloquy. You'll have to read it without a warm up or we'll be forced to move on to someone else. I take it you are familiar with The Taming of the Shrew?'

'Of course.' A piece of paper was thrust into my hands. I was going to have to audition if I didn't want to lose my chance to speak with her. I just needed to buy enough time to get her attention. Shakespeare is a favourite of mine so I took a deep breath and began to read. I went slowly and gently. I'd been taught at school that you should read Shakespeare as if you were having a conversation with a friend, never overacting. As I ran over the first few lines my confidence grew and I looked up into the bright lights. Years of being in court had given me the confidence to project my voice and look up when reading aloud. When I'd finished there was a moment of quiet and then a single pair of hands began to clap. They continued until the lights came up. My eyes adjusted and I could see a woman a few rows back in the auditorium. Her hair was greying but tied back in an immaculate bun. I watched carefully and saw the tell-tale shake in her hands, although it wouldn't have been noticeable if I weren't looking for it.

'That was very good. Have you played Katherina before?' I opened my mouth to extricate myself from the situation before I lied any further when her assistant came back in and cut me off.

'I'm sorry Miss Roman; I have Mr Fortune on the phone for you. He's asking to speak to you immediately. He apologises but says it's a matter of importance.'

'Very well, Jake. Wait outside please; we'll call you back in if we need you.' I suspected that my day was over. I hadn't anticipated Jake calling Daniel whilst I was still on stage. I hated to be lied to and imagined how Sabina would react when she found out the truth.

I sat down on the corridor floor and the young man who'd expressed his admiration for my leathers flopped down next to me.

'She's a tough audience, huh? Don't take it to heart, she just doesn't let anybody get away with less than perfection. When I auditioned to join the company two years ago she screamed at me for my enunciation. I thought it was the end of the world. She called me back, told me I was in and gave me a lecture about sloppy speech for the next two hours. She's a pussy cat when you get to know her. It's Eve, right? I'm Xander. That hair colour is divine. Who's it by?'

'Um, that's just my natural colour.'

'Get out of here! I just love it. And that accent, you're Australian right?'

'English.' Xander squealed at me and then hugged me in a way that made me grin from ear to ear. I held back a laugh; he was a caricature of a sitcom character.

Jake poked his head out of the door and called me back in. I stood up and held my hand out to Xander. 'It was a pleasure meeting you Xander. If I'm in California long enough I'll try to come and see you on stage.'

'Don't say goodbye yet, I'm sneaking in to see what she says.'

'I wouldn't bother, honestly, I suspect it will be brief and humiliating.' Xander wasn't taking me quite literally enough. He squeezed my hand and pushed me through the door, following close behind.

'Oh, honey, we all feel like that when we audition. Just keep smiling and believe in yourself.' I walked back down onto the stage. Before anyone could say anything I thought I should apologise.

'I just want to say I'm sorry. I wasn't ready for today and I handled it badly.'

'No need to apologise, my dear,' Sabina cut across me. 'Daniel explained that you've had no time to prepare or have any head shots taken since you arrived in the States. I was in your situation myself, many years ago, so I understand how hard it is to move half way across the world to pursue a career. He also said that you have his full backing. He asked me to tell you that he'll do all the paperwork, nothing to worry about. He really is an excellent agent, you're very lucky.' I stood with my mouth open. Words completely failed me. Far from being found out, Daniel had apparently taken a leap of faith and backed up my story.

'Thank you.'

'Don't thank me, thank yourself. You read beautifully and you're a perfect choice for the role of Kate. If Daniel Fortune says you're up to the job then I have no doubt that you are. He'll prepare contracts; Xander can give you the tour now if you have time. I'd like to meet here again tomorrow, ten o'clock if that suits you?'

Jake was tapping his foot by then, quite loudly, on the stage. 'I'm sorry Miss Roman, we still have a lot of people to see for the other roles. If you don't mind we should get started again.' He led me off the stage. My face must have been a picture.

As Xander pushed me through the exit door I managed to say, 'I'm not quite sure how all this happened. She's made a mistake.'

'Oh, have more faith in yourself.' Xander picked me up and whirled me around. 'Welcome, welcome, beautiful English Eve. I'm so excited, come on, I've got to show you your new home!' I pleaded a need for the restroom and hid myself in a cubicle. I finally stripped off the leather trousers and took stock of what had happened. In the space of an hour I had an agent and a job in a professional theatre company. I rummaged in my bag for a comb to sort out my hair and found Daniel's card. I would call him later and sort out the technicalities. For now, I wasn't going to look a gift horse in the mouth. If I were honest, I loved the feeling of being on stage, immersing myself in a different character, forgetting my own problems. People would pay their life savings for the chance I'd just been given.

Xander showed me around the whole theatre, from the offices and bar to the backstage areas, dressing rooms and green room. The Circle Theatre puts on plays in the round and the Golden Bough itself, with a traditional theatre layout holds an audience of up to three hundred. More impressive than both of those were the photos Xander was showing me of the Forest Theatre, outdoors on Santa Rita and Mountain View. Built in 1910, the amphitheatre can hold an audience of five hundred and forty people at a time. It looked breath-taking. I was totally and utterly terrified. What the hell had I got myself into? Performing the lead in one of Shakespeare's best loved plays in front of that many people? I really had to go back and tell the truth.

'Xander, I have to go. I can't do this. I'm just going to let everybody down. I don't have the training or the experience. I need to see Sabina right now.'

The bubbly blonde beside me looked serious for the first time. 'What you need is to come with me,' he said. 'Give me an hour of your time. Then if you really want to, I'll take you back so that you can give up the best opportunity of your life.' Put like that, I felt like an idiot. Xander was being so sweet that the least I could do was let him show me whatever he had in mind. We left the theatre and hopped into a little car parked outside on Casanova Street. Xander drove as if he were about to fall off a cliff. It was odd seeing someone so confident suddenly look so afraid. We drove a few blocks inland out of the town then started to climb a hill at the edge of Carmel. We soon pulled up next to a sign for the Forest Theatre. We walked some way to the auditorium and Xander motioned for me to sit down. A semicircle of tiered seating looked down onto a bare stage. I whistled appreciatively. It was big and scary, but also magnificent.

'Don't tell me you haven't fallen in love with it already, because you'll be lying,' Xander said, very softly, the smile back on his face. He looked like a naughty school boy. He knocked into my shoulder with his own. 'Come on, say something.'

'I don't think anything I say would do it justice. You're right, no-one could help but fall in love with it. I'm just not good enough for this. I'm not really an actor Xander. My being here is an accident. I wanted to see Sabina and the only way was to audition.'

'There's no such thing as an actor. Just people who pick up scripts and make believe they're someone else. You're either good at it or you're not, and you must be or you wouldn't have got the role. It'll be fun, I promise, and I need someone to do this with. There are too many people taking themselves terribly seriously in the acting world. I promise to help you if you'll promise to give it a go. What do you say?'

'You'll rehearse with me, help me learn my lines? Tell me when I walk on stage with my skirt tucked into my knickers, things like that?'

He didn't answer me. He just jumped up, grabbed my hand and pulled me down the aisle between the seats to the stage. I looked out into the auditorium and imagined a sea of expectant faces. Stood there, Xander's arm slung casually round my shoulder, the terror left and I felt the growing seed of excitement in my stomach. 'I knew you wouldn't be able to resist once I got you here,' he beamed.

'Yeah okay, don't gloat.' I poked him in the ribs. As much as I was enjoying just being here it was also wonderful to have a conversation with someone. 'Thanks Xander, now take me somewhere I can buy hot food. Dinner's on me, if you're hungry.'

'Are you kidding? I'm always hungry. Being an actor's great but it sure don't pay all that well. Let's go get ribs, we'll diet again tomorrow!' As we got to his car I offered to drive. He looked like it was his birthday. 'Dinner and a driver? If you were a man I'd propose right now.'

'I don't need a proposal, but I do need a recommendation for a hotel tonight. I'm never going to make it into the city and back for tomorrow morning at ten. I also need a store to buy clothes and a toothbrush, I had no idea I was on a road trip.'

'Follow me Eve MacKenzie for indeed I can fulfil your every need.' Xander bowed as he got out of the car. If he was like this off-stage I wondered what he'd be like in front of an audience. Arm in arm we walked into a little diner to eat the best ribs I'd ever tasted. The combination of food, milkshake and Xander's company was a remedy for anything and I laughed so much that by the time I paid the bill I was wiping tears from my eyes.

As we walked up the block to a general store, Xander looked me up and down.

'You're alright, you know that? It's even better now that I'm getting used to your accent and I can understand what you're saying. Why don't you stay with me tonight? I've only got a small apartment but there's a pull out bed that's really comfortable.'

'Xander, you've only just met me. It's so generous, but I'd feel bad putting you out.'

'You're not, I just want someone to drive me around. Come on, we'll watch a movie, eat popcorn and pretend we've known each other for years. Say yes?' I did. We bought all I needed and drove a few minutes out of town to Xander's place. It was great not to be in a hotel and I found myself longing for home comforts. If I were taking a job for six months I'd need somewhere more permanent to stay. I had a lot to do, starting with figuring out what to say to Sabina the next day.

By half past nine the next morning I was waiting at the theatre door. I'd phoned Daniel first thing and he'd acted as if he'd known what would happen all along. He'd already got a copy of my contract with the theatre company and an agreement for him to represent me. He was also arranging a few things I hadn't even thought about like union membership and an application for a work visa. At precisely ten o'clock Sabina came through the door, leaning heavily on crutches. A young woman walked behind her, carrying a variety of bags, hats and jackets.

'You can put all that down in the green room for me Elise, thank you. Eve, come with me.' I followed her progress up the corridor. She was slow on the crutches and I knew Parkinson's was a disease where sufferers have good and bad days coping with the symptoms. I found myself in a tiny office where every inch of every wall was crammed with photos, newspaper cuttings and magazine columns. It was a tribute to the Sabina Roman who no longer acted.

'Forgive my vanity. Remembering who I once was gives me the drive to get out of bed in the morning when my hands shake so badly I can't lift a glass without help. Please, sit down.'

I sat on the edge of the chair. The woman in front of me seemed frailer than the day before, now that I was up close. She was trying hard to control the shaking that gave away her condition. Her strength was admirable. Many would have chosen to stay at home in privacy and comfort.

'So, you're English. Where were you trained?' Her eyes were as sharp as needles waiting for me to answer. There was absolutely nothing wrong with her cognitive functions.

'London.'

'Which drama school?' My heart skipped a beat. I couldn't lie any longer and the person before me deserved better.

'I didn't go to drama school. I'm not trained. I was improvising yesterday.' I waited for the response. She did nothing but look me up and down for what felt like an age.

'I know, Daniel told me.'

'He did? But I thought...'

'He told me that you were no actress by profession but that he would be your agent if I cast you. You were lucky that I'd heard you audition before I spoke to him. His view, and I agree, is that audiences will find you intriguing. You can act, I have no doubt.'

'Why didn't you say anything?'

'Because I wanted to see if you would tell me the truth, unprompted, this morning. Also, I am curious enough to want to know what is so important that you would fly all this way to meet me.'

'I'm sorry I wasn't more direct with you yesterday but I didn't know how else to get you to see me. I'm looking for Adela

Karas. I was told she was your nurse for some years, that she came over here with you from Slovakia. Is that right?'

Sabina looked down at her hands. She was very still for a moment and then stared up at the wall of images. She pulled a dog-eared photo down off the wall and handed it to me. It was in colour but badly faded by time. I could tell it was Sabina in a wheelchair, surrounded by photographers. Behind her, and only partially in shot was a dark haired, dark eyed woman smiling down at her patient. I ran my fingertips over the image. Adela had been beautiful. She looked kind and warm. When I took my eyes off the picture I saw that Sabina was crying. I knew that I was too late.

'She died a year ago. Cardiomyopathy set in after a virus and her heart just couldn't keep going. She never complained, not once. It makes me sick to the stomach to think of all the days I'd whined about how awful my disease was. Adela was like a sister to me. Now this theatre is all I have. What is it you wanted to know?'

'It doesn't matter now,' I choked back tears. 'I was hoping she could give me some answers. She was my...' I didn't know how to finish that particular sentence so I tried again. 'There was a mistake on some papers I found when my adopted mother in England died. Adela's name was given as my birth mother but I spoke to the midwife from the hospital in Brezno and I know that can't have been right. Adela was the last person who might have been able to tell me what happened. I've wasted your time. I apologise.' I tried to stand and leave but found myself sobbing. Sabina thrust a handkerchief towards me and I took it gratefully as I regained my composure.

'Oh, my dear. I'm so sorry you missed her. I don't think that a single day went by when she didn't think about her baby. '

'You knew about it?' I sobbed and looked up at Sabina.

'Adela took care of me for nearly three decades. She had secrets, of course, but then so did I. She would have given all she had for just one look at you. Handing the baby over for adoption broke her heart. She never recovered. Coming here with me was, I think, the only thing that stopped her from taking her own life. Let's not sit in here and talk about this. Adela and I made a habit of visiting the seafront once every day; she said it was good for me. It was just her excuse to go down there and watch the waves but I never minded, it made her so happy. If you don't mind pushing an old cripple along we'll take the chair. I won't make it on the sticks. Bring your jacket, the front can be breezy even in June.' Sabina phoned through to Elise who organised the chair. I'd wiped away my tears enough to go out in public and we set off the few blocks to take in the view. When we reached the sea Sabina pointed out a bench and I sat next to her wheelchair as she looked out at the ocean.

'I don't understand. The midwife told me Adela's baby was born with Down's syndrome and yet I know I'm the baby she handed over for adoption because of the medical report and the burns on my feet. Do you know what happened?'

'I only know what Adela told me. I have no reason to doubt that you are the baby she handed over for adoption. There was such a scandal about what Branimir did that she felt the best way to protect you was to have you adopted in another country. She contacted an agency who found an English couple who, as I recall, had lost their only child.'

'That's right, a baby girl.'

'The baby Adela gave birth to at Brezno hospital was a little girl. It took the doctors a couple of days but they knew something was wrong with the baby and eventually they diagnosed Down's syndrome. Branimir was saddened at first but Adela never gave it a second thought. Branimir saw how much she loved the baby and he overcame his anxiety and accepted it. About a month after they'd left the hospital Branimir picked the baby up from her cot early in the morning. It wasn't yet light, as Adela recalled it. They lay in bed together, cooing and smiling at the child between them. As the sun rose and the light entered their bedroom they saw the baby's face clearly. Gone were the tell-tale signs of the Down's syndrome. The eyes were closer set and more alert, the nose more prominent and well defined. But not just that. The baby they saw that morning had a shock of deep red hair.' Sabina paused to stroke my hair as she said it. 'Her eyes were a vivid shade of green and she seemed older and more awake. Adela told me how she reached out to pick the baby up and comfort her only to see Branimir backing away across the room. He was a superstitious man from an old and very traditional family. He said that demons had come in the night and changed the child. Adela pleaded with him to be calm, give it some time and let his heart soften towards the baby. Branimir was obsessed though, he wouldn't rest, reading folk law and listening to myths about changelings. I'm afraid he lost his mind after a few weeks. Adela came back from buying eggs and milk at a local farm to find Branimir holding the baby's feet, your feet my poor child, over the fire. She grabbed you and did all she could to sooth the burns. Then she left and never returned to that house with you again. She moved back to her parents place for a while and from there she organised the adoption. You know about Branimir?'

'I do. At least now I know why. I've been scared that I was going mad, that it was something I'd inherited from him. I had all the pieces of the story but just hadn't been able to put it all together. I wasn't sure if I'd been put in the wrong cot at the hospital or stolen by Branimir to replace a baby who'd died. There's one more thing I don't understand. The midwife told me that at the hospital Adela named the baby Zora. On the papers I have the name is shown as Eve. Did you know?'

'I didn't know the name they gave you at the hospital but it makes sense. Zora means sunrise. They hadn't had the naming ceremony when they discovered their baby no longer had Down's syndrome. Before Branimir finally lost his sanity they held the service but Adela insisted your name be changed to Eve. We were both quiet for a minute. Out at sea I could make out banks of fog rolling in towards the land. 'Walk me back would you, please?' said Sabina. 'If I get caught outside in that sort of weather it'll put me in bed for a week.' I turned the wheelchair away from the waves and back towards the theatre.

'Did Adela ever say what she thought happened? I can understand why Branimir took it so badly, I think I would. From what you've said Adela just seems to have accepted it.'

'I know what you mean. For years I thought she was driven by the necessity to keep the baby, you, at any cost. She knew that if she told the authorities it was not her baby it might be put into an orphanage. As time wore on and she talked about the story with less raw emotion there was something else. It was as if she were not surprised by what had happened. I can't explain it any more than that and she never discussed it. I loved her too much to ask.

She lost a child, a husband and had to leave her country. She never saw her parents again.' We were back at the theatre now. I pushed the doors open and picked up my bag.

'Thank you Miss Roman. You've been more help than you can imagine. I wish I could have met Adela. She sounds extraordinary. I'll leave you in peace, you look tired.' I took the liberty of kissing her on the cheek. 'I'm sorry to have been less than honest yesterday. I'd best get back to the city.' I turned to leave and was taken aback by the sharp voice that crackled in the air behind me.

'Don't you dare walk out of that door! What I've told you today changes nothing. I gave you a job yesterday, and I did so on your merits. As far as I'm concerned you are playing Katherina in my production and you have made a commitment to do so.' I took in a deep breath and frowned.

'But, I assumed that when you knew the truth about who I was...'

'Adela would have wanted you here, where I can keep an eye on you. It's the very least I can do for her after all she did for me. I assume you have nowhere to stay in Carmel. I own a small ranch a few miles away, nothing luxurious by Californian standards but easily big enough for you to have your own space and privacy. You shall stay with me for the next few months. I can help you prepare for the play and you can keep me company. It's lonely out there by myself. My new nurse is fine but she can't make conversation worth a damn. I won't take no for an answer. Make what arrangements you have to in the city. I'll be expecting you tomorrow night. I'll have Elise email you the address.' She turned and wheeled herself away up the corridor. At least I would have an opportunity to find out more about Adela.

The motorbike was due back with the hire company today so I started the long drive up the coast. By the time I handed the bike over I was ravenous from lack of food. I went back to my hotel, ordered room service then emailed Naomi and told her about my extraordinary new job. Once I'd packed my few belongings I fell into bed. After an age of tossing and turning, I slept.

I could hear a voice telling me to wake up and rolled onto my side to see Perun's face. I knew I'd awoken within the dream, sat up to clear my head and saw that I was outside. I lay on a grassy bank next to a stream, back in the forest. Boughs of trees overhead provided shelter from the night sky. Perun sat up behind me, his body burning hot and ran his fingertips down my arms. It was so much easier to give in rather than continuing to fight him. His lips touched my bare shoulder and I realised I was naked except for my locket. He trailed his tongue around the back of my neck to my right earlobe where he bit gently as his hands moved to my nipples. He brushed his fingers back and forth across my breasts until the sensation drove me to push back in his arms so that he lay me onto the grass below. In the moonlight I looked at his body and saw that it was as perfect and unmarked as his face. He looked like a waxwork model. His flesh was firm and smooth, muscles rippling beneath the skin. I felt my own desire pushing reason away and threw my head back so that he could kiss my neck. His body slid across mine and I arched my back at the sheer pleasure of flesh meeting flesh. His hand took mine and pulled it down to his groin. He shuddered as I took hold of his penis, thrusting firmly but slowly up and down and he leaned down and snaked his tongue into my mouth. Looking into my eyes he smiled as he plunged his fingers deep inside me, parting my legs with his and overwhelming any resistance I had left. My breath was raw in my throat and I felt dizzy. I waited to feel him entering me, arching my body to meet him and I felt water splash onto my face. When I opened my eyes to see where it came from I saw the woman with the red hair hidden in the branches above. Tears were coursing down her face, one hand with its back hard against her mouth as if to stop her from crying out loud. I jerked my body to sit up but Perun's weight upon me was too great and I couldn't move. She shook her head at me and I knew she was cautioning silence. What I saw in her eyes, though, was unspeakable sadness. I summoned all my strength and shoved at Perun’s body. As he tried to push himself into me I drove a shoulder hard into his chest and knocked him sideways. He must have seen the horror on my face and instinctively turned to look where she had been but he was too late. For the first time I saw some character in that blank beauty. He growled and the sound that came out was more animal than human. The anger and frustration made him close to feral. He whipped his hand around to pull me to him again but I was ready for him this time. I grabbed a stick and plunged it into my leg to wake myself up.

I was shaking in my bed when I came to and not only through fear. I had been in the throes of a desire so strong that I'd abandoned myself to a man I wasn't sure I trusted or liked. The dream was more vivid than anything I'd ever had before. I ran my hand over my face and found that it was wet. I could have persuaded myself that it was sweat only my sheets were dry. Were these the tears of the woman from my dream? I was losing touch with reality. Daylight was reaching under the curtains and I was grateful not to have to return to sleep. I shifted out of bed to shower and winced as I put weight on my leg. When I looked down I found a bruise, blood still spreading under the skin. It was round with jagged edges and in exactly the place where I'd jabbed myself. I took the locket from around my neck. Whatever Perun wanted with me, it was starting to feel more like a hunt than a game.

Fourteen

I'd checked out of my hotel by ten and returned to the motorcycle shop to take out a long term hire on the bike. I was going to need a way of getting around for the next six months and the bike was perfect in the balmy climate. The hotel was sending my cases by courier, arriving late afternoon. Daniel had emailed various documents which I'd already printed off, signed and sent back. By noon I was back on the road again and much more confident on the bike for a couple of days' practise.

I finally found Sabina's ranch after trekking around a labyrinth of roads in the centre of Point Lobos State Reserve. On the outside the buildings looked old, blending in with the landscape over many years. Inside the ranch was modern and warm, with hardwood floors, bare oak beams, high ceilings and an open plan layout. Sabina wasn't there when I arrived so I was met by a housekeeper who showed me to a smaller building across the lawn. There was a two bedroomed guest house in the grounds that appeared to be mine for now. The bed had been made up and there was food in the fridge although I was invited to take evening meals with Sabina in the main house. My lounge had an open fire and the bathroom featured a huge picture window facing down into the valley below the gardens. You could lie in the bath and stare outside for miles with no-one overlooking you. There was a phone connection with an intercom button to the main house. I realised this must have been where Adela had lived. I hoped that the trees and mountains had made her feel at home rather than being a painful reminder of Slovakia. You could hear nothing but the birds and the wind, it really was idyllic. On the other side of the main house I'd seen stables and the cars in the drive suggested some staff were on site. I unpacked my bags which had already arrived and took a quick shower. Sabina wanted me at the theatre at five in the afternoon looking presentable for a press release, so I put on some white jeans and a tailored, denim shirt. On a whim I slipped the locket back over my head. Twenty minutes later I'd arrived in the centre of Carmel. As I pulled up I could see photographers setting up outside the front of the Golden Bough Theatre. Xander was waving to me from the side of the building. I slipped in through the stage door and he hugged me like a long lost pal.

'Hurry up, there's someone here to do your hair and make-up. Sabina always makes a huge fuss when we have a new member plus it's great publicity for the play. Always helps ticket sales if we've just had a splash in the papers.' He ushered me into a room where a woman was waiting with a variety of pots, brushes and sprays. Xander kept me entertained while I was pushed and pulled around. Fifteen minutes later my eyes looked larger, my hair was polished and my lips were pouty. There was a knock at the door and I was summoned to see Sabina. With no time to spare we were off to show the press an Eve MacKenzie I barely recognised as Sabina announced the cast for The Taming of the Shrew. I smiled and posed for the cameras. It gave me a chance to see something of the former Sabina Roman. She had a way of lifting her jaw and opening her eyes wide to catch the light. Next to her I felt like a fraud. The press loved the English girl image and asked a barrage of questions about home. I said as little as I could until Jake appeared and said time was up.

We stayed at the theatre and had our first full cast meeting. Scripts were handed round as were questionnaires about clothes and shoe sizes for the wardrobe department. For the next twelve weeks I'd be in a rehearsal hall trying to learn lines and figure out how I was going to pull this off. Xander was playing Grumio, the fool. I managed to avoid any difficult questions from the rest of the cast about my acting experience by asking endless details from all of them about Carmel, where they'd each trained and anything else I could think of.

Sabina was expecting me for supper and the last thing I wanted was to be late on my first night when she'd been so kind. I kissed Xander and waved goodbye to my new colleagues. Life felt exhilarating and in spite of my nerves I was excited to be starting out on rehearsals. Naomi had already emailed to insist that she and Tim would fly out for the opening night. Over dinner, I told Sabina all about life in England and she explained what to expect from rehearsals, translated a few technical terms I hadn't heard before and told me a little more about herself and Adela. Over their years together they had become much more like family than employer and employee. Sabina's pain on losing her was still very raw.

The next morning I found copies of numerous papers on my doorstep, courtesy of Sabina's housekeeper. They were the regional and local dailies for San Francisco and Carmel, carefully flagged with the publicity and photos from yesterday. I thought I looked like a rabbit caught in headlights but Sabina reassured me that it had all been a great public relations success. That day the first rehearsal was spent blocking. This was all new to me but we just went over entrances, exits and where I should stand during each scene. I could see Xander trying hard not to grin each time we caught one another's eye and it made the experience much less intimidating. Still, I'd reread the play the night before and was terrified by the amount there was to learn. Three months really didn't seem enough.

At lunch time Xander and I made our way down to Carmel beach to stroll and eat. We kicked off our shoes and walked bare foot along the sand, gossiping about the various cast members and what other productions they'd been in. I was busy tidying away my sandwich debris when I heard Xander shout out. He grabbed my arm and raised one foot off the floor. Blood gushing from a deep wound and I saw that he'd stepped on a broken bottle half buried in the sand. I took his weight and helped him sit to get a better look at the injury. I cleaned it with some salt water and found a nasty gash. The blood flow was serious and we'd have to stop the bleeding before he could walk back up the beach. I ripped off the shirt I was wearing over the top of a white tee and bound it tight around his foot.

'Wait here, I'm going to run back up the beach and find a first aid kit from one of the bars, I'll only be ten minutes,' Xander grabbed my arm and held me back. 'Are you kidding? This is the first day of rehearsals. Do you have any idea what Jake will do to me if I'm late back on the first day? Honey, I'd sooner lose another pint of blood.'

'Xander, that's crazy, you're injured. They'll understand.'

'No, you don't understand how hard it is for an actor to get a decent job. If I mess this up I'll spend the next year doing school theatre and honestly I'd rather bleed to death right now than go back to all that. Now get me up and back there, you hear?'

I put his arm around my shoulders and we started to hobble over the sand but within ten meters the shirt was no longer doing its job and blood was flowing freely through the fabric. I didn't even have a mobile with me to call Sabina and let her know what had happened. I sat him down on the sand again and stared at his foot. I felt like an idiot for what I was about to do but it had to be worth a try, even if just to satisfy my own curiosity,

'You're going to think I'm completely nuts but just go with it, okay?'

'I have no idea what you're talking about but as we have only ten minutes to be back in rehearsals I don't care what you do.'

I pulled off the makeshift bandage. Rolling my eyes to the sky and wondering just how deluded this was, I wrapped both my hands around the wound and focussed on Naomi, how I'd managed to make her better before. Xander looked as if he were either about to run away screaming or burst into hysterical laughter, I wasn't sure which. I let go and apologised.

'I'm sorry, I thought it was worth a go. I did say you'd think I was nuts. I need to run and get help, sorry but you'll have to be late this once.' I stood up and started to walk away, my hands covered with congealing blood and my face red with humiliation.

'Eve, wait.' I turned back to look at Xander. He was pale, shaking and staring at his foot. 'Just how the fuck did you do that?'

I sprinted back and threw myself at his foot. The wound had stopped bleeding and was scabbing over already. I pressed on it gently and it felt firmer than before, the depth of the cut obviously decreasing. I had no idea what to say to Xander so I opted for action rather than a debrief.

'Great, if you can walk we can just make it back in time. Lean on me.' I hauled him up and luckily he was still in enough discomfort to stop him talking. It gave me a couple of minutes to consider what to tell him. I hadn't really believed it could work and I was still trying to understand the implications. As we arrived at the theatre I handed him back his shoe.

'Thanks', he said, not quite meeting my eyes. 'I'd better go and clean up.' He hopped into the men's room and I waited outside. I had to give him some sort of explanation before the rumours got out of hand. By the time he came back out he was wearing the shoe and barely limping. I went to talk to him but one of the theatre staff stopped me.

'Miss MacKenzie, there was a man here asking about you. He said he was a friend.'

'Did he give you his name?' I was waiting for Perun to show his face again although this wasn't really his style. On the other hand, I didn't know anyone else in California.

'No, I told him you were living at Miss Roman's ranch so he could get a message to you there.' She looked concerned that she might have done something wrong. I smiled to reassure her.

'What did he look like? Just so I can figure out who it was.'

She blushed ever so slightly and glanced down. Whoever it was had clearly made one hell of an impression. 'I'd say he was in his late thirties, maybe early forties, kinda hard to tell, easily six foot tall. He had the nicest green eyes with a deep voice and this little smile at the corner of his mouth. He seemed sort of old fashioned, too. He walked with his back real upright and this sway to his hips. Listen to me goin' on, I'm sorry, is he your boyfriend?'

'No, don't worry, he's not my boyfriend. Although he certainly sounds like one to watch out for!' I laughed as her face lit up.

'Well, I sure wouldn't kick him out of bed. Y'all have a good afternoon, now.' She disappeared into the offices and I turned back to Xander who was waiting for me.

'Xander, we need to talk.' I wasn't sure what I was going to say but I had to come up with something.

'You bet your sweet ass we do, but not right now. Come on, everybody's waiting for us.' I followed him in and spent the rest of the afternoon figuring out which side was stage left and stage right, then being measured up for costumes. I wondered who the man asking questions had been. Not Perun, for sure, the description wasn't even close. I guessed after all the publicity it could have been a journalist although they would have left a name or card. When the day finally ended, Xander grabbed my hand and told me to meet him in The Blues, a little cafe-bar up the street. I brushed my hair and threw on some fresh lipstick then left by the stage door. As I turned the corner I saw Perun waiting in the shade of a tree.

'You found me,' I said as I walked up to him.

'I never lost you,' he replied and I believed him. 'I just thought you needed some time to settle down and take it all in. And of course, you know about Adela now. Are you ready for some answers or do you want to carry on running away a little longer?' I didn't answer him because I didn't know what to say. I knew from my experience with Xander today that there was plenty left to find out. 'I'm not here to hurt you, Eve.' He pushed a strand of hair out of my eyes and I felt the familiar stirring of lust when he touched me. 'I know you're scared but you don't need to be. I'll see you tonight.' He brushed his lips against my temple in a parting gesture and left before I could argue with him, not that I would have. I'd been waiting for him to reappear.

When I reached The Blues, Xander had already got drinks and was sat waiting for me at a table in the corner where we wouldn't be disturbed. He wasn't going to be put off as easily as I'd hoped. Xander raised his glass to mine with a ceremonial clink.

'Here's to your first day as a professional actress. May fame and fortune be yours and may I always have you nearby in times of crisis. Now, spill it! That was the weirdest thing I ever saw.' He leaned forward, eyes shining with anticipation. I took a long, slow sip of beer.

'I don't know what to say, Xander. I have no idea how I did that.'

'So are you like a faith-healer or a white witch or something? How did you know to try it at all?'

'I'm not an anything and would you keep your voice down? Look, I've always been able to make people feel better when they've been ill although I've never tried it on a wound like that before. Maybe it's a sort of energy? Honestly, if I knew how I did it I'd tell you.' He was obviously disappointed by my lack of secret magical knowledge.

'Well, I don't care how you did it, you got me back there on time. And you did great today, by the way. I don't know how you came to be here but I'm sure glad you are. Just one thing, can you cure hangovers because I am going to the party of the year this weekend?' I laughed and thought how much less fun this would all be without him. 'Seriously, if you want to talk about it, I'm right here. Now I'm going home to learn my lines and I suggest you do the same. Read them out loud in front of the mirror; it'll help. Just before you go I wanted to show you this.'

He shook off his shoe and turned his foot over. Where the wound had been was the faintest red line, barely noticeable. He didn't say anything else, just slipped his shoe back on, winked at me and left. When he'd gone I examined my wrist where the burn had been. There was no mark at all and if anything my wrist was whiter and smoother than before. It was time to find Perun and get some answers.

When I got back to the ranch I was pleased to see Sabina riding into the front yard. On horseback she looked happier and younger than I'd seen her. A man helped her down, crutches at the ready, so that she could get into the house. He led the horse away and I went after her. The ride had tired Sabina out and she was planning on eating in her rooms. I can't say I was sad to have the evening to myself and I decided to have a walk around the rest of the ranch to get to know my surroundings better. To the east of the main house were the stable blocks. I could see at least eight horses as well as a store for feed and equipment. Beyond that were some tiny cottages providing staff accommodation for Sabina's nurse, housekeeper and ranch hands. She'd never married and had invested all her love and money into the ranch. It was a beautiful place, close enough to civilisation not to be isolated but far enough away to have a sense of peace and space. I spent some time with the horses. I'd never learned to ride but they were fabulous animals. I considered taking a longer walk but then remembered the amount of work I had to do on my lines. I went home, picked up the script and settled down on my veranda.

As I sat reciting passages out loud over and over again, the last rays of useful light were fading from the sky. I closed the book and put it down beside my chair. As I did so Perun walked up the steps towards me.

'You're later than I expected,' I said, not to let him have the advantage.

'Let's take a walk, the woods are at their best as the sun goes down.' He held out his hand to me and I took it with only the faintest unease. I saw no sign of ill-intent in his eyes. If he wanted to do me harm he'd have done it by now. We walked down the little pathway through the trees that led to a mountain trail. I hadn't thought to bring a flashlight but there was still a good hour of dusk before blackness. There was a half moon rising in the distance, shining pale yellow and intermittently hiding behind clouds. It wasn't quite clear enough to see the stars. We climbed the trail for fifteen minutes or so then sat on some rocks overlooking the valley to see the lights of the ranch in the distance.

I settled back against a fallen tree, head tipped up to the sky. I had sat myself far enough from Perun that I wouldn't be affected by his touch. It would be all too easy to be seduced by him but what I wanted tonight was his knowledge.

'I'm ready,' I said. 'You've made your point about belief. Now you need to give me something to believe in.' He held out his hand to me. 'No.' I said. 'I don't want to touch you. When you do that I don't know what's real and what's not. You came to find me and I'm here, so tell me whatever it is that's so important.' I drew my knees up and crossed my arms defensively. Perun didn't try to move any closer.

'Your mother needs you. Your true mother, not these humans who have failed so miserably to help you realise your true potential.'

'This is insanity. Talking about humans as if I were something other than that. You're wasting my time, none of this is real.'

'She is dying, Eve. I came to help you find your way to her before it is too late. We knew you wouldn't believe any of it unless you took this journey for yourself. After all you have been through, everything you know, how can you continue to deny the truth?'

'Just tell me about my mother. I don't want it to be too late. How do I get to see her?' I was willing to trust him to the ends of the earth if that's where my real mother was. I felt a longing like nothing I'd ever experienced before, the desperation to be in a place where I truly belonged. A sudden realisation hit me. 'I don't even know her name.'

'She is called Anousk. I can't be sure how much time she has left. We don't have illnesses in the way that humans suffer them, we simply reach a point where our time runs out and we move on. There is no way to slow it, no medicine. She has had a long and fulfilled life, except for the pain of losing you. Now she wants to hold you again before it's too late. It will mean sacrificing your life here as you know it, and you must come willingly or not at all. We have been waiting for you.'

'Who is we? There's so much I don't understand. Where can she be that I can't simply travel to see her now?' As I began to weep Perun opened his arms and I let him soothe me like a child.

'Your people are the Vilya. It is the same as this world, different cultures, races, all colours and creeds. We have laws and customs so that we live together peacefully. I've been sent as a messenger.'

'And what are you?'

'Humans have a crude term for us. They call us demons.' I looked up into his face to see if he was mocking me. 'It is no joke, but you have to understand that the meaning has changed. When humans first used the term “demon” it meant a state between human and god, a creature who had moved on from this life and become something more advanced. Folklore and so-called religions over centuries reduced the meaning to a creature of evil to scare people into belief and compliance. When religions needed a scapegoat to explain mental illness or unexpected pregnancies they terrified people with stories of demonic possession, making their followers more devout through fear. We were an easy target. And yet it's much more complicated than that. Like every culture, there is no black or white, only shades of grey. The power you used to heal your friend today works in many ways.' His voice had lulled me so when his hand flew out and came back holding a mouse, wildly scratching at his fingers to escape, I screamed involuntarily. 'Put your hand over mine,' he commanded, the once gentle voice now insistent.

'I don't understand.' I held back, not knowing what he intended.

'If you want to understand who you are you need to know what makes you different from the people around you. Now do it.' I thrust my hand over his and he held it firmly in place. 'The energy you use is drawn from your emotions and your experiences. What makes you angry?'

'I don't know, the same things that make everyone angry, mindless violence, injustice, suffering. What do you want from me?' I tried to pull my hand from between his and found that I couldn't.

'Not everyone, just you. What about the Dragon's Cave? Tell me what happened there with that ignorant prick who thinks so highly of himself.'

'Marcus? I don't want to talk about that. Please, let go of my hand.' He ignored my protests and continued.

'Why did you let him touch you like that? Why didn't you fight?'

'I didn't let him do anything. He wouldn't get off me.' My temper was starting to boil. I didn't like to be held when I'd asked to be released. 'How do you know about that? I haven't spoken about it to anyone. You have no idea what it felt like to be mauled by that bastard and I don't want to talk about it. Now let me go!' I felt pain shoot through my core as if I'd been punched and I wrenched my hand from his, falling backwards. Perun stepped over the top of me and knelt with one leg either side of me. He uncovered his upper hand and showed me the body of the mouse. It was uninjured but perfectly still, as if sleeping. I knew it was dead.

'You did that,' he said. 'Your rage. When you do good things, like helping your friend on the beach today, you feel a sense of satisfaction and calm. When your energy becomes destructive you feel the pain you felt just then. The energy comes from within you; it's drawn from your emotions. If you are tired or unbalanced you won't be able to control it. We can teach you how, show you so many more possibilities than you have here.' I looked down at the tiny creature. It hadn't occurred to me that I could do both harm and good. I reached out to touch it but Perun discarded it before I made contact.

'If I come back, can I help my mother, give her more time maybe?'

'You can help her pass on in peace, seeing for herself that her daughter is safe and well.'

'Then take me there. I don't care what the sacrifice is. There's nothing here that means enough to stop me from going. Take me with you.' Perun reached out and stroked my hair. He smiled and for the first time I saw his own agenda showing clearly in his eyes. It didn't matter. I had more to gain than to lose and if he had his own reason for helping me then so be it. I pushed my body against his, my arms round his neck. 'Take me there; I'll do whatever you want. I understand what you're asking of me. If I never come back here again, I can live with that.'

I heard the footfall only when it was immediately behind me. I span my head around without letting go of Perun. It must have looked like the middle of a passionate embrace. The man who stood in the near dark was no-one I knew. He kept his voice soft and whatever he saw or didn't see, he showed no emotion when he spoke.

'Miss MacKenzie, Miss Roman asked me to come and find you. She was concerned that you shouldn't be walking up here after dark. It's easy to get lost. I'll walk you back down to the house, ma'am.'

'I'm fine, thank you. I appreciate Miss Roman worrying about me but I have unfinished business here.' To my surprise Perun took my hands and pulled them firmly from his chest. He was staring at the man who had appeared so quietly. I couldn't understand why he didn't do or say something to help me. There was so much more to talk about. 'Perun, tell this gentlemen that everything's fine.'

Before he could respond the man sent by Sabina had taken one small but meaningful step forward. 'I think it would be best for everyone if you came back now, don't you? It wouldn't be polite to keep Miss Roman up worrying.' He gestured to the path and although he may have been speaking to me, he was looking at Perun. His head was cocked slightly, as if challenging him to disagree. The air was electric with understatement.

'Go,' said Perun. 'We still have time.'

'But I need to...'

'You need to rest,' Perun pushed me slightly towards the man who held out a steadying arm. I refused it and tried to keep my feet firm on the path in the near dark.

'When will I see you?' I called back to Perun, but his figure had already faded from sight in the dark. If the man escorting me home had any questions about where Perun had gone he kept them to himself. I remained silent on the way back down but inside I was furious. That Sabina could be so controlling as to send this man to find me was a step too far. Just because I was living on her property did not give her the right to have me guarded. I hadn't even realised she was watching where I was going. First thing in the morning I intended to pack my things and find a new place to stay. As soon as I found Perun again I didn't think I'd have much need for lodgings any more. I had limited time to find my mother before I lost her forever and I'd just lost the first precious opportunity I'd had to do so. By the time I reached my house the man started to wander off towards the staff accommodation without so much as a word.

'Just a moment,' I was too angry to bother with manners. 'If you were so eager to put an end to my evening you can go over to Miss Roman's house now and tell her that I'm fine. You can also tell her that I'm an adult who doesn't need a minder. I don't appreciate having her watching me like that.'

The man sauntered infuriatingly slowly back to me, standing just a couple of paces away. 'Well now, it looked to me as if you did need a minder. Heaven only knows what sort of trouble you might have gotten yourself into. And as for telling Miss Roman anything, I think the less she knows the less likely she is to be upset. I used my own initiative about coming to find you although I'm pretty sure that if she had seen you go then her orders to me would have been the same. You might want to be more discerning about the company you keep.' I couldn't restrain myself any longer. I stepped forward and slapped the man across the face as hard as I could. His head turned but his body stayed routed to the spot. 'I'll bid you goodnight them ma'am.' He nodded his head as I stood there fuming. I ran inside, slamming the door like a petulant teenager. Who the hell was he to talk to me like that? And as for making the decision on his own to come after me, I would speak to Sabina in the morning and have him sacked. I grabbed the small bottle of whiskey from the kitchen and poured myself a larger glass than was sensible. I wanted to drown out my own thoughts for a moment. Nothing Perun told me had made any logical sense and yet I'd felt the truth of it when he was speaking. I swallowed the drink down in one gulp and my rage bubbled back up in my veins. I threw the glass as hard as I could and it smashed against the wall into tiny shards, then I covered myself in a blanket on the couch and let the liquor pull me into sleep. I could hear the distant ticking of a clock, held tightly to the locket around my neck and wondered how much time my mother had left.

Fifteen

When I awoke I had about an hour before needing to be on my bike into Carmel. I hadn't decided yet if I was going to carry on with the play. In the light of last night's discoveries it all seemed kind of futile. My head was aching and my body felt dirty and dusty. I grabbed black coffee from the kitchen and ran a bath. Twenty minutes of soaking later and I started to pull myself together. The sun lit up the bathroom through the picture window and it looked as if today was going to be glorious. I got out of the bath and walked to press my hands against the glass. From here, it was as if nothing existed except nature. No other houses, aerials or roads were visible. I took in a deep breath and tried to recompose myself. As I dropped my shoulders and breathed slowly out I let my head drop and opened my eyes. Standing staring openly at me, leaning back against a tree as if he owned the place, was the man who'd interrupted my conversation with Perun last night. I screeched, threw a towel around my dripping body and ran down the stairs. By the time I'd thrown the door open and stormed out he'd walked forward to meet me. He stood with one foot up on the veranda, eyebrows raised and chewing his bottom lip. He was trying to keep himself from smiling and I just saw red.

'I don't know who the fuck you think you are, but I am not going to put up with being spied on by the hired hand.' I don't swear like that unless I've really lost control and this time I was well past the point of no return.

'When you've calmed down enough to be rational, you should know that Miss Roman sent me over because you weren't answering your phone. You also didn't respond when I knocked the door so I was waiting to see if there was any sign of you before I kicked it down.'

'Oh, and is this like last night when Miss Roman sent you to get me? You know, I could have done without the self-righteous lecture yesterday, especially coming from a man who stands and stares at naked women through their bathroom window.'

He threw his head back, hands on hips and looked into the sky as if summoning the patience to deal with a small child. I don't lose control very often but when I do it's not pretty. Part of me wanted to throw myself on the ground and kick my legs and the rest wanted to run away and hide in a cupboard.

'I'm going to say one last thing and then I'm going to leave you to work this out on your own. I wasn't spying on you and I didn't know that was your bathroom. I had no idea you were going to appear in the window naked, and while I'm on the subject, maybe you shouldn't have been standing at the window without anything on. But let me reassure you that the glass is reflective enough for me to see virtually nothing, not that I'm desperate enough to stand around and look at women through their bathroom windows. I'm afraid I'm the old fashioned kind of guy who's only interested in women's bodies when they're being shown to me willingly and in private. Given the company you've been keeping I can see how you might have the wrong idea but I keep higher standards.' I opened my mouth to retort but by then my stupidity balloon had started to deflate. He carried on before I could interject anyway. 'Now I apologise for last night but I genuinely believed I was keeping you safe. Miss Roman has, in fact, asked to see you this morning and she's waiting for you on the east veranda with coffee. Shall I tell her you'll be over shortly?'

By then I couldn't speak. Humiliation has a way of shutting me up. I just nodded. He was wearing a cowboy hat this morning which he tipped at me with a simple 'ma'am'. As he sauntered away, I wondered if he was the man who'd been asking about me yesterday at the theatre. The description fit him perfectly. I didn't dare shout after him to ask, having just accused him of spying on me I probably shouldn't chase it down with a question about being some sort of stalker. I went inside and dressed for coffee with Sabina.

It was a good fifteen minutes later when I made it over to her house. Sabina was looking at her watch when I sat down. She didn't say anything but I apologised for my tardiness and explained that I'd had a late night trying to learn my lines. It was close enough to the truth that I didn't feel too guilty then I changed the subject by asking if she got out riding very often.

'You know, I haven't been on a horse in two years. Then yesterday a young man applied for a job as a rancher and managed to fix me up a saddle that keeps me properly secure. I can't tell you how good it felt to be able to ride again, that's what I bought this place for after all. He's quite something, as well. You could do a lot worse for company if you don't have anyone back home. Do you ride?'

'No, I love horses but I never learned.'

'Well, now's your chance.' The housekeeper bustled between us collecting coffee cups and Sabina's breakfast things. 'Oh, Maryanne, send the new man over to us would you. I'd like Eve to meet him.'

'Oh I'd better get going to the theatre. I don't want to be late.'

'It'll only take a minute and nothing's going to start until I get there, is it?' With that, predictably, the man I was hoping to avoid for the next several years rounded the corner and smiled at Sabina. Her face lit up when she saw him. 'There you are James. I'd like you meet Eve, my absolutely charming house guest, who is also about to take the lead in the play I was telling you about. Now, Eve has never learned to ride. Would you mind?

'It'd be my pleasure to teach her, Miss Roman. How about later this afternoon?'

I felt like the worst kind of idiot. This was not a situation I wanted to be in at all. I smiled as sweetly as I could at Sabina. 'That's so kind of you, but you don't have to go to that trouble. I have my lines to learn and I'm not sure what time I'll be back today anyway.'

'Oh nonsense. We'll have finished blocking your scenes this morning, you can be back here by two and run over your lines in the evening. It's important to think about other things as well or the play will grow stale for you. James, could you organise some riding gear for Eve and meet her at the stables to get her fitted out later?' Sabina stood and grinned as if she'd won a prize. 'I think you two will get along famously. Now, I must get going.'

There are times when you wonder how life gets so complicated. I needed time to find Perun again and make sense of what he'd told me last night. In the cold light of day I was relieved we'd been interrupted. The last thing I remembered was all but begging him to let me see my mother, whatever the cost. This morning I wanted more space to make that decision. I had the shoots of a new life here, good friends back in England and I had no clear idea of how final the sacrifice was he'd talked about. I cleared my head on the ride into Carmel and by the time I arrived I felt calmer. I focussed on the job at hand and had a lively, fun morning. Surprisingly, I found I was able to throw myself completely into character, not a huge leap from the behaviour I'd exhibited with James earlier, so at least I had something to draw inspiration from. Sabina was full of praise and sent me home with a smile on her face for my riding lesson. Xander threw me off my game during coffee break by asking if I could give him Botox treatment just using the power of my mind. I told him that he was an idiot and stole his bagel to teach him a lesson. After what I'd learned I could do to the mouse last night I was more worried I'd end up taking his face off. Xander seemed remarkably unfazed by what happened yesterday. I, however, had some way to go before coming to terms with everything Perun had told me.

As I pulled my bike into the garage James' silhouette appeared in the doorway, hip leant against one wall, legs crossed at the ankle. He was wearing a v-neck white t-shirt, close fitting jeans and looked for all the world like a Levi advert come to life. He was holding riding boots in one hand and a hat in the other. When I got close he held them out without even bothering to look me in the eyes.

'You ready to swap the leathers for something more comfortable?' he asked. He spoke so slowly and softly that I wondered if he ever rushed or got riled. It was hard to imagine him losing control the way I had that morning. I took the kit out of his hands and hung up my leathers.

'Will this take long? I have other things I need to be getting on with.'

'Let's just see how the horses take to you. They may not want you riding on them; tend to be good judges of character.' I guess I'd asked for that. I determined to build bridges for Sabina's sake. I owed her that much.

'Look, James...' I couldn't find the right words for the apology and I was going red as I fumbled with my strap.

'Do you need some help with the hat, Miss MacKenzie?'

'No, and for goodness' sake would you please call me Eve? I think we can drop the formality as you've already seen me naked.' I'd smiled as I said it but he ignored my attempt at humour. Then I remembered that in my fury I'd slapped him the night before. I had some serious work to do to put this right.

'Alright, I'm sorry, really I am. Could we please just start again? The person you saw last night and this morning, that's not really what I'm like. My behaviour was inexcusable, I know that, but there's a lot going on. I can't explain it any better but I hope you'll accept my apology and give me another chance.'

'You don't need to apologise for any of it. You said yourself; I'm just the hired hand. I'm sure you can take care of yourself so I'll do exactly what I've been asked, teach you to ride and stay out of your personal space. Now, do you know how to mount a horse properly?' He wasn't going to be won over quite so easily and I couldn't say I blamed him. I put on my game face and decided to get this over with as quickly as possible. There was one last question I couldn't help but ask and I regretted it before my brain had connected with my mouth. 'I know this is going to sound crazy, especially after everything else, but did you by any chance go to the Golden Bough Theatre and ask about me yesterday?' He looked me full in the face, hands on hips, shaking his head ever so slightly. I gabbled on. 'It's just that the man described to me didn't leave his name but the description fits you perfectly. God, I'm sorry, I've done it again.'

He pushed me up into the saddle and adjusted the reins for me. He didn't bother to answer my last question and I cringed as he walked around the horse making sure I was safe.

'This is Tempest. He will go where I lead and do what I say. Today is just for you to get used to the feeling of being on horseback. You don't need to do anything except hold those reins lightly and sit with your back straight. He'll do all the work. This might be a more enjoyable ride for us both if we agree not to talk. We're going up the mountain path and around the river on the other side. It'll take about two hours but I have some water with me if you get thirsty.' With that, he mounted the stunning black stallion beside Tempest and we walked on slowly through the pasture and up the mountain trail.

We rode for about an hour until I could feel the muscles in my legs and backside starting to pull. We'd come down the far side of the ridge to the river's edge and James reined in his horse to a stop. Tempest did the same. He was incredibly good natured. I'd passed the time in contemplation and barely noticed how far we'd come. He helped me down and led the animals to water. When they were safely tied to a log he sat down in the long grass and held out a bottle of water. I stood sipping and watching him from the corner of my eye as he relaxed in the sunshine. His large hands showed the physical work he did and he was slim and well-toned. I guessed that riding kept him as fit as any gymnasium. He was just about the quietest man I'd met in my life. I coughed once very gently to get his attention but he didn't move a muscle.

'Is there some sort of plan for the afternoon? I do have other things that need my attention, you know.' He didn't answer immediately so I just kept on talking even though I wished I could stop. He just wasn't bringing out the best in me. 'I'm sure that when Sabina asked you to give me a riding lesson she didn't plan on you sunbathing for half an hour in the middle of it.' He sat up so that he rested back on his elbows and met my eyes with a level stare. His voice was only just audible over the babble of the river.

'And I'm sure that she would want me to rest her horses after an hour's climb so that they don't get injured. They need time to drink and rest their muscles. If you'd like to report me for taking a break at the same time then you should feel free to do that. Otherwise, may I suggest that you give your own legs, and perhaps also your voice, a rest as well?'

Properly chided I sat down next to him, stretched my aching limbs then lay back in the grass. 'Listen, I don't know why I'm behaving so badly. I guess I like to be in control.' I waited to see if he would bother conversing with me and put an arm over my eyes.

'It didn't look like you were in control with that man last night.' I couldn't deny that. I was virtually on my knees to Perun.

'Yeah, well, he has something I want.' I opened my eyes again to find that he'd rolled onto one side and propped himself on his elbow, staring down at me.

'What would that be?' His eyes searched mine and for a moment I thought he was going to reach out and touch me.

'He knows how I can find my mother,' I replied. James didn't move but he turned his head and looked away from me.

'That must give him an awful lot of power over you. Aren't you scared?' I thought about it for a moment.

'A bit, but more than that I just want to see her. I've never met her. It's all a bit, um, complicated.' The skies overhead were darkening and the wind had picked up. It was nearing four o'clock and although rain hadn't been forecast it was obviously on its way.

'Don't get upset, there's no need,' he said.

'I'm not upset. I just need to make some decisions.' I stood up. I'd come close to confiding in this stranger and the last thing I needed was more complications. 'Are the horses rested enough yet, only we should probably be getting back?'

'The horses are just fine where they are. You're getting wound up for no good reason. Take a breath.' He held one hand out to me and I took a step away from it.

'I don't know why you think I'm getting upset but I can assure you I'm not. I'd like to get moving again, is that okay?'

'Not while you're like this. Look at that sky. You're going to bring on a storm if you're not careful.' The sky was looking threatening but I was in no mood to be told to calm down. 'Control yourself, Eve. Let me help you.' He took a step forward again and I avoided his touch. I felt sick to the stomach and my head was spinning. I tripped on a tree root and went down on my side before I could catch myself.

'Goddammit!' I screamed. Thunder rumbled across the mountains and I grabbed at my ankle, burning with pain from the twist. James bent to see the damage but the last thing I wanted was help from him. 'Leave me alone.'

'No,' he said. He knelt and lifted the ankle in spite of my protests and raised it onto his knee while he pulled off my boot. It was swelling already. 'We need to get you back. It's not broken but you should get some ice on it. Put your arms round my neck, I'm going to lift you back onto the horse.' I ignored the offer and tried to stand on my own. It was infuriating, being dependent on him, especially when he was the reason I'd fallen in the first place. I felt my anger start to boil. As it did a bolt of lightning hit the trees above us followed by a crash in the woods close by.

'Eve, I know you're confused but you need to listen to me right now. You're causing this storm, you have to calm yourself down.' Rain had started to pour and the temperature was dropping. I was trapped in the mountains with a man I barely knew and he was scaring me. I grabbed the nearest stick and pointed it at him like a dagger.

'Leave me alone,' I screamed. 'You don't know anything about me. Just get back on your horse and go; I'll find my own way back to the ranch. I don't know who you are or what you want but you sure as hell didn't turn up here out of the blue.' I was ready to swing the branch and do as much damage as I could. The rain was so heavy now that we were both soaked to the skin.

He turned his head and I followed his eye line. The river was rising dangerously fast. He left me and sprinted for the horses, untying them both and hitting them hard on their hind quarters so they galloped beyond the reach of the water and away from us.

'Are you trying to kill us?' I screeched, hobbling towards him. 'You can't let them go! How the fuck are we supposed to get home? Is this what you wanted, to get me into the woods alone? You're going to tell me who you are and what you want, right now.' He strode up and grabbed my arms, holding me fast and shouting to make himself heard above the gushing torrent. 'I'm exactly who I've said I am and I'm not sure what you are but I do know this. If an incubus wants you then you are in a lot more trouble than you can imagine. You have to control your emotions right now because this storm will take us to a place I don't want to go.'

'Stop saying that! It's insane. This is not my fault!'

'I don't care if you believe me or not, just get a grip before it's too late.' I started to scream, well beyond reason or comprehension. The river had burst its banks and I didn't care. I wouldn't have cared if it carried me away. My world had spiralled out of control and the worst of it was that I knew every word James said was true. I wasn't meant to be here, someone had been given my place in a world that should have been my home. The pain was unbearable. I could still see James but it was like watching through a telescope, he was separated from me by a dimension and I felt like I was being ripped away. I held out my hand to him, throwing down the stick away I'd been brandishing. Too late I tried to control the tide of my emotions.

'Eve, don't do it, you can still stop this.' I felt James throw his arms around me and I fell backwards with him clutching me as if I were nothing more than a rag doll, a sick merry-go-round sensation invading my head.

I stared into his eyes, and the world was a blur. 'What's happening? James? Don't leave me. Don't let me go.' Then there was only darkness and silence.

Sixteen

Light was flooding into my head as if I were racing through a tunnel. I was in exactly the same place as when I'd lost consciousness except there was no evidence of the storm's destruction. The river had subsided and sunshine burnt through the clouds. I tentatively moved my head to one side but felt no pain where I'd expected to find myself black and blue. James lay to one side of me and I scrambled over to him, hands on his throat to check for a pulse. His heartbeat was strong and he was breathing normally, so I left him to walk to the river bank. There was no sign of the horses and I prayed they'd found their way safely back to the ranch, for Sabina's sake. I drank from the river, the water cold and clear, with none of the mud that must have washed down from the mountain top. The whole place was untouched. All the tension had lifted completely and I felt as if I'd slept for hours. James was starting to come round and I went to sit by his side, stroking his forehead with a cool hand and studying his face properly for the first time. It was tanned and symmetrical but made beautiful by the tiny lines around his eyes. His mouth was a soft line in contrast to the square jaw and straight eyebrows. I ran a finger over his lips and jumped as his mouth opened to draw in a sharp breath. He sat up, hands running over his body to check for the injuries that should have been there, exactly as I had done.

'Are you hurt?' I asked. He stared at me, as if I were a stranger.

'You don't know where you are, do you?' His voice had returned to its customary softness but had taken on a sadness that made me ache. He stood in one fluid motion and held his hand out to me. I took it and let him pull me up. 'This is where he promised to bring you. They call it Manitu, their word for the spirit of nature. You called down a storm and brought us here. I hadn't realised how little you knew about it all. I'm sorry, I thought I'd be able to keep you safe and now it's too late.'

'But we haven't gone anywhere, it's all the same as it was. And we're both fine, uninjured. I don't understand what you're talking about. You called him an incubus, just before the storm knocked us out. Do you know Perun? Can you help me find my mother?' I saw tears form in his eyes but they didn't fall. 'James?' I whispered, but he'd recovered his equilibrium already.

'I don't know Perun but I know his kind. They are the Perelesnyk, a race of incubus and succubus that take their power from humans for their own ends. They seduce people to control them but it's not about sex at all, it's about possession. Whatever he wants, it certainly isn't to help you. I'll do all I can to help you but right now we need to find a way back. This is a shadow world we're in. It may look the same as ours but it doesn't belong to humans and there's no safe place here for us. If we stay too long we won't be able to get back, at least not with our sanity in place.'

'James, I can't go. If this is where Perun wanted to take me then this is where my mother is. He said my people were the Vilya and that my mother is dying. This may be my only chance to see her. I have to find her. Please?'

'I don't believe your mother would've sent an incubus as a messenger. There are many different races here who desire power exactly as we do. You don't want to end up in the middle of it. If Perun was so keen to help you find your mother then you need to find out what he had to gain from it. I'll help you, but you have to repay that help with some trust. Can you do that?' I nodded and smiled at him. 'You look like them, I should have seen it before.' He held my face in his hands and studied me like a new species. For a second I thought he was about to kiss me but he dropped his hands and bent to pick up his water bottle. 'Come on, we need to find shelter. This place may look idyllic but it's wilder than you know.' He walked ahead of me through the woodland until we came to a path. The landscape was familiar in shape but it was as if the colours had been set too high on a monitor, everything was sharper and brighter than before and after a while it hurt your eyes. The sound of footsteps approaching from behind took us both by surprise. James reached out and pulled me down in the undergrowth. Seconds later three young males sprinted along the path past our hiding place. We lost sight as they rounded a bend leading up into the next hill. They had been carrying animals slung over their backs, the kills of a recent hunt. Their hair was long and their skin the deep tan colour of constant outdoor living. I felt more wonder than fear but James' face was less certain. After a few minutes of stillness and silence it seemed safe to move again.

‘Wait, how do you know where we're going or even if we're going in the right direction?' We were in uncharted territory without so much as a compass. I was starting to sense the enormity of what we were trying to do.

‘If you've ended up here it's because this is where Perun wanted you to be and if he wanted you to see your mother then she's nearby. Think back. How did you come to be in Carmel, with Sabina? Nothing is accidental. He helped you find this place, didn't he? Bit by bit he's influenced your movements. All we can hope is that he doesn't find us before we find her. After that you’ll need to find a way to reopen the doorway you dragged us through and get us home. Whatever you were when you were born, you are more human now than them. Let's get moving before we lose the light. Take my hand.' I did. It was warm, strong and I drew the strength I needed to walk for the next two hours until the first stars showed. In the valley below I could smell wood smoke like earthy perfume rising up the mountain’s sides and see distant firelight.

'What do we do now? I'm not sure I'd know my mother even if she appeared right in front of me.'

'We'll have to go down there, watch and listen, find out what we can. Until we know we're safe we have to stay out of sight.'

'Won't they know we’re there? Since I got here my senses have been running on overdrive. Aren't theirs the same?'

'Not if they're feasting. They have an ability to lose themselves in a way that humans can't unless they're drunk or drugged. They won't be on their guard, as far as we know they’ve got no reason to think we’re here.'

I stared at James. 'You've been here before. But you said you were human. Are you one of them?'

The bitterness in his voice was enough to stop me asking questions. 'I'm nothing like them. I've been here before, against my will, and I paid too high a price for leaving. We're running out of time. Let's get moving.' He shouldered his back pack and left the mountain path, going directly through the woods. The slope was steep but at least it was sheltered. The going was slow. I was constantly stopping myself from slipping and painfully aware of every twig snapping underfoot. After a while the glow of the fires was much closer and I could smell the meat cooking on the spits. In spite of the danger, the food made my mouth water and I felt famished. Everything was more powerful here, the colours, the light and my response to it all. Nagging at the back of my mind was the fear that going back to the world where I belonged was something I might not be able to achieve, or even want, for very much longer.

James' hand across my mouth stopped me daydreaming before I walked straight out into a clearing. He pressed my body back against a tree and I nodded to show that I would stay still. A circle of women were before us, silently chopping great platters of fruit. As we watched they finished their work and began taking the food along a small pathway leading to a fire. We'd come closer to the group than we'd realised. The women were attractive and petite but they looked strong. I yearned to touch them, to see if their skin felt the same as mine. As the last of them started along the path the woman at the very back of the line stopped in her tracks and turned round. Just in front of her someone else glanced over her shoulder and called out but she waved her on and returned to the clearing. She set down the platter she'd had on her shoulder and cleared up the discarded fruit peelings and stones from the ground. When the line of women was completely out of sight she looked towards the place where James and I were hiding.

'What is it that scares you so much you will not show yourselves? You have nothing to fear here.' Neither of us moved or answered. She waited to see if we would come out and then moved directly in front of the bushes. 'I am Ellette from the family of Vilya. I will not harm you. I know you are there, strangers. Let me see you.' James released his hold on me and I went slowly out. As I moved closer I saw her eyes widen briefly in surprise and then narrow with suspicion. She took a step back and raised one hand defensively.

'You cannot be here. We did not bring you. Which of the families has done this?' She regained her confidence and took a step in my direction. James stepped between us, sensing the rising conflict. I was too shocked by her reaction to do anything but freeze, open mouthed.

James put up both his hands in a gesture of compliance. 'We're here by chance and no-one but you knows it. I am James and this is Eve. We need help and a passage of safe return to our own world. If you know a way to help us we will do all we can to leave without upsetting your family.'

Ellette didn't take her eyes off me to even acknowledge that James had spoken. 'She does not come here by chance, not now. Our rivals seek to take the throne from my family because they say the blood line is tainted and then you appear, without warning, claiming innocence. You will bring down a war on all our heads. Do you not know what the cost of this will be?'

I stepped forward. 'I don't know who you think we are but we're not here to cause any sort of trouble. We came into this world through a storm I couldn't stop because I was so desperate to find my mother. We won't hurt you or your family. I just need your help.' There was shouting from the fire at the far end of the path and revellers began to run down the pathway. With the speed and strength of a lioness Ellette pushed me and James back into the bushes. We stayed quiet as the others passed us and then Ellette put her hand over my heart. She picked up my own hand with her free one and put it over her own chest.

So softly I could barely make out the words she whispered. 'Has the human world dimmed your senses so much that you do not know your own blood? I am your sister, Eve.' It was all I could do not to cry out loud. It seems ridiculous but it had never occurred to me that I might have siblings. As I felt her heart beat beneath my palm I knew it was true. I threw my arms about her and held her tight. She returned the embrace but was tense in my arms and I could feel her watching over my shoulders.

'Follow me but be silent. I will take you somewhere we can talk.' She took me by the hand and led me through trees, into the rocky outcrops at the base of the mountain. James was watchful behind us, keeping his distance. Their mutual wariness made my skin prickle. At last we reached the entrance to a small cave. Ellette pulled me inside and indicated a rock to perch on while she made a fire. I couldn't take my eyes off her. Whatever else happened here, just knowing I had a sister made the journey worthwhile. To have been able to hold her and talk to her was a miracle. The look on her face told me she didn't feel quite the same. James sat next to me and Ellette watched us from across the flames. Once the flames were well fuelled she finally began to speak.

She explained that the various families in Manitu, of which the Vilya were just one, had long since stopped warring for power and agreed that each family in turn would rule for a five year period. The oldest child of the matriarch would take the throne. The Vilya's descendant would be next in turn and in just a few weeks the coronation was due to take place. I was only half listening and feeling increasingly desperate to see my mother.

'I'm sorry, Ellette, all I want to do is see Anousk. I understand that things here are complicated at the moment but Perun told me she's dying. How much time do I have?' Ellette's head shot up from where she was poking at the burning wood.

'It was Perun? He came to find you? That makes sense. If the Vilya cannot take the throne then it passes to the Perelesnyk. You are in more danger than I thought. We have to get you back to your own place, there's no time to explain all this.' James stood up immediately and nodded his head. I stayed right where I was.

'When you've both stopped making decisions for me there are some things I need to know and I'm going nowhere until I have answers.'

'Mother is not dying any more than you or I. Perun used your worst fear to manipulate you and he did it well.' Ellette was terse with me and I didn't like it.

'How do I know you're not just saying that to get rid of me? The only way to settle this is for me to see her myself. Why should I trust you any more than I trust Perun?'

Ellette's anger made her face glower a deep red and I could feel her energy filling the cave. 'There's more at stake here than just your happiness, sister; other lives hang in the balance. This isn't some childhood fantasy. If Anousk knew you were here she would ask you to go as quickly and quietly as possible. You need to do as I say.'

I faced her full on, my own emotions running just as high as hers. 'And you need to get out of my way. If you won't help me then I'll find someone who will. I don't care what Perun's agenda is, I've had everything I ever believed in stripped from me. I have no idea who or even what I am. Don't tell me what's at stake.' A noise outside the cave broke the moment. James pushed me to the floor and Ellette flung herself into the shadows of the cave wall. There was silence for several seconds as we waited for whoever was out there to show themselves. I felt the unbalancing sense of premonition as James reached out to pull a burning bough from the fire. I grabbed the nearest heavy rock and felt sweat pouring down my back.

With a scream, a figure came hurling into the cave and towards Ellette. James thrust the burning branch towards the oncoming body as Ellette rushed forward to intercept. She knocked the branch from James' hand as the flying body landed on top of her.

'Ellette, I found you. You were hiding and I found you first. Mother is looking for you.' The young woman, rounder in body than the other petite females I'd seen earlier, lay on top of Ellette, hugging her.

Ellette was breathless and shaking with relief and surprise. 'It's alright Zora, you found me, well done. Let me up, angel.' The woman moved so that Ellette could sit up. As she did so she noticed James and me. Evidently the extraordinary senses of the Vilya did not extend to her. She turned around to look at us in the light and as she did so my brain finally processed who she was. Her face, lit by the most brilliant smile, had the tell-tale almond shaped eyes, small chin, and flattened nose typical of Down's syndrome. Zora had kept her human name. Adela would have been pleased to know that her child was alive and thriving. This was the final proof of my parentage. She walked over to me and raised her hands to my face.

'Why are you crying?' she asked. I put my hands to my cheeks and brushed away tears I hadn't realised were there. 'You're too pretty to cry. I'm Zora. I don't know you. What's your name?'

I choked back my tears and smiled at the guileless woman-child before me. 'Hello Zora, I'm Eve,' I said. 'You're much prettier than me. We're just visiting. Is it nice here?'

I scanned her face for any sign that she might know who I was but there was only joy. 'Oh yes, we live in the forest. Mother says it's beautiful because I light it up when I smile. I think she's being silly.' She turned to Ellette, distracted by the thought. 'Is she being silly Ellette? She laughs when she says it.'

Ellette walked over and stroked Zora's hair, very gently, as one would handle a tiny animal. 'No, my darling Zora, mother's quite right. She laughs when she says it because you make her so happy.' Ellette kissed her on the cheek and stood with one arm around her waist.

Zora remembered me again and came to whisper in my ear. It was still loud enough for us all to hear but she thought she was quiet and we maintained the illusion with her. Her innocence was so disarming that I could do nothing but smile at her.

'The man next to you is very sad inside,' she said. 'You should hug him and make him happy.' I looked at James and then back at Zora. I too whispered so I didn't give the game away.

'That's my friend James. Don't worry Zora, he's not sad. We just need to find a way home.' She looked at me as if I were a very small child who had misunderstood.

'He's not sad because he wants to get home, you silly thing. He's sad because he's been cursed.' James didn't move a muscle but his body was tense. I reached out instinctively and took his hand in mine. As I did so Ellette put her arms around Zora and pulled her face round to emphasise her point.

'You should go back and tell mother that you won, you found me first. But you'll lose the game if you tell her about Eve and James, my love, so you must promise not to tell.'

'I don't want to lose the game. I'll go back to her straight away, Ellette, I promise.' She kissed my blood sister and was as excited as a five year old on Christmas morning. How lovely it must be to live in a world where you can be made content so easily. For a moment I envied the simplicity of emotion that kept her protected from reality. She took my hand as she went to leave. 'I dreamed of you once. Whatever you decide, it's all right.' She kissed my cheek with a hard hug, stood on tiptoe to peck at James's mouth as she passed by and then raced from the cave before either of us could speak again.

'You knew her,' Ellette said. I nodded. 'Then you know you were changed with her as a baby. You were mother's first born daughter. She owed a great debt to the human woman Adela and agreed to take Zora so that she could keep her healthier for longer in our world. She paid a terrible price for doing so and was never allowed to cross into your world to find you.'

The image of my mother being separated from me without even knowing if I was alive or dead all these years was unbearable. 'Then let me see her, Ellette, before I have to go back.' Ellette turned away. There was a long silence.

'If you go to her, if you touch her here in our world, the touch reverses the change. You were sacrificed as a changeling to repay a debt to a human. If you have any physical contact with mother and take your place in our family again you will push Zora out of our world and back into yours, irreversibly. It would devastate mother, to think of Zora out there in such a cruel place, without us to protect her. Zora would be driven crazy. You've seen her. She could never understand what was happening. You will destroy two lives to make your own complete. I am truly sorry, I can feel what a heavy burden you carry, but I will not let you near our mother. Please try to understand.'

'I don't understand, I can't. Why was I given away? How could she have loved me and sent me away? There must be some way of making this right. I promise not to touch her, I only want to be near her, just for one minute. Ellette, please?'

'And force her to send you away again, without so much as holding you? Neither of you would have the strength for that and your emotions are too wild to risk it. She would be forced to choose between one child in agony and another who could never protect herself. There is no right or wrong here, it is about causing the least harm. Perun brought you here to prevent Zora's ascension to the throne. The Perelesnyk deny that she has a right to rule, not being of our blood. If they manage to displace Zora and you refuse to take the throne in her place then they will reign as the next family in line. Only they could be so devious. They must have moved the very planets to lead you here. I'm sorry for what they've done but I won't let you or Zora be hurt any more. You must go back Eve, it is the only way to stop this destruction.'

'But how could Zora rule, anyway? As extraordinary and sweet as she is, she has the mind of a child. She won't be able to understand the decisions she'll have to make.'

'She makes decisions by following her heart. There are worse ways to rule than that. She is the purest of us all and she has to be kept safe. Perun will do whatever it takes to take power.'

'You know what? You're just as bad as Perun. He was using me for his own ends and now you want me to leave for yours. Does no-one care about me?' I smashed a fist into the wall of the cave and a violent gust of wind behind me hit my back like a whip.

Ellette took a step closer, her voice placating. 'Calm yourself sister or your anger will alert our enemies to your presence.' I looked out into the night and knew exactly what I wanted.

'Your enemies, Ellette, not mine.' I turned before she or James could register what I was doing and jumped out of the cave onto the path. It was as black as pitch beyond the firelight and I stumbled over rocks and roots as I found my way into the cover of the trees. I could hear their voices calling after me, pleading with me to return but I hadn't the will to listen. It felt as if a knife were being twisted in my guts. I ran as far and as fast as my legs could carry me until I saw light through the trees once more and slowed down. It wasn't right that I shouldn't even set eyes upon her. I'd travelled so far to find her, there was no way I could go home without having some tiny memory to show for it. I crept through the undergrowth as silently as I could manage to watch more closely. When I was nearly at the clearing I stopped and hunkered behind a tree. Without warning a hand went around my mouth and pulled me backwards. I should have known that James wouldn't be far behind me. He seemed to have an uncanny knack of knowing where I was. I forced my body round ready to protest and choked back a scream of surprise when I saw Perun's face. He pulled me towards him and kissed me roughly on the mouth, leering as if he were drunk.

'I knew you would come eventually. Follow me, you must meet some of your people. They have waited a long time for your repatriation.' He took my hand and led me into the centre of the circle. This was not the gathering where we'd found Ellette but I recognised the Perelesnyk, all of whom had the curious perfect features of Perun, unlined and unmarked. James had called him an incubus and since then I hadn't had time to ask any more about it. I recalled the kiss on the train that was the catalyst for this whole chain of events and knew with certainty that none of it was coincidence. Still, these people were welcoming me back, accepting me as one of their own. Whatever their agenda, at least I'd been afforded the dignity of recognition. In the centre of a group of young men and women sat a female, holding court. She rose to her feet as I approached and a hush settled over the crowd. She stared at me for some time and then slowly raised a hand towards me. I stared at the outstretched hand and began to sink to my knees in a gesture of humility. In a heartbeat the woman had stepped forward, grabbed my hand with her own and pulled me back to my feet. I felt a moment of fear quickly replaced by surprise as the night air was filled with shouting and cheering from the crowd.

'Eve, we feared you had been lost to Manitu forever. Welcome home, child. Let me see you properly.' She stepped back and looked deep into my eyes. I didn't know whether to laugh or cry. The woman held my face between her hands and raised her voice above the cheering. 'Eve has returned. We were told she was beyond our reach and yet here she is. Perun, you were right, she has retained her true nature even after all those years in the human world. Tonight we celebrate, welcome Eve back to her rightful home, and tomorrow we undo the brutal sacrifice that was made and return her to her proper place.' She held my hand aloft and the crowd became frenzied. I felt an uneasy exhilaration at the response of the crowd and yet I too was smiling and gripping hard to the woman's hand. Right or wrong, someone wanted me; someone felt that I had been cheated from my life exactly as I felt cheated. That one bit of empathy was worth putting aside my scepticism to bask in the warmth of being wanted.

The woman gently let my arm back to my side but did not release my hand. With the speech over, the crowd began celebrating in earnest, carousing, singing and dancing as Perun walked over to me. The woman smiled at him and put her free hand on his shoulder.

'Perun has not eaten or slept, he was so worried for you. He feared you were being poisoned against us. I am so glad you found your way to him. You and he have a bond. Do you feel it Eve? You must have done, to be drawn here to us.' I wasn't sure where this was going. I had stumbled into the middle of the Perelesnyk by accident, not through some mysterious bond. I nodded, smiling, and then realised I didn't even know her name.

'Forgive me,' I stuttered. 'I don't know what I should call you. Please don't be offended.'

'Do not let me hear you apologise again, not for anything. Here, in Manitu, you were born to be a ruler. After the cruelty, the injustice you suffered, you should never have to apologise to any of us. I am Mandalina, matriarch of the Perelesnyk. I am honoured to finally reach out and hold you in my arms. Now come, it must have exhausted you to get here. You need to eat and drink. Tomorrow we will take you to the Council of Families and repatriate you with your mother. For tonight, Perun will keep you safe. You two can have all the time in the world together now.' She leant to kiss my cheek and Perun slipped his arm around my waist as she disappeared into the night. I felt the odd sensation of both warmth and a chill when he touched me. He led me to where platters of food were laid out in the grass and the chance to regain some strength was welcome.

'So you made your way home. I hadn't expected you to be able to find us alone. Tell me about your journey.' Perun's fingers worried at the bark of a branch, slicing off tiny shards with his long finger nails and I realised he had been taken by surprise at my appearance. The gesture made me cautious and when I gave him a brief version of the last few hours I omitted any mention of James or Ellette. Perun put his food aside and leant closer to me when he spoke again. 'So you saw or spoke to no-one? It must have been frightening for you, not knowing where you were.'

'There were hunters running through the wood. I hid when I saw them but it showed me the pathway. I walked for an hour or so and then saw the camp.' His concern about what company I'd kept made me nervous for James, although I was sure he'd be safe enough with Ellette guarding him for the night. 'Tell me what will happen tomorrow. What's the Council of Families? I would love to be able to go and see my mother straight away.'

Perun held his hand out to pull me to my feet. 'Come, you need some rest. We will give you shelter here tonight and take you to see your mother tomorrow. It can be dangerous out there in the full dark, even for us. If it were safe we would have taken you to your own family already.' He took me to a tent made from huge leaves hanging across interwoven branches. Inside, the floor was a bed of moss and a tiny candle provided light. 'Put your questions aside until the morning. We are your friends Eve. It was me that brought you back, remember? You can trust me.' I had my back to Perun and was admiring the structure of the canopy when Perun brushed up against my back, sliding his hands over my hips. His touch sent chills up my spine. I don't know if it was my heightened senses or wariness at being amongst strangers but I was hit by a sense of foreboding like looking over the edge of a perilously high cliff. Perun was wrapped up in his own thoughts and unaware of the fact that I was frozen motionless.

'When you have stood before the Council and taken your rightful place in Manitu, perhaps then you and I will have the chance to know each other better. Our families can be bonded in a way that will bring peace. You and I are the future, Eve. The bond that brought you to me can only get stronger. Now sleep. I shall come for you in the morning.' He kissed me once on the nape of my neck and it was all I could do not to shiver. I said goodnight quietly without turning around, knowing that my face would betray me, and he slipped out of the tent oblivious.

I sat on the soft floor, legs shaking and a wave of nausea overwhelming me. I put my head in my hands and took a few deep breaths, desperate to fall asleep and dim the voices screeching inside my head but that would be the worst thing I could do. There was so much I didn't know and I had limited time to make some serious decisions. On the one hand I had an opportunity to meet my true family, find my proper place and answer all the questions burning me up inside. The Perelesnyk, who had accepted me unconditionally, were willing to make it all happen and yet they left me cold. Perun reminded me of a crocodile. When he touched me it was like being swallowed whole. I knew that Ellette would urge me to think of Zora and it was dreadful that what I did could devastate the lives of others but no-one, no-one at all, was thinking about me. I was the one who was sent to strangers to be raised. Surely I should be entitled to some sort of restitution. I decided to take matters into my own hands. I blew out the candle and sat quietly, listening to what was happening outside. There was no noise nearby so I pulled back the leaves a little to see out. The foliage shielded the ground from moonlight giving me the cover to creep out unnoticed. The revellers had quietened from earlier. I found a safe place against a tree and waited for my eyes to adjust to the blackness. I could hear raised voices in the distance, two men and the softer tones of a woman, Mandalina, I thought, in another tent. I slipped off my shoes and stepped as silently as I could to listen.

I made sure there was no light behind to cast my shadow against the tent wall and ducked down low.

'If you present her to Anousk without first warning the Vilya, you risk starting a conflict and losing the sympathy of the Council.' The man who spoke was older than Perun. His voice was edgy and tense. When Mandalina cut in her tone was soft but left no doubt who was in charge.

'That's enough. I have heard all you have to say and I value your wisdom, but there is no way we can warn Anousk without risking her refusal to see the girl. Once she does that, all is lost. I will not see a human take the throne. She has no right to dictate how the Perelesnyk will live.'

'And this woman, Eve, what makes you think that she will rule any better. Perun said himself she is all but human, now. We may displace one only to find the other is worse.'

'I can control her.' Perun's frustration with the older man was tangible. 'Her desperation to see Anousk will ensure that she does not leave Manitu again. Everything she valued in her world is lost; I've made sure of that. Once she is on the throne I will finish what I've started. She is mine for the taking. Human women are so ready to be seduced, it will hardly be a challenge. The Perelesnyk will rule for two consecutive sessions, once as husband to the ruler and afterwards in our own right. As long as we get rid of Zora we cannot lose.' I bit down on my hand to silence my rage.

'And Anousk?' The older man spoke again. 'You know it will destroy her to lose Zora. What makes you think she will not seek vengeance?'

'Anousk will have her first born daughter back. I have no doubt that her grief will be terrible. She will be in no fit state to do anything but lick her wounds for a very long time. And if Eve becomes too much like her mother and Perun cannot control her as he thinks then I'm sure she can be persuaded to revisit the human world. She still has ties there. Once she does that we will be next in line to take the throne. Now leave me, I need some quiet before the morning.' I stood to move away from the tent before Perun exited, afraid he would sense me so close by. As I did so a branch poked hard into my back and I gasped as it cut my skin. In a heartbeat there was silence inside the tent. I stood completely still, running not an option when I would break hundreds of twigs beneath my feet in just a few metres.

Without warning hands grabbed me from the branches above and I was lifted into the darkness. Even as I struggled I heard Ellette's voice telling me to stop and I recognised James's profile against the moonlit tree trunk.

Perun appeared below us. He stood for a few moments and then called to Mandalina that all was well. I relaxed as he left and the hands that held me let me loose to find my balance. I began to speak but Ellette shot her hand back across my mouth before I could make a sound. Her voice was a low growl in my ear.

'No, not here. Keep as silent as you can until I tell you it's safe.' I nodded to show that I'd understood and then we climbed out of the boughs and through the trees, away from the Perelesnyk's encampment. It was a good half hour before Ellette stopped moving. In the dark I had no way of guessing how far we'd come but I didn't begrudge her caution. We halted at a river to drink. The night was quiet around us and there was a large open stretch of grassland so that we could see anyone approaching. A vast tree marked the river bend and Ellette pointed up into the foliage.

'You will sleep there tonight. It is safe and well hidden. The lookout has been deserted for years and it is comfortable enough.'

'I didn't tell them I'd seen you. I'm so sorry Ellette. You were right about Perun. I know I shouldn't have run off. Please believe me, I didn't go looking for them. I stumbled into their camp looking for the Vilya.'

Ellette walked towards me with a curious look on her face. 'It makes me proud that you have such a strong love of your mother in spite of all you have been through. I am not angry sister, only glad you are unharmed. It's late. James will keep you safe.' She stepped closer to me so that only I could hear her words. 'He was beside himself with fear for you. Accept his guardianship, Anousk will like him.' I smiled at that. 'I must leave you now, the family will be anxious for news.' I caught her arm as she went to leave.

'So, you'll tell Anousk that I'm here? What made you change your mind?' She looked thoughtful for a moment.

'Necessity. The Perelesnyk have become too much of a threat to keep this from mother. She will be pleased to have news of you after so many years.' With that she pulled me into a hard hug, kissed my cheek and quickly wiped tears from her eyes.

'One last thing,' I said. 'What was it that Anousk owed Adela that made her change me for Zora?'

Ellette shook her head. 'I cannot answer that. Their reasons are known only to them. She has never spoken of it. I'm sorry.' She walked away, taking James gently by the arm and leading him to the tree where we would sleep that night. I was lost in thoughts of Anousk while they chatted in hushed voices, vaguely aware of James glancing over at me. When Ellette's voice became more insistent I broke out of my daydreaming and walked towards them. Their conversation stopped and Ellette shook James's hand in farewell. Before I could speak she had run off into the forest, turning back just once to wave to me. I thought I saw the faint shining of tears on her face again. By the time my attention was back on James he was already in the lower boughs of the tree, holding out his hand out to pull me up.

Seventeen

The lookout was high in the branches and when we finally reached it I could feel the muscles in my arms straining. A door in the base of the shelter pushed inwards and we hauled ourselves up. James had refilled his bottle from the river and Ellette had given him some food to keep us going until morning. There were windows in the lookout with views across the grassland, river and forest. The stars were shining so bright it looked as if you could touch them and animal pelts had been left to keep out the cold night air. There were no seats or beds but the floor was covered in a woven mat which was soft and warm. There were worse places we could have been spending the night. James secured the trap door with a heavy piece of wood and for the first time in hours I was able to relax. It occurred to me that if getting up into the lookout was that dangerous then getting back down would be nothing short of lethal. When I expressed my concerns James just shrugged.

'That's not something you need to worry about tonight, is it?' he said.

'No, but my shoulders are agony already and I feel like I've run a marathon. Until today I thought I was reasonably fit.' James hauled some of the pelts down into a pile on the floor and indicated for me to sit. When I'd made myself comfortable he handed me food and water. There were vine leaves filled with spiced beans then figs and berries afterwards. We ate in silence, taking in the wild beauty of the night-time landscape. I finished, wiped my hands and stretched myself out in the warm animal hides. When I turned to speak to James I caught him staring at me. He had a curious look on his face and I wondered what he and Ellette had been discussing before I'd interrupted them.

'You okay?' I asked him.

'I'm fine,' he replied, quickly. 'How are those muscles feeling now?'

I reached up and rubbed at my shoulders. 'Well, if I were at home I'd be in a hot bath with a glass of wine to self-medicate. But under the circumstances it could be worse, I guess.' I smiled at him and to my surprise he smiled back, slowly and tenderly. He met my eyes for long enough to make me feel a fluttering of self-consciousness in my stomach and I had to look away before the heat rising in my cheeks became visible. When I raised my head to look at him again I found him settling behind me and felt a shiver of electricity as his hands slid over my back. His hands were so big that they covered my shoulders completely and when he began to rubbing my aching muscles the warmth I felt was nothing to do with the animal furs covering me.

'Is that better?' His voice was so low that I could barely hear him. I managed to nod rather than speak, unsure how husky my voice might sound. His fingers held me still whilst his thumbs pressed small circles either side of my spine. I found myself chewing my bottom lip with the effort of controlling my breathing. His hands travelled further down my back and found the place just below my shoulder blades where all the touch receptors in my back joined. His finger nails scratched my skin lightly as he pressed insistently until I cried out and my body jerked forward without warning.

'Sorry, I didn't mean to hurt you.' Pain was the last thing on my mind. Every nerve in my body felt as if it were scorching.

'It's fine' I replied. 'Just a bit sensitive.' I reached for the bottle of water and took a long swallow. I held it out to him without looking at his face. As he took it his fingers brushed mine and I felt my stomach drop with a desire so strong that it rocked me where I sat. His arm reached round my waist and I closed my eyes, leaning my head against his chest so that he couldn't see how he was making me feel.

He laid me back onto the bed of pelts and stretched his body out next to mine. I rolled onto my side so that I could take a few deep breaths and slow my pulse. He slid his right arm under my head to provide a pillow and shifted his body behind mine, his left arm around my waist. The lust stirring in me was so overwhelming it was like being tortured. I willed myself to sleep but after a couple of minutes I knew I couldn't stay still like that, feeling his body hot and hard against my back. I opted for conversation as a distraction.

'I know so little about you. What are you doing here, with me?' I turned very slightly round towards him so that I could see his face out the corner of my eyes. He gave a quick smile and tilted his head up at the ceiling.

'Well, that's probably too long a story for a night that's already slipping by but if I'm honest I suppose I'm settling a score.' His left hand was stroking my arm slowly up and down as he spoke. He didn't even seem to be aware of it.

'A score with whom?' I let my body relax back against his. I wanted to see his eyes but the darkness showed only the greyest of silhouettes.

'The Perelesnyk. They took someone very precious from me a long time ago. I swore I'd do all I could to stop anyone else suffering the way I did.' He was as matter of fact as ever which only made his grief more apparent. I turned over where I lay so that we were face to face, ending up closer than intended but neither of us moved.

'Tell me,' I said. He smoothed my hair, tracing the line of my cheekbone and jaw with his knuckles. The gesture made me shiver and this time I didn't bother to hide it from him. He ran one fingertip around my lips and my nipples hardened as he touched his mouth to mine.

'I lost the woman I loved and the chance to ever love again. I forfeited everything you're looking for and I don't want the same to happen to you.' He swept my hair away from my neck and lowered his lips to skim from my ear down into the curve of my collar bone.

'I don't understand,' I said and slipped my right hand up his chest to grip his shirt. 'James, I can't think straight when you're doing that.' He pulled his arm from behind my head back so that his fingers slid into my hair, tilting my head backwards and grazing his teeth against the soft flesh of my neck. His other hand pushed against my hip bone to roll me onto my back. Before I could slow things down he was on top of me, one leg resting between mine. I could feel the steady pressure of his thigh pushing into me and it was all I could do not to thrust against him. His free hand slid to the front of my shirt and one by one I felt him undo my shirt buttons. He pushed himself up on an elbow to look at me as he opened my shirt and bra.

'Why do you need to think about anything right now?' I opened my mouth to speak but all that came out was something between a cry and a moan of pleasure. He let his hand continue its course down my stomach until he reached my jeans. He tilted my head back so that I was looking him straight in the eyes as his fingers opened the buttons and slid inside my clothes. He moved straight on down inside my panties, found my clitoris and circled it with his fingertips. I tried to open my legs further for him but was constrained by my clothes. I frantically pushed at them and in an instant he was up on his knees pulling my jeans and underwear off in one move and throwing them away. I sat up enough to lose my shirt and bra. In his face I saw the same carnal wildness that I was feeling. I lay back down on the fur skins watching as he stripped and knelt back down before me.

He straddled my body, one knee either side of my thighs, and brought his head directly over mine. I ran my hands over his arms and chest, feeling the coiled spring of each muscle quivering with pent up energy. I knew he was waiting for some sort of consent. His face was so beautiful in the half-light, just the tiniest glint from his eyes and the heat of his skin against mine. I ran one hand around the back of his neck and pulled his lips to mine. It was like being filled with sunlight. His tongue teased and licked the inside of my mouth and I shifted onto my side so that he could explore my body better.

This time when his hand moved between my legs it didn't stop. His fingers slipped into the wetness of my crotch and thrust inside of me. I took hold of his hand and pushed him even further, unable to get my fill of him. With his thumb he brushed over my clitoris until I could feel nothing else. I didn't breathe or move, I felt him tense above me, just watching and then a wave of pleasure exploded through me. My body shuddered in waves until my throat was hoarse with crying out. James lifted his mouth from mine and moved between my legs. When he entered me we rose and fell with one another in a rhythm that made me feel as if the world were spinning around us. He gripped my hand with his own, whispering my name over and over, his face buried into my neck. I had the strangest feeling that we were falling, that the earth had left us. When he finally came it was with a roar like a battle cry. He wrapped his arms around me so hard that I lost my breath and the stars I'd watched earlier seemed to be bursting inside my head. I called his name and felt my face wet with tears as one by one the stars faded and I fell into a sleep from which I wanted never to wake.

Eighteen

As I awoke I felt a stabbing pain in my back and when I came to my senses enough to investigate I found it was a tree root. A weight on top of me had me pinned to the floor and that panic shocked me from my stupor until I realised it was James's body wrapped around me, making breathing difficult. I dragged myself out from beneath him, blinking to adjust my eyes to the daylight and then took in the fact that we were no longer in the treetop shelter. I spun round to check James was unharmed and saw that he was starting to wake up. I was still naked and began hunting for my clothes. My jeans were caught a couple of branches up and as I climbed to retrieve them I could just make out the lookout far in the canopy above. At the river bank I took a handful of water to revive myself, then grabbed another and dashed back to James, wiping his face to bring him round.

'James, wake up. Something's happened. We've been moved during the night. James!' He opened his eyes and I paused for a moment reliving the detail of the night before. Unfazed by his own nudity, he reached out and took my hand.

'Eve, you're not in any danger now. We're home.'

'Home?' I repeated. 'You're wrong. We fell asleep up in the lookout. There was no storm; I didn't get angry; no-one brought us back through to our world.' James sat motionless. As I stared into the distance I saw my shirt in the grass and ran over to pull it on, looking around as I went. The river was still there, the large tree cradled in its bend and the forest spreading out around us. Still, I knew he was right. The colours were duller, the foliage more sparse. It all felt less vital, less alive.

'But we were so high up; we can't have fallen and survived. It doesn't make any sense.' James was get himself dressed.

'There were enormous branches supporting the lookout floor and I was ready for it. I was able to get you down safely most of the way. Near the bottom I lost my footing and we fell. I'm sorry.' The reality of the situation hit me. I felt sick to my stomach and leant over, clutching at my middle, trying to get enough oxygen to stop myself passing out. Before I knew it I was on my knees in the dirt.

'No, this can't be. I was going to see her this morning. After all I've been through, I was going to meet my mother. This cannot be how it ends.' My eyes were blurred with tears of rage. James reached for me but I hit him roughly away. 'No, don't touch me. I have to get back. Ellette will be there waiting for me.'

'You can't go back. You know what a terrible price everyone will pay if you do. Let me help you.' A terrible anger swelled inside my chest. I raised my face to his and could see the depth of regret in his eyes. Not enough, though. Not nearly enough to placate me. My voice was a growl I barely recognised.

'You knew.' I took a step further away from him. 'You knew what you were doing. That's what you were discussing with Ellette at the base of the tree.'

'Eve, don't make this harder than it already is.'

'How dare you. This was not your decision to make. And last night? What a bloody idiot I was, believing that you and I...'

I couldn't find the words for that. It had all been a sham; I'd been betrayed and humiliated. I turned away, unable to bear the sight of him. My anger was a block of ice inside me.

'Tell me how it works.' I hissed.

'Why don't you let me get you home and then we can talk as much as you want?'

'What I want is for you to answer me, right now.' He must have seen the blank determination on my face because he sat on a tree trunk a few metres away and in that soft voice confessed his conspiracy with my sister.

'You move between here and Manitu when you are beyond your normal consciousness; rage, pleasure, grief, terror. Ellette thought that it would be the easiest way to get you back safely.

You must believe she didn't mean to hurt you. She's protecting her world and the people she loves. I didn't want to see you used by the Perelesnyk to do something you'd regret so I agreed to what she suggested.'

'And everything last night was to get me back here? That makes you no better than them, doesn't it? At least with Perun I know what I'm getting into.'

'Eve, that's not true. Do you think that last night could have happened if we didn't both...' Before he could utter another word I cut him off.

'Don't! Don't you dare pretend it was anything other than a device! Well, I may be back here for now but I know how this works. You and I are done. I don't want to be anywhere near you for one second more, understood?' I walked across the meadow and found my shoes as I shouted at him. 'From now I'll do what I want, when I want and if that involves Perun, or anyone else you don't like, then you and I are going to end up on opposing sides. Stay away from me.' I didn't wait for a response although I suspected he'd realised that trying to talk to me was futile. I walked towards the river and followed the flow of the water. Eventually it would lead me down out of the mountains to Sabina's land.

I don't know if he followed at a distance. I didn't turn round to check and the water drowned out any other sound. It was midday before I got home and I hadn't even considered the impact that being missing for so long would have had. I had no time to prepare myself for the welcome from Sabina, desperate since the horses had made it back without their riders. We'd been gone twenty-four hours and searchers had, of course, found no sign of us. Sabina was up on unsteady feet to hold me before I could say a word and I realised I couldn't explain where James was. Fortunately, he was closer behind me than I'd known and whilst I was still in Sabina's arms he appeared across the back fields. He reassured her that we were both uninjured and then improvised a story about a flash flood. He explained that we'd had to take shelter in a cave overnight which had got blocked by debris. I said nothing, just nodded in agreement. Once Sabina was certain that no-one needed medical help and the emergency services were stood down, I managed to persuade her that all I wanted was a hot bath and bed. James offered to walk me home but I ignored the pretence of friendship, unable to talk to him directly. I felt his eyes follow me as I made my way along the path. Tears fell down my face with every step and that short walk felt longer than the entirety of the last day.

I slammed the door behind me, curled up on the kitchen tiles and felt nothing but a vacuum of grief which I thought would swallow me whole. I don't know how long I stayed there, knees pulled to my chest and eyes shut to the world. I must have slept after I'd burned out every tear I had because when I woke it was night-time. The worst of it was that in spite of losing an opportunity to see my mother, and knowing that my own sister had betrayed me, what hurt most was that my love-making with James was just a cheap seduction planned by someone else. There wasn't a single thought in my head that I wanted to remain conscious for and I only bothered to stand long enough to find whiskey and a large glass. I poured it without ice or water, drinking so much in one mouthful that I made myself gag. I made a fist with my hand and forced it down, keeping on and on until I finished it then filled the glass to the top again. I drank until I could feel numbness over-whelming me and then dragged myself to the couch. My laptop was still plugged in and the little light was blinking. I knocked the mouse and my emails lit up before me. I could just make out that there was a message from Naomi but nothing made any sense. I was dimly aware of clicking the reply button and then I was typing before I could stop myself. Unconsciousness took me soon after and I let go of the world and the horrible pain inside me, falling into alcohol induced stupor on the sofa. I can honestly say that I slept the sleep of the dead. Not one dream, image or conscious thought interrupted the next twelve hours. When I finally surfaced I paid the price for my self-induced oblivion and ran to the bathroom, vomiting. I sat on the bathroom floor, crying and emptying the contents of my stomach for the next two hours.

I rose shakily to my feet when my stomach had finished punishing me and caught my eyes in the mirror. I was whiter than white except for the blackening circles around my eyes. That was the first moment in my life when I thought suicide might be a viable option to stop the merry-go-round of pain and confusion inside. The dawning realisation that I needed help jolted me into action. I grabbed the phone and quick dialled the first person whose number came up, rambling for three or four minutes before hanging up. I'd spoken to someone but I wasn't even sure who and at some point I simply gave up.

The next thing I knew, a cool flannel being wiped on my forehead. I opened my eyes and found Xander staring at me as if he'd discovered a new species of insect. He must have realised I was coming round, because a second later he was bear hugging me so tightly it hurt.

'You stupid, stupid bitch. Don't you ever scare me like that again.' Xander was babbling and I had a vague memory of phoning him before everything went blank. I was propped up in bed and dehydrated like I'd never been before.

'Xander, let go, I can't breathe.' The grip loosened a little but he didn't let go completely. 'I'm sorry, I'm really sorry. Tell me what happened. Could I have some water before anything else, please?' I tried a weak smile but the panic was still evident in Xander's eyes and I saw, for once, that he wasn't exaggerating the drama of what I'd put him through.

He disappeared into the kitchen and returned shortly with ice water, hot tea and buttered toast. I hadn't figured on him having a maternal side. He opted for changing the subject and talked non-stop for the next hour about the reaction at the theatre when I'd gone missing.

After a while I drifted back into sleep and was vaguely aware that my agent Daniel Fortune had come to see me. By the time I surfaced one of Sabina's housekeepers was sitting at my bedside. She bustled out to fetch me some dinner and I did my best to eat the pot roast she brought. When I woke the next morning the sun was streaming through the window, opened to let in some fresh air. Another of Sabina's staff must have come over because I could hear dishes clattering in the kitchen and someone humming a tune. I put on a robe, ignored the horrors in the mirror and went to say that I was fine and they could leave.

When I got to the doorway I was sure I was hallucinating. Stood at my sink, putting wild flowers into a makeshift vase, was Naomi. She froze mid-sentence and I looked to see who she'd been speaking with. Just outside the door, reading a newspaper on the veranda, was Nate. I couldn't speak or move. I was crying before I could talk and Naomi was holding me in her arms in a flash. When she'd satisfied herself that I was in one piece, Nate came in. He opened his arms slowly, obviously unsure how I'd react. It was all the invitation I needed and I let myself be folded up in the safety and normality of him until I was sure I could speak without sobbing. I gave them the same version of events that James had given Sabina and they were full of questions about the flood and life on the ranch. Nate looked at his watch and said he had to go, explaining that he'd set up meetings with colleagues in San Francisco as an excuse to get over to the States at such short notice.

'So now I actually do have to go into the city for a couple of days to see these people. I'll be back for the weekend, though. Naomi's staying to make sure you don't get in any more life threatening situations until then,' he teased. I walked out to his hire car and remembered why I'd been so charmed by him. I was stunned that he'd come all this way to see me and more than a little grateful for the attention.

When I went back to Naomi she was waiting on the veranda with an empty chair pulled up next to hers.

'That looks like you mean business,' I said. She didn't smile as I'd expected. I sat down and waited for her to speak.

'I want the truth about how you are,' she said.

'Not great obviously, but I'll get better.' She didn't look convinced. 'Naomi, you don't have to worry, it was just a storm and we Brits aren't used to quite such dramatic weather.'

'That's not what I meant.' She stared hard into my eyes. I looked away even though I knew I shouldn't and she reached for my hand. 'I was talking about your email. That's why I'm here.' My face must have given away my confusion. 'You don't even remember writing it, do you?' The chance to lie convincingly was long gone so I shook my head. When I met Naomi's eyes they were filled with tears. She had a hand pressed against her mouth and took a moment before she could speak. When she did her voice was shaking. 'You said you wanted to fall asleep and never wake up. You said you'd lost everything. You talked about someone called James in a way I've never heard you talk about any man and said you'd been betrayed beyond what you could bear. Bits of what you wrote were incomprehensible but mostly it was just desperate. I've been worried sick, not knowing what state you'd be in when I got here. I didn't tell Nate about the email, just the official version. But I need you to reassure me there's nothing else going on, that I don't need to be really worried about you because I never, ever want to be scared like that again. Do you get it?' I did get it. I didn't want to read the email I'd written because I thought it might push me into an even darker place than I'd been. I reassured my friend that we would talk but that I needed a bath and some clean clothes to make myself feel human again before I could handle it. She agreed and we went back into the house together. I felt a little light creep back in where the darkness had been.

Naomi produced a light salad, some bread that she'd baked in the afternoon (even jet lag couldn't get her out of the kitchen) and then suggested that we go for a walk around the estate. She saw my hesitation immediately.

'We won't go beyond the fences, but you've been in this house for three days now. You need some fresh air. Come on.' I couldn't argue with the logic and I was longing to clear my head. Arm in arm we left the veranda and wandered around the side of Sabina's house down to the paddocks.

'I'm so grateful you came. I'm just sorry I lost the plot so badly. I think it's all been too much, you know, the last few months. Ever since I found out about the adoption my whole world has turned upside down. I feel a lot better having you here. How long can you stay?'

'Chambers have given away all my cases for two weeks but that's as much as I could get away with on late notice. If you need me though I'll stay as long as it takes.'

'I'll be fine. Two weeks with you here will be heaven although I'll have to diet for a month to pay for it.' Naomi looked relieved to see me joking.

'You could do with some home cooking. You've lost weight since you came here, I swear I can see your ribs.'

'Yeah, well I've got to fit into my costumes and I can't suck my stomach in all the time I'm on stage.'

'You know, with all the drama, I'd forgotten about that. So how is the new career? I always thought you were destined for more exciting things than the courtroom.'

'I've barely started yet; Sabina must regret ever casting me. I seem to have done nothing but cause trouble since I arrived.'

'I'm not regretting it at all, my darling. Now do introduce me to your friend.' Sabina had appeared behind us, moving quietly on her crutches, having spotted us from her house. I kissed her cheek in greeting and introduced Naomi. The two of them hit it off immediately, bound by their mutual concern for me. We made our way back across the meadow to Sabina's porch where a pitcher of iced tea was waiting. We talked about life as a lawyer, Sabina's acting career and I switched off when they discovered each other's love of cookery. As I watched the sun go down over the trees I heard Sabina suddenly call out.

'James, there you are! Come and meet Eve's friend Naomi.' I tried to make my face neutral before I turned round. For some reason I'd been certain he'd have left the ranch after all that had happened. It hadn't occurred to me that I'd have to see him again. I heard the soft fall of his boots up the veranda steps and watched him tip his hat to Naomi in greeting. To my horror she began thanking him for bringing me back to her safely.

'I'm not sure Miss MacKenzie shares your feelings on the subject I'm afraid, it was my decision to trek into the mountains that got us into trouble to begin with.' Naomi was murmuring about how ridiculous that was. 'How are you doing now ma'am? Recovered from the experience I hope.' I looked him in the eye and, to be fair, saw nothing but genuine concern. I tried to hide some of the bitterness I felt before Naomi picked up on more than I wanted her to.

'I'm fine. A couple of days rest was all I needed. Now that I look back on it none of what happened was worth making such a fuss about.' I forced a smile and he returned it with more ease than me. Dissatisfied with the impact my comment had on him, I continued. 'In fact, I'm feeling so much better since Naomi arrived that I'm going back to rehearsals tomorrow. I've left everyone waiting too long already.'

'Oh darling, you don't need to do that,' Sabina interrupted. 'We've been going through the scenes with your understudy reading in. You should take a few more days to recover. You've had a dreadful experience.'

'Not at all. To be honest, being trapped like that was more an exercise in conquering boredom than anything. I shall be back at the theatre in the morning. I hope you won't mind if I bring Naomi along to watch, I can show her Carmel when we've finished. Now, we'd better be getting to bed, I want to be back on top form and I certainly can't go out in public with my hair and nails this much of a mess.' We said our goodbyes and Naomi left Sabina promising to swap recipes the following evening.

'Cup of tea?' I asked Naomi as we walked back into the kitchen.

'What the hell was all that about?' Naomi blurted. 'You can't go out with your hair and nails in such a state. I've never heard you come out with such rubbish. You're the least vain person I've ever met. And going back to rehearsals tomorrow? After everything you've been through, you've got to be kidding me.'

'I just figured staying busy would be the best thing to do. I can't sit around here feeling sorry for myself and I have a responsibility to the rest of the cast. I thought you'd be pleased, positive outlook and all that.'

'I would be pleased if I believed it was real. It just seems like it came out of nowhere.' She put the kettle on, clattered mugs around for a few moments and then continued. 'Now that I think about it, it didn't come out of nowhere. This new positivity, if that's what we're calling it, only appeared when James spoke to you. Talk, MacKenzie, there's something you're not telling me.' She placed two steaming mugs of tea on the table, put her head in her hands and stared at me.

'You're imagining it,' I countered.

'That's a load of crap and you know it. Are you in love with him?'

'No, I am fucking well not in love with him.' I reacted more angrily than I should have and the extraordinarily sharp Naomi, whom everyone underestimated, seized on it straight away.

'Then why the overreaction? No-one could blame you for falling for him. I'm engaged to be married to the most wonderful man in the world but I can still appreciate how someone like James would make you feel. Toned body, that sense of quiet control, great accent, sexiest walk I've ever seen. The two of you thrown together like that. I can only imagine...' I finally lost patience.

'You can't imagine. You don't know what it was like. I know he seems perfect but the truth is very different. He's manipulative and controlling and will stop at nothing to do whatever he thinks is right. And it doesn't matter what his body's like or his eyes or his voice or anything else. I found out the hard way that he can't be trusted, okay?'

Naomi sat still for a moment, contemplating.

'Wow,' she said. 'I knew there was something going on but I had no idea he'd affected you that badly. I won't tell Nate, you know, you didn't promise him anything and he came here not expecting anything. So what happened?'

'Nothing happened, I just...' I didn't know what to tell her although some sort of explanation was owed. 'You're right, there was a connection, or at least I thought there was. I misread him, that's all. Maybe it's just my pride that's hurt. I think I made a fool of myself, you know how I am about that.' I put my cup in the sink so that I could get out from under Naomi's stare.

'He didn't seem to be the sort of man who would be into playing games, quite the opposite and he looked genuinely concerned about you.'

'Well, all I can tell you is that he didn't turn out to be what I expected at all.' I knew from the resignation in Naomi's voice that she wouldn't push this any further tonight. I made my excuses and sloped off to bed. I could hear Naomi in the guest room on the phone to Tim and envied the reliability of her relationship. I shifted my thoughts to Nate. It was time to have a good long think about what I really wanted from my life. Perhaps Nate was exactly what I needed. Maybe it was time to stop running away from commitment.

Nineteen

If it did nothing else, seeing James forced me to return to rehearsals as promised and I threw myself into the role of Katharina, the shrew, with a passion I hadn't previously felt. Naomi was filled with endless praise and I began to believe I might actually be able to pull the whole thing off by opening night. For the next week I was spoilt with Naomi's chatter, home cooking, and the attentions of Nate who returned from San Francisco with the news that he'd arranged to stay for the next month. It was a surprise but not an unwelcome one. I quickly settled into a routine with people around twenty-four hours a day to keep me busy. I would catch a glimpse of James every other day or so although he was careful to stay out of my way. There were no signs of Perun and I took to reciting my lines out loud every time I found my mind wandering onto the painful subject of what had happened in Manitu. With each passing day it seemed more like a bad dream than anything else. Naomi was becoming increasingly attached to Sabina, would sit next to her during rehearsals and could be found pouring over recipe books with her in the evenings. The two weeks' vacation passed all too quickly and before I knew it we were in Nate's car to the airport to see her off.

As sad as I was to see Naomi go, I knew she was missing Tim and eager to get back to work. I hugged her at the departure gate. Just as I was about to let her go she pulled back and whispered in my ear.

'The thing with James. I didn't ask you any more but Sabina says he hasn't been the same since. She says he seems lost. I just thought you ought to know.' I didn't say anything. I couldn't. Whatever Sabina and Naomi had been discussing, they didn't know what he'd done to me. I'd be lying if I said the mention of James didn't make me curious but I could rely on Nate. It was about him now. He was the one who'd come running, unbidden, just when I needed him. I wasn't about to fall back into old habits and reject someone reliable just because I imagined something more exciting around the corner.

'I'll miss you so much,' I said. 'Be here when the play opens. Promise? Besides, Sabina has practically adopted you. She'll never forgive me if I don't get you back soon.'

'Just try keeping me away.' She smiled and kissed my cheek. 'Call me, day or night, whenever you need me. Love you.' With that she was gone. I watched until she was out of sight then Nate took my hand and we walked back to the car in silence.

'I thought we'd go for a picnic,' he said. 'All packed and ready.' In the back seat of the car I noticed a picnic basket and rug. He knew I'd need something to take my mind off Naomi's departure and had chosen exactly the right thing. 'Know a good beach?'

'I certainly do,' I replied, setting the navigation unit and tuning the radio to something upbeat as we set off for the coast. A few miles north of Santa Cruz is Bonny Doon beach and from the way Xander had raved it seemed like the perfect secluded getaway. We found it easily enough although negotiating the path down the cliff with a picnic basket was more challenging. I thought I could run down the bottom few metres but slipped at last moment, landing heavily in Nate's arms. I laughed as he brushed sand out of my hair. When I went to pull away he held me to him for a moment. I thought he was going to kiss me but he smiled that sweet smile of his.

'As much as I'll miss Naomi, it'll be good to have you to myself now,' he said and released me so I could get my footing on the beach. Whilst Naomi was there Nate had stayed in a separate room to me. It wasn't something we'd discussed, just the way it had worked out. I'd been grateful, needing my own space. I wondered if he'd be sleeping in my bed tonight and felt some nerves at the prospect. We paddled for a while but the water wasn't warm enough for much more and then settled to eat our picnic. Nate had been thoughtful about everything and I found myself wondering if I shouldn't just pack my bags, fly home with him, let myself be taken care of and forget this endless search for belonging.

When we'd eaten almost everything in the basket we lay back on the blanket and stared at the clouds. As I closed my eyes I felt Nate's hand slide across my belly and then he kissed me. I don't know if I wasn't expecting it or if it was too soon but I jerked my head away. I swore quietly under my breath and wished the earth would swallow me up. Nate had been about as perfect as anyone could ask for the last two weeks and here I was ruining everything.

'Nate, I'm so sorry. You just took me by surprise. I guess I'm still a bit jumpy, it's nothing to do with you.'

'That's okay,' he said. 'No pressure, I wanted you to know that I still feel exactly the way I did when you left, that's all. Would it help to talk about what happened?'

'I don't think so,' I muttered. Telling him about James was a certain way to close my door to a future with Nate forever. 'Could you just hold me for a while, instead?'

'Of course,' he said, but I recognised the slight downward cast of his eyes as disappointment. He felt my unwillingness to be intimate with him. As he held me I had my back to the sea and felt him tilt his head to one side. Curious, I followed his eye-line and saw a completely nude young woman walking straight in front of us and down to the water. I could understand why Nate was staring; she had a stunning hourglass figure and skin like milk. I was slightly taken aback that his attention was elsewhere and then he broke the moment with a laugh.

'I had no idea what sort of beach you were bringing me to. Presumably we're not obliged to join in?' Nate was looking further along the sand to where other naked sun worshippers were braving the chill in the air.

'Oh hell, I had no idea! My friend Xander comes here all the time. He didn't tell me about this. No wonder we managed to avoid all the tourists. I'm going to kill him!' I busied myself putting picnic things back in the basket and as I looked up I saw the girl reappear in no hurry to get back to her towel. She emerged from the surf, skin healthy from the sun and breasts that would never need surgery to perfect them. I turned to Nate to make a joke and caught his face, completely captivated by the girl's beauty.

Silenced, I looked back to her. She was staring at us, wringing the water from her hair, smiling unabashed. It was the first time I'd studied her face and as I did I registered the line-less perfection of the Perelesnyk. A wave of nausea, so strong that it cramped my stomach, gripped me. She watched, beaming still, as I doubled up on the rug. I couldn't let Nate see what was happening and I did my best to hide the way I was affected. I needn't have worried, he was still open mouthed at the girl's unashamed nakedness. I knew I was being sent a message that they were still watching, able to follow wherever I went. I threw the last of the items into the basket and put a hand on Nate's shoulder to break the spell.

'Come on, I think we'd better go somewhere we're more at home.' Nate shook his head to wake up and I caught the blush on his cheeks when he realised he'd been staring. 'Ready to brave the walk back up the cliffs?'

'Sure,' he said. 'Good idea. Let's get moving.' I walked in front carrying the rug but twice when I glanced back I saw him following the girl's progress up the beach. I felt a flash of irritation then reminded myself of my reaction to Perun the first few times. So much for being able to walk away from it all. I thought they'd have relented by now; they knew from my disappearance that I wasn't willing to help them. I had to stay calm. Getting stressed and angry would only make me vulnerable, which was exactly what they wanted. As much as I longed to return to Manitu, and I certainly planned to soon, it was a journey I was going to make on my own terms, when I was good and ready. My anger started to rise and I chased it down with banal thoughts of what to cook for dinner. Having agreed on fajitas, we stopped at a store to get supplies, arriving home in the early evening. Nate went off to shower whilst I cooked.

When Nate came into the kitchen he was still dripping wet with just a towel wrapped around his waist. I whistled appreciatively, and he slipped his hands around my waist. I leaned back against him as I stirred thin strips of beef in the pan. He dipped his head to my neck and began kissing just below my ear. I didn't stop him; the last thing I wanted was a repeat of the awkwardness that afternoon. I told myself that it was natural to feel reticent and that if I just went with it I would soon get in the mood.

I turned round in his arms and kissed him back hard, but I was pretending a passion that I wasn't feeling. Nate was obviously pleased by the response and pushed me, gently enough against the kitchen cabinets. I could feel his frustration by the hardness under his towel. His hand moved over my breast and I shuddered. I wasn't ready for this at all and now I didn't know how to stop it. Nate took it as a sign of longing and suddenly he was undoing my shirt and trailing his lips down to my breast. I couldn't carry on anymore and pushed him away.

'Nate, stop, I'm not ready for this yet.'

He looked incredulous, standing with his hands on his hips. But you kissed me; you let me do all that. You knew where it was going. I know you've been through a lot but you're not a child, Eve. Is there something else going on?'

'No, I don't even know what you mean. There's nothing else. I just need some time. I explained it this afternoon, I thought you understood.'

'I understand you were trapped in a cave and it was scary and that you had a really bad time. As sympathetic as I am, that doesn't seem to have any relevance to the way you're behaving now.'

'Listen, I need you to let me deal with this in my own time.'

'I thought you wanted me to stay here. What did you expect when Naomi left? That we'd carry on sleeping in separate rooms? I'm a patient man but I'm not a saint.' I couldn't offer any better explanation, nor could I tell him when I might be in the right frame of mind to pick up our relationship where we'd left off. Evidently, my face told him all he need to know and he disappeared into the guest bedroom. I turned off the cooker and threw the food into the sink. Nate came back fully clothed, bags in hand.

'I'm going to stay in Carmel for the night. I'll text you when I've found a hotel so you know where I am if you want to talk. I'm not punishing you, okay? I just don't think I can spend the night here knowing you don't want me to touch you. Good night.' I didn't say a word, partly because nothing I could say would make the situation any better but mostly because I knew he was right. I heard his footsteps fade into the distance and the faint roar of an engine a few minutes later as he left the ranch. I locked the door for the night and caught movement out of the corner of my eye in the woods. I stepped out onto the veranda thinking that whatever it was would be scared away by my presence. Quite the reverse was true. After a few seconds I saw Perun step out from under the canopy to face me full on in the moonlight. I had no idea what to do. Running was pointless, they could find me wherever I went. I still didn't think they meant to do me any physical harm, quite the opposite, it was in their interests to keep me safe. The ringing of my landline made me turn my head away from Perun and in that split second he disappeared. I stepped back inside and locked the door. He knew where I was and if he wanted to talk he'd be back soon enough. Having established that the caller was Naomi letting me know she'd got home safely I tried to take my mind off Nate and Perun by watching television. It didn't work, I couldn't concentrate on anything and reading was impossible. I toyed with the idea of finding James to tell him that Perun had reappeared but quickly decided against it. The last thing I needed to do was layer on more complications. Whatever was happening would have to wait until morning.

I heard my phone buzz to signify a new text and decided not to bother reading it. Instead I lay on my bed and tried to run through my lines. I fell asleep with my head resting on the script and awoke to the sound of thunder. I was freezing cold and stiff. I pulled the covers over me and stared out of the window at the rain that was just starting to beat down. I closed my eyes again but sleep wouldn't come this time. I had the increasingly nasty feeling I'd missed something, like when you forget what you're saying in the middle of a sentence. I got out of bed to get some tea and found myself staring through the window where I'd seen Perun earlier. There was no-one there now and I was grateful Nate hadn't seen him when he'd stormed out earlier. Of course, Perun probably had seen Nate.

I was pouring boiling water across my hand, overflowing from the cup, before I completed the thought. I was such an idiot. The girl on the beach wasn't there to send me a message, she was there for Nate. I ignored the burning pain in my hand and sprinted to the bedroom to throw on whatever clothes were at hand. If Perun was using Nate to get to me I had no time to worry about finding James to help, it might be too late already. I jumped on my bike with the briefest glance at my phone. As promised, Nate had sent a text with his hotel details and I set off at breakneck speed, hoping the noise of the storm would be enough to cover the scream of the engine.

In spite of the treacherous conditions it was the fastest I'd ever made the journey into Carmel. When I reached Nate's hotel I looked again at the text message. He'd given me his room number so I was able to bypass reception and given the state I was in that was just as well. My heart was thumping and I jabbed my finger repeatedly onto the button for the elevator. I gave up on that as I saw the door for the staircase and sprinted for the second floor. I leapt out into the hallway, breathing hard. If I were wrong about this Nate was going to have an awful lot of questions about the state I was in. Too late to debate it now. I tried to keep my footsteps quiet as I made my way down the corridor looking for room 226. When I found it I put my ear to the door. I could hear nothing at all and it seemed as if I must have let my imagination run too wild this time. Just as I'd made up my mind to walk away a loud smash came from inside the room and I knew that my instincts were right: Nate was in trouble. I hammered on the door as hard as I could. There was silence again and I repeated the hammering, knowing that whoever was in there would have to open up before I woke the entire floor. I could hear a man's voices cursing and then the door was flung open. I looked into Nate's eyes and saw the shock on his face as his eyes travelled involuntarily to the girl in his bed. He began apologising and explaining how he hadn't planned this but his frustration from earlier had got to him. I heard very little of what he said, the girl and I had not broken eye contact since the door opened. She knew that her role had been played to perfection and I knew that my assumptions from earlier were correct. It was the girl from the beach, sent by Perun. She made a point of standing slowly so that I could take in her nakedness. Finally Nate recovered his senses and asked her to leave.

She took her time slipping her clothes on. Even then Nate couldn't keep from glancing back to watch only now I felt nothing but pity for him. This was all my fault. He'd become a pawn in the game and I was responsible. I was just glad that no harm had come to him, having pictured much worse when I heard the lamp smash although I didn't let my mind dwell on how that had happened. Nate finally stopped babbling and looked at me.

'Say something,' he whispered. 'Slap me or shout at me or something.' He sat on the edge of the bed and put his head in his hands. 'I don't know why I did it. I saw her in the bar, recognised her from the beach and then she came over. We had a drink and the next thing I knew we were up here. God, Eve, I'm so sorry. Tell me what I can do to make this right?'

I knelt in front of him. I couldn't explain what had happened but I could do something to make him feel better; I could tell him the truth.

'Nate, look at me,' I took his hands in mine. 'You don't need to feel bad. You left tonight because of the way I've been behaving and I don't blame you. Forget the girl, I don't care about her. I care about you, though, so there's something you need to know. I slept with James, the night we were trapped. I was afraid and cold and, well, it just happened. I didn't tell you because I thought we could make a go of things. That's why I've been acting so strangely with you. It's me that should be sorry for this whole bloody mess. You came here to help and I've done nothing but hurt you.' He didn't say anything but at least he hadn't pulled his hands from mine. 'Whatever we had, it's not working here. I'm not the person I was Nate, and until I sort myself out I think I'm just going to end up damaging anyone I get close to. Honestly, you've had a lucky escape.'

I stood up and gave Nate a few minutes to take in what I'd just told him. I poured him a brandy from the mini-bar and took a sip myself. He took the glass gratefully. Ever the gentleman, he pulled himself together faster than I would have managed in the circumstances. We finished our drinks in silence, recognising the futility of recriminations or apologies.

I left about fifteen minutes later. Nate would be leaving on the next flight he could get. My journey back to the ranch was unremarkable and by the time I arrived I had no memory of the drive. I felt sick to my stomach as I walked back to the house, pausing with my key in the lock. Nate wasn't the only one who deserved an apology. James had tried to warn me how dangerous the Perelesnyk could be. He may have taken matters into his own hands and made a decision against my will but at last I saw Perun would stop at nothing to get what he wanted. I didn't bother to check my watch or make myself presentable, just threw my keys and jacket on the kitchen table and set off through the dark to the staff quarters on the far side of the ranch. There was no light on in his cottage but I knew from Sabina where he lived. I was sure she'd passed me the information to try to start some sort of intrigue, little did she know.

I knocked softly on his door and waited. It was only seconds before it swung open. His face looked like thunder and I thought he was about to start yelling when he dragged me into his arms, holding me so tightly I couldn't move. I could feel his heart thumping in his chest and allowed myself a moment to close my eyes and remember how he smelled. When he pulled away he took me by the arm and kicked the door shut behind us.

'I heard your bike leaving. I knew there was something wrong. Are you hurt?' I shook my head, surprised by how emotional he was. He gestured to a crumpled old sack of a chair by the fire and I sat down as he lit kindling and got the flames going. 'You want to tell me what happened tonight?' He stretched out on the floor, long legs in faded jeans, bare chested and completely unselfconscious. I moved my eyes to the hearth before he caught me staring and watched the flames flicker around the logs, the warmth spreading through the room. I told him everything that had happened that day and he stayed quiet until I'd finished. When I'd explained what I thought was going on, only leaving out my confession to Nate, I moved myself onto the floor so that I could look him straight in the eyes.

'I came here tonight to say sorry and I know it's long overdue. It's taken me a long time to see how dangerous the Perelesnyk are, but now I know you were trying to protect me from whatever they have planned. I still wish it could have worked out some other way but I wanted you to know that I get it. I didn't before; I was blinded by my own needs. I'm glad you stopped me from finding my mother, you were right.' I slid my hand onto his right cheek softly as I kissed his left. He closed his eyes and said nothing. He didn't try to return the touch and I was glad, it was a gesture of conciliation rather than anything else. I rose and walked back to his front door. As I was reaching for the handle I heard him sigh deeply.

'It's vengeance, the reason I'm helping you. I didn't want you to go through the same thing that happened to me. That's why I'm here.' I watched him, not moving in case I broke whatever spell had made him start to talk. He gestured to his side and I retook my place on the floor.

'I told you that the Perelesnyk are incubi, meaning they seduce humans. The female, called a succubus, does the same. That's what the girl is you found with Nate tonight. They're sometimes called night demons or storm demons. They can fly at night which is why it's been so easy for them to follow and find you. In most ways they detest humans but they can't breed without them, that's why they spend so much time here.'

I ran my hands through my hair, the heat spreading around the room now. 'I still don't understand how you got involved in all this?'

'The succubi look for human men to impregnate them when they're fertile. They find a man whose defences are down, drunk or frustrated, and they take advantage when resistance is at its weakest. They work the same way as any predator. I was just nineteen years old when I got married. She was my school sweetheart. We'd known each other forever, I guess. We'd both been brought up with old-fashioned values and had decided to wait until our wedding night to consummate.' He stopped to pick up the fire-irons and turn over the dwindling logs. 'Our wedding was beautiful, a small church way out in the country, just close friends and family. In the evening we went off in a little car I'd saved a year to buy and drove to Fort Bragg where a friend of her parents had a little place. We were going to walk along the beach, go riding, lock the door behind us and pretend the rest of the world didn't exist for two weeks.'

'So what happened?' I said when he seemed to have lost himself in his memories. He almost jumped when I touched his arm and I withdrew my hand.

'We got to the house late that night, been driving for hours, must have been two in the morning. It had been a hell of a long day but I'd been waiting what felt like a lifetime to make love to my wife and I didn't care what time of the day or night it was.

Anyway, she said she had a headache and hoped I didn't mind if she just got a little sleep, start fresh the next morning. I don't know where it came from but I got angry. I was overtired and like most nineteen year olds, overwhelmed by my own testosterone. Like an idiot I accused her of making excuses and told her she was leading me on. There's not a day goes by that I don't hear every stupid word I said to her over and over in my head.' His voice wavered for the first time and tears shimmered in his eyes. I looked down at my feet, feeling like an intruder. He shook his head and continued.

'I stormed out only stopping to pick up a bottle of whiskey from the kitchen. I walked down to the nearby beach, threw stones in the water and got as drunk as I could as quickly as I could. Next thing I knew there was a woman, taking her clothes off ready to go skinny dipping. I didn't make a sound, just watched her. I knew I should've turned and walked away but after being rejected, or so I was telling myself, I thought it was fair enough to just watch. Then she turned round and beckoned to me. That's all it took, all the will power I had. I ran down the beach, dropping my clothes as I went. By the time I reached her I was ready for anything. She didn't say a word, just swam around me, giggling, touching me under the water. I was almost crazy with frustration. We got out of the cold water and ran under the cover of the trees. She started running away, teasing me, hiding behind the trees. She'd let me catch her for a few seconds, kiss me, put my hands in places I'd never touched a woman before and then she'd run off again. Before I knew it I didn't recognise where I was, the trees, even the moon looked different. I was drunk with alcohol and frustration and lost all sense of time.'

'She'd taken you into Manitu,' I breathed. 'What happened?'

'At last I ran into a clearing and found her just lying there waiting for me. No more games, she was naked and more perfect than any woman I'd ever seen. I lay down next to her and kissed her and it was like drinking wine. I never wanted it to end. Only it felt like I was out of control all of a sudden, like I was drowning in her. It was exciting and terrifying at the same time. Then I thought of how my wife would have looked, how she would have tasted, what her body would have looked like naked, laid out on the ground like that. That flash of guilt, maybe I was sobering up, I don't know, but it made me want to get out of there as quickly as I could. The succubus must have felt the change because all at once she was on top of me trying to force her body onto mine. When I saw her face it was pure animal, no softness, no humanity. I hit her. I've never hit a woman in my life but I was so full of rage and guilt that I lashed out. She wasn't expecting that and it gave me the chance to get up and run. I could hear her calling after me, crashing through the undergrowth but I just kept going.' James sat forward clutching his knees with his arms. His muscles were tensed so hard that his arms were shaking. I almost didn't want to hear the rest of the story.

'As I ran through the forest I could hear the sound of the waves in the distance. I knew it must be the path to the coast so I followed it as fast as I could. Then I could hear another voice, my wife, calling and calling my name. I was naked and dirty with another woman's sweat on my body but all I wanted was to throw myself into her arms and ask her forgiveness. Every time I thought I was getting close to her I ran into a dead end of thickets. In my rage I screamed and tried to push my way through a thorn bush scratching the flesh off my arms as I went. I could see nothing but a haze of red in my temper but as I got through to the other side and calmed down the scenery looked normal again. I stood still and listened for my wife's voice and then heard her calling. I burst through the trees and there she was, just reaching the top of a cliff path a couple of hundred meters away. I screamed to her at the top of my voice and I must have scared her because she slipped. I saw her spin round to the sound of my voice and then the stones under her feet were kicking up dust. I ran towards her but it was like swimming in mud. She fell backwards and her hands were grabbing for something, anything, to hold onto. There was nothing there. She must have hit the cliff face two or three times as she fell, I heard every tiny noise. It was as if the sea had become silent for that minute just to punish me, to make sure I'd never forget. She was dead when she hit the bottom. I scrambled down the cliff face and held her and begged her to forgive me, to come back.'

His face was streaked with tears, as was mine. 'James, you don't have to go on. I understand now, I'm so sorry, please don't put yourself through this.' He grimaced and I saw more anger and hatred in that expression than I have ever seen on the face of any person.

'The succubus appeared behind me. She was laughing and laughing. She told me that humans were foolish and pathetic, choosing to deny themselves pleasure out of guilt. I remember telling her it wasn't guilt, it was love.'

'In the cave with Zora she said something about a curse. What happened?'

'She was furious that I'd rejected her. The curse was no more than I deserved. She said that if I ever found love again then that woman would die just as my wife died. She cursed me to a lifetime alone. Funny, really; that punishment is probably the only thing that stopped me from taking my own life. It made me feel as if some sort of justice had been done.'

We were both silent for a very long time. There was nothing I could say, no words that could be of any comfort. When the fire died I fetched blankets from the bedroom to slip round our shoulders then made coffee. I had so many more questions but we both needed sleep. When we'd finished our drinks I took him by the hand and led him to the bedroom. He lay down without speaking and I crawled behind him, wrapped my arms around him and closed my eyes. I wondered if he'd be able to sleep but soon the rhythm of his breathing slowed and deepened. I slept fitfully, dreams of falling waking me two or three times. I opened my eyes to find bright sunshine filling the room and James sitting on the edge of the bed watching me. I sat up to see how he was this morning and was relieved to see he was himself again. I showered while he made breakfast, both hungry in spite of the night we'd had. Afterwards we went back to my house so I could change my clothes before we went for a walk. James knew I had more to ask him and the reappearance of the Perelesnyk last night was something that couldn't be ignored.

Twenty

We got through the next hour with small talk and little eye contact. The sunshine, for once with barely a cloud in the sky, lifted both our spirits. Sabina waved us a cheery good morning as she took her breakfast on the veranda but didn't call us over. I read more than a little curiosity in her eyes at the sight of the two of us out together so early and knew she was imagining a very different night than the one we'd spent together. My heart lurched unexpectedly at thc thought. This was a man who could never hold a woman in his arms and think of a future with her. How futile would the world seem if that were me? Tears sprang to my eyes and I dashed them away before he noticed. There had been enough crying for a while.

The horses began to trot towards James before he'd even called them and they waited in line at the fence for some attention as we walked between the paddocks. He looked younger to me than he had before and I wondered if it was because I was seeing the bereft nineteen year old who would always be stuck in that moment of time, constantly punishing himself. As we jumped across the stream that ran through the lower meadows he reached for my hand automatically. I must have hesitated before taking it and he looked at me quizzically.

'It's okay you know, it's not catching.' I laughed and the gloominess was gone. I felt a tingling sensation across my skin. A light breeze picked up and the sun seemed warmer. The colours of the leaves were bright and sharp and for a second I wondered if we'd wandered unwittingly into Manitu. When I glanced ahead, sitting on a boulder as still as could be, was Ellette. Her hair looked on fire in the sunshine and I wondered if mine was the same. I don't know if she was concerned I would still be angry or that I might turn and walk away but she did nothing, just sat there and waited for us to reach her. Without thinking I was scrambling up the river path as fast as I could and her eyes were wide with surprise. I threw myself at her and held her fast. In the stupor of the last few weeks I'd done my best not to think about what had happened in Manitu but it finally registered that I had a sister, real family, a blood bond. Whatever she'd done, all I wanted was feel her in my arms and be grateful she existed at all.

'Ellette, I'm so happy you're here. Thank goodness nothing happened to you, I was worried Perun might have figured out who helped me escape.' I kissed her warmly on both cheeks and she smiled, nodding over my shoulder to James.

'Sister, I am glad to see you safe. We must talk quickly. No-one knows I am here. James, will you walk with us?' She did not let go of my hand and I felt the odd combination of excitement and trepidation as we walked under the trees for cover.

'Is it mother? Has something happened to her?' I asked.

'No, not mother,' she paused and looked at me quizzically. 'Has anything happened since you got back, have you seen or heard anything from Perun?'

I briefly recounted the events of the last few days. She didn't seem surprised by what I'd told her.

'It was Perun's last desperate attempt to make you so enraged that you would pass back into Manitu. He must have thought that seeing your lover Nate with the girl would distress you so much that you would lose control. How did you manage to control yourself so well?' she asked.

'I don't know,' I stuttered. It was something I'd been wondering, too. 'I suppose I didn't really feel angry, just sorry that Nate had been dragged into my mess.' James was staring at me. It was obviously a question he'd been wanting to ask me. I felt too embarrassed to tell them that the relationship was already over before Perun had stepped in. The Perelesnyk had overplayed their hand and may have ended up doing me a favour. 'Why do they want me back, anyway? I assumed they'd have given up once they knew I wasn't going to help them willingly.'

'If Perun can present you to the Council, willingly or not, you would be the oldest daughter of the Vilya alive in Manitu and first in line for rulership. Willing or not, blood ties among our people are strong, and being there so close to mother, with your whole family around you....Perun must believe that once you experienced that, nothing in the world could make you leave again. He is almost certainly right, which is why James and I did what we did the last time we met. I am sorry we lied to you Eve. It has caused me more pain than you could know.' In my sister's eyes I saw she was telling me the truth.

'Ellette, you didn't come here to make peace, although I'm pleased you have. What's wrong?'

'Zora has gone' she said and her face was downcast when she spoke. 'Late last night she vanished from her bed. She has never done that before. She does not like to be alone for long and she has not returned this morning. We can find no sign of her anywhere and we cannot track her. Someone must have covered the trail, Zora is so unaware of herself that she can never hide from us. Now it makes sense. When Perun's plan to get you back to Manitu failed they did the only other thing they could. They took Zora. If she is not presented before the Council they can stop her ascension to the throne and power will pass directly to the Perelesnyk.'

I swallowed hard. Ellette was obviously desperate with worry and I couldn't imagine how our mother must be feeling. 'What will they do to her?' I asked. The thought of her being harmed was sickening, she was so innocent and trusting.

'I do not know,' said Ellette. 'They will have to keep her hidden and cannot risk her being able to tell the Council what happened. She will be terrified by now, she has never been separated from mother,' she stood abruptly. 'I must get back, we have to continue searching. The ascension ceremony is at sunrise after two more moons. Forgive me for not spending more time with you. I must tell mother what I know.'

I took in the full implications of this. 'You mean she knows, about me? She knows I was there before trying to find her?'

'Yes, when Zora disappeared last night I knew I had to tell her everything. She wept with joy to know that you are well and strong. I have to go Eve, we are running out of time.' I leapt to my feet and went after her.

'You can't let them take her place. They have no right. There must be something you can do to stop it. Won't the Council listen?'

'There are already other families who believe Zora should not take power with human blood still in her veins. I cannot make an accusation against another family without risking war and I will not shed bad blood after good. I have a long way to travel for the ascension and I still have to do all I can to find our sister.'

'Where?' I said. 'Where will it be?'

'The Rock of Ages. You call it by another name. El Capitan at Yosemite? All the families will travel there from every corner of Manitu,' she stopped long enough to repeat my gesture of kissing both cheeks. 'I promise I will come back and tell you what happened. For now, you must let me go. Stay safe, Eve. I cannot lose another of my kin,' and with that she disappeared into the trees as if she were an animal, barely rustling the leaves.

James had hung back, waiting until I was ready to go home. He took one look at my face and I heard him whistle softly under his breath.

'Oh, now there's a new look and I don't think any good will come of it,' he waited until I was level with him and we walked back towards the ranch. It felt good to find that the part of me that was always up for a fight still alive and kicking. James knew exactly what I was thinking. The next time I looked he was grinning from ear to ear and the sight was beautiful. I grinned back and felt my blood pulse with adrenalin. By the time we'd reached the lower paddock I knew exactly what I had to do.

'So, are you coming with me to Yosemite?' I said. James pulled his hat down over his eyes as he always did when he was thinking.

'You sure you know what you're doing?' he asked. I didn't have an answer so I just shrugged my shoulders. 'You know, I never thought I'd miss the hot-headed, ill-tempered little madam you were when you first came here but I guess you were more endearing than I thought.' I raised my eyebrows at him and before I could retort he pushed me against the wooden fencing, one arm around my waist and his other hand with his fingers entwined in my hair. 'Please, just for once, don't argue,' he muttered and I felt his lips on mine, soft and dry, his body a wall of heat against me.

He kissed me until we were both breathless and when he pulled away I found myself as carefree as I had been a year ago.

'You know, we are under some time pressure here,' I said.

'Well then, you'd best go get ready. I'll fetch the jeep. Better tell Sabina we'll be away all weekend before she calls out the troops.' We walked back up towards the lodgings and his fingertips found mine for a second before we parted to prepare for the journey. It was a tiny gesture but it made me painfully aware of the sort of man he really was. There was a reason I hadn't been the least bit angry with Nate. I clamped down hard on those thoughts and steeled myself for a battle I had no idea how we could win.

Minutes later I had a rucksack packed with food, water and a change of clothes. I emailed Naomi to say I was going on a retreat for the weekend and not to worry if she couldn't get hold of me. Then I spoke to Sabina as James had suggested. She asked who I was going away with and when I'd told her it was James she winked and wished me a wonderful weekend. She also confided in me that Daniel Fortune was coming over that night and said it was a shame we couldn't double date. I was glad she'd finally given in to his request for dinner and crossed my fingers that we'd make it back to find out how it went. It was the first time it had occurred to me that we might not. I guess if you thought too hard about consequences then nothing extraordinary would ever happen. James and I didn't speak as we climbed into the jeep. There was a map on my seat and the sat nav unit was already programmed.

'Do you actually have a plan?' James asked as we got on the road.

'No, but the least I can do is buy the Vilya more time to find her. You sure you want to do this? I mean, it's not your fight. I understand why you're here but it's my family and you don't owe me anything, far from it.'

'I was having dinner in a restaurant in San Francisco with some ranchers I was working with, when I saw this beautiful young woman,' he glanced at me. 'You couldn't really miss her, hair like redwood and a body that moves like a cat. As she walked out it was clear that something was wrong and then I saw the face of the man she was with. I knew he was one of them, another one here to take what they want without caring what damage they leave behind. Since seeing you that night I made it my mission, foolhardy or not, to find you and do whatever I could to keep you safe.'

'So it was you at the theatre, asking about me?' He just smiled. 'How did you find me?'

'Well, your face was all over the papers that week as the newest member of the Pacific Repertory Company so that was the easy bit. I'm not sure I've done too good a job of looking after you since then. But I'm here now and I'm not going anywhere until I know you're out of harm's way.' He put the radio on, finding a country and western station that made me feel about as far from London as a girl could get. Dolly Parton and Kenny Rogers were singing Islands in the Stream and I shut my eyes to pretend I was on a different journey with this man, where we weren't heading towards a land so wild I had no way of knowing if we'd make it out alive. Then something deep inside my head finally put together what I'd been missing for so long.

'Found me from the newspaper photos,' I said.

'Hey, I wasn't exactly stalking you,' James replied. 'You were all over the papers.'

'No, not you. Perun. Before my first trip to Krakow I'd represented the same soldier the year before. There was loads of publicity, I was asked for interviews, there were pictures in the paper and on TV. That's why Perun targeted Albert Cornish in the bar. He knew I'd be asked to defend him again. None of it was an accident, from the very start.' James said nothing. He'd been trying to warn me for such a long time. I'd been such a bloody fool for not seeing the whole picture earlier. A horrible thought occurred to me.

'He needed me to find out that I was adopted. My mother's accident...you don't think?'

James took one hand off the steering wheel and covered mine to stop it shaking. 'You'll probably never know and it won't change anything now. There are some people we can still help and that's what we're going to do. At least now we won't underestimate the Perelesnyk. You need all your energy to get through the next forty-eight hours so just think about that, okay? When it's all over you can sit and put the pieces together. For now, I'd rather you just concentrate on making it back in one piece. I don't want to lose you as well.'

Twenty-one

It took us just short of four hours to get from Carmel to Yosemite, stopping a couple of times for fuel and coffee. By the time we hit the entrance to the National Park we realised we had no idea where to stay the night. We had about thirty-six hours until the sunrise that marked the ascension ceremony in Manitu. Although we knew we were low on time it seemed safer to bed down in a cabin at Yosemite that night and cross over into Manitu at dawn. The less time we were there before the ceremony, the less likely it was the Perelesnyk would find out their plans were under threat. The last thing I could do was risk putting Zora in more danger than she already was. Yosemite Village was busy but James managed to find us a tiny lodge for the night. We grilled food outside and sat watching the stars before falling asleep on our bunks. James didn't kiss me again and I kept my distance from him so that we weren't distracted; we had enough to deal with planning for the days to come. I fell asleep trying to figure out how I was going to get us into Manitu the next morning. One thing was certain in my mind, given the curse the succubus had put on James it was way too risky going there the way we'd come back last time.

At four in the morning James was shaking me awake. It was still dark outside but the sky had that dark blue translucency before it lets first light through. We packed up and left everything we could in the car, keys and all. Backpacks on and torches in hand we began the trek to El Capitan, the three thousand foot high granite monolith that had dominated the valley for one hundred million years, named by the American Indians to whom this was home. By the time we'd walked through the valley to get to the foot of the mountain, daylight was showing us the path. We stowed our torches and sat down to rest. The place was deserted and I knew it was now or never. An hour from now climbers, riders and hikers would be appearing from all sides.

'How are we going to do this?' he asked. 'You've got to take me through with you and as far as I can figure that means I have to be close to you when you go.'

'I thought about it last night. I need you to tell me something and I'm sorry to ask.'

'That's okay,' he said. 'Whatever it takes.'

'I want you to tell me her name, your wife.' James looked away, this was the last question he'd been expecting. 'When you told me what happened you only referred to her as your wife, you never said her name. I need to think about all the people the Perelesnyk have hurt and how they need to be stopped but I don't have a name for her. Do you mind?'

'No, that's fine. I call her my wife because that's all I had, those few short hours when she was just mine. Everyone else who knew her can call her by her name but for that short time she was my wife. I'm the only one who can say it. That's why.' I put my hand over his and wished I could do more to take his pain away. It helped me, though, feeling that raw emotion, seeing his grief. 'Constance,' he said. 'Although everyone always called her Connie. I hope it works.'

I nodded and turned my back to him. He put his arms around me while I closed my eyes and tried to lose myself in the memories of all the pain, mine and others'. At first nothing would come, I was so wrapped up in what I was trying to achieve that I couldn't focus on the faces I needed to see. I shook my head to clear my thoughts and James whispered in my ear.

'The train wreck when you were travelling from Krakow. You remember the storm? That was them, their first contact with you. Can you see the faces of the people travelling with you?' I nodded but this was the one memory I'd been avoiding and I didn't want it in my head, even now.

'Did they scream, the people in your carriage? Did they have time to scream?' James felt me try to pull away from him but he held me still and carried on, his voice low and insistent in my ear. I felt the warm flow of tears on my cheeks and tried to turn my head away from him.

'Did they die straight away or did it take a while after the accident? What happened Eve? Could you help any of them or were you too scared?'

'Stop it, please, I can't think about that.'

'It wasn't your fault Eve, it was Perun. It was their first strike to make you weak and vulnerable. It's what they do and they'll stop at nothing. There were children on that train and they threw their lives away as if they were trash. Did you watch them die or close your eyes?'

As unwanted as they were, the pictures came rushing back into my head as if I were right there, right then. I recalled walking through the train to my carriage and saw the faces of twin girls, no more than five years old, playing with their dolls as they waited for the train to leave. A young mother in the carriage next to mine had been trying to find a quiet corner to breast feed her baby away from curious eyes. A teenage boy and girl in my carriage had been making eyes at each other since we pulled out of the station. A sob burst from me and I rocked forward, the pain in my stomach shocking and unbearable. I was sick before I knew it was going to happen. I was dimly aware of James still holding onto me but I was too far gone to take any comfort from it. I felt Perun's lips on mine and heard the sound of the storm swirling and all at once there was ripping metal and screaming and blood and fire.

I forced myself to relive events with Marcus in the Dragon's Cave and how he'd pushed me to the floor and then time shifted again and I was seeing the horror on Nate's face when he opened the door to find me standing in the hotel corridor. Finally I found myself with Constance. I could see her as if I'd been right there, her relief when she heard her new husband's voice calling to her and then the terror as she scratched all the nails off her fingers trying to find something to stop her falling down the cliff to her death. I felt her sadness from deep inside me as if she were giving me what I needed to get us into Manitu. The curse that these demons had put on James finally sank in and I knew the one man I wanted was the one I was destined never to have. The last thing I heard was Zora's voice calling to me, not crying but just terribly lonely and confused. I could hear a woman screaming over and over and then realised it was me. James's arms were wrapped vicelike round my waist as I kicked and struggled to be let go. The depth of my sorrow and anger took me down into a blackness from which I couldn't imagine escaping. At last, when I could take no more, a void descended and relieved my agony.

I knew we'd made it to Manitu before I was even conscious, the whole feeling of the place was different and much more extreme than the first time. James took longer to come round than me and I made sure he was comfortable before walking round the small clearing to check that we hadn't disturbed anyone or anything. The last thing we wanted was to alert anyone to our presence before absolutely necessary although I needed to let Ellette know where we were. As much as I prayed that Zora had been found safe already, in my heart I was sure that wasn't the case. We had twenty-four hours to figure out what to do and how to do it. I sat down and rested my back against a tree. In the tranquility I let my mind reach out to Ellette. She'd had no problem finding me when she needed to and I suspected that given time I would be able to do the same. It took a while but finally I could bring Ellette's face into vision, clear but dreamlike. I could hear her voice and feel the softness of her skin. I tried to call out to her but she didn't seem to hear me. Frustration broke my concentration and her face swirled into a cloud of colour. James's voice startled me.

'Hey, wake up! Eve?' James was kneeling in front of me. However awful it had been getting here, we had a job to do before anyone else got hurt. James pulled me to my feet. 'I'm sorry about what I said to get you here, seeing you in that much pain was...' He broke off unable to find the words.

'Don't,' I said. 'You did what I couldn't. Let's find Zora and make it all worthwhile. We should get somewhere with more cover, it won't be long until the families start to arrive to make camp for tomorrow and I still haven't quite figured out what we're going to do.' We picked up our backpacks and walked into the undergrowth, following a small track up the mountainside until we found shelter. We stopped, ate and drank, then found a small inlet in the rock to stow our packs where they'd be out of sight. It was lucky we moved when we did. Minutes later we heard voices in the distance, with occasional shouting and laughter. A large crowd was on its way to the base of the mountain. James and I peered out of our small shelter and I could see a line of tall blond haired people, thin and willowy.

'Who are they? They aren't Vilya or Perelesnyk.' I wanted to put my head out for a better look but James pulled me back. Over the course of the next twenty-four hours the valley would fill up with the different families and I was excited by the prospect of seeing them all.

'They must have been travelling for days or weeks to be here,' James whispered. 'Look, there's another group coming around the base of that outcrop.' Dusky-skinned men were carrying wood, meat and pelts, their torsos painted with what looked like pale clay in intricate patterns. I was trying to see what the women in the family were like when I was distracted by what I assumed were small animals scampering through the undergrowth along the base of the cliff where we were hiding. I heard James swear under his breath and took a closer look. They were people, smaller than us, but running on all fours like foxes. Everyone was heading towards the Rock of Ages so at least I was certain we were in the right place. I sensed that Ellette was behind me before I'd glanced over my shoulder. Alongside her were two other young women, with the same deep red hair as mine, staring at me as if I had two heads.

'Sister,' she said in a hushed voice. 'I felt you come through searching for me. This is too dangerous. What are you doing here?'

'Buying you some time. Are you any closer to finding Zora?' She shook her head and the girls with her looked nervous. 'We've come to help, Ellette. No one else knows we're here. I won't let Perun win, he and his family have done enough damage already. And don't worry, I'm not here to see mother. We need a way to move around with you without being recognised. I had no idea there would be so many people.'

'There will be thousands by nightfall, although with every family represented there will be enough races here for you not to be recognisable. Take my hood, and don't forget that you are one of us sister, you do not stand out in Manitu. You are Vilya. It is James who will be recognised as human and he is in danger. Very few will tolerate a human watching the ascension ceremony,' she spoke to one of the girls who disappeared from the shelter, running. 'We will bring clothes that will help hide you. We picked up Zora's trail a long distance from home but lost it again at the river. The Perelesnyk can fly at night. They are able to carry others with them for very short distances. I believe they took her across the river to break her trail. There are no bridges for hundreds of leagues from where we lost her trail and the current is too strong for us to swim.'

'I can help,' said James. 'I'll be able to find a way across the river; you just have to take me to the narrowest stretch you know. Eve should come with us though, she can't stay here alone, it's not safe.'

'I'll be fine,' I replied. 'Just help them find Zora. You'll need as much manpower as you can get to construct a crossing for the river without it being obvious that many Vilya are missing from the ceremonial group. I just need to know some more about what'll happen at the ascension.' Ellette held me close.

'I didn't want to ask for your help, you've been through so much already. Thank you for coming, sister. I will keep your man safe if it costs me my life.' The girl who had left the cave so abruptly returned, thrusting clothing towards James who threw them on and looked at me. He didn't saying anything, didn't need to. Ellette whispered to her companions who nodded and then she and James were heading for the trees without so much as a goodbye. For a second my strength failed me and I desperately wanted James to come back, then I recalled Ellette's words. I was one of the Vilya. I had a family to protect and there was no time to be afraid. The two other girls were sitting down and motioned for me to join them. I had to find out every detail about what would happen at sunrise tomorrow and work out a way to stop the Perelesnyk from completing their coup.

We talked the rest of the morning away and I found out about the other families. The system was tribal in structure but democratic in its procedures. Power passed from family to family by crowning the matriarch's oldest child. Because Zora and I were changelings the position was unique. Ellette had been right when she said there were other families who sympathised with the Perelesnyk's view that a child of human blood should not take the throne. Humans, for the most part, were considered primitive in Manitu. Our world was accessed when necessary but other than that we were thought of as destroyers of nature; war mongers with no understanding of the value of the world. I could sympathise with some of that but it was a terribly one dimensional view. If the Vilya could not put forward their oldest child tomorrow then the Perelesnyk would be entitled to present theirs. It was no surprise to find out that meant Perun taking the crown. The Council was composed of the most senior male from each family, two hundred and eleven in total. Ellette had told the two young women to do whatever I asked and to reveal my presence to no-one. I needed to be hidden overnight somewhere I'd have easy access to the ceremony in the morning and that wasn't going to be easy.

By the time the girls had told me everything that could possibly be useful, dark was starting to descend on the valley providing enough cover for us to make our way out of the mountain shelter and into the forest. We'd agreed that the only safe place for me to stay tonight was in the Vilya's camp where at least I wouldn't look out of place to onlookers from other families. I put on their traditional clothes, covered my face and wondered how I could avoid contact with everyone.

Their camp was a series of small tents that looked like upturned boats in a line along the river side. The mood was sombre as I'd expected, which at least meant they were all distracted and quiet as we made our way through. I was to have Ellette's tent for the night. She was a senior daughter so she wouldn't be sharing with anyone and I could await any word of their progress finding Zora. We bypassed the main meeting areas and were within about twenty meters of my tent when a voice behind us called out.

'Serenta, I've been looking for you. I was worried that you too had disappeared. Where have you been all afternoon?' The girl next to me froze momentarily and then recovered enough to step in front of me before replying.

'I am so sorry to have worried you, Anousk. Ellette asked me to stay part way along her trail to bring back word of Zora. I have only just returned.' I was sure my heart must have been audible outside my body and I felt faint with the buzzing of blood through my ears. My mother was stood no more than a few arms lengths in front of me. I could hear her voice. A dozen steps forward and I could touch her. It was dark enough that I risked raising my head a fraction to try to peak out from beneath my hood. I wanted so badly to see her face with my own eyes.

'Who is that with you, child? We need to make sure that everyone is back in camp before we sleep. It is too dangerous for anyone to be left out there alone.' If I were discovered now it would risk everything. Ellette had made it clear that Anousk could not bear to lose Zora and I wasn't here to cause more pain. I grabbed the arm of the other girl next to me who I thrust forward. She recovered her senses just in time to stop Anousk's curiosity in its tracks.

'They are attempting to cross the river tonight, Anousk. They believe they can track Zora on the other side. They have headed for Tormund bend where the river is narrowest.' She walked forward and took Anousk by the arm. 'Come, let me tell you about it in your tent where prying ears cannot overhear. All our party is safely returned. You do not need to be concerned tonight.' Anousk allowed herself to be led away to hear the details of the day and I finally stole a glance at her.

It was like looking at myself in the future as I hoped I would be. Her hair had kept its deep red tones, cheekbones a little higher than mine, skin with a slightly more colour from the wind and sun. But her face was pinched with fear and sorrow. I could see the exhaustion from maintaining her public composure but there was no mistaking the underlying grief. I was desperate to comfort her but I knew the sight of me, right then, would do more harm than good. This society was no different from mine, there was good and bad, coveting of power and unacceptable prejudices. I watched until she disappeared into the shadows then made my way to the tent. It was dark but warm with a bed roll on the floor and fresh water, vegetables and fruit had been left for me. I forced myself to eat even though I had no appetite and lay down. There would be a signal to rouse the Vilya in the morning, as it would still be dark when the family had to make their way to the Rock.

As I drifted asleep I heard Zora crying again. I tried to reach out to her in my mind but there was no blood tie and it didn't work the way it had with Ellette. I had only a few hours left until I did something that might change me and my future forever. I hoped I wasn't making a dreadful mistake.

At the sound of the horn in the small hours I quickly put my hood back on in case anyone entered Ellette's tent unexpectedly. There was little I could do in readiness since we'd left our backpacks in the mountain shelter. After a few minutes a voice whispered to me and the tent flap pulled back to reveal one of Ellette's companions from yesterday passing me fresh water and what smelled like sweet porridge. I took it gratefully and she stayed with me as I ate. The camp was quiet apart from the sound of scurrying feet. There was still no word from Ellette. The Vilya were about to face the dawn with no first born to take the throne. I suspected the atmosphere was very different in the Perelesnyk camp.

A hand thrust more clothes into the tent, a long white gown, too large for me but it would have to do so that I could look like one of the Vilya women for the ceremony. I put it on and wondered how I looked. I had a pang of missing Naomi, imagining what she'd say if she could see me now. I wasn't sure I'd ever see her again. Leaving Manitu may not be an option, given what I had to do. It was still pitch black outside although there was increasing candlelight and if you listened carefully you could hear the sound of many feet treading through the forest, making their way to the valley of the Rock of Ages to prepare for the ceremony. The ascension was supposed to happen at first light and there was little time to spare. I had to stay well hidden from the Perelesnyk so I put my hood back on over my robe and waited until we were last to leave our camp. I kept thinking that any minute James would appear, bringing Zora with him, saving the day. Behind us, though, there was silence.

What I saw when I reached the clearing stopped me in my tracks. The valley was filled with tiny torches, the light a strange yellow green from the surrounding trees, and the shadowy movement of thousands of bodies. It was remarkably peaceful given the numbers. I could see a central spiral of flat boulders making what looked like a prehistoric snail shell on the ground. Over the next few minutes, while the Vilya took their places, I hung back behind the tree line. One by one, the stones were claimed as seats by the elder male from each family. The Council was gathering. I could see my mother towards the front of the

Vilya, a shawl over her head, not talking to anyone. By now she must have been fearing the worst and I didn't blame her.

I'd had a glimpse yesterday of the amazing diversity here but that hadn't prepared me for the sight this morning. Perun had told me that we were often referred to as demons, at least that seemed to be the closest generic term humans had and I could see why. There was skin of every colour and texture, hands that looked almost webbed, people so tall they appeared stretched and others with faces that were closer to animal than man. Yet here they were, sat together peacefully, waiting for a process that they had agreed upon to create a fair society where no one family dominated and everyone had a voice. Superficially it seemed idyllic and yet I knew that the Perelesnyk had plotted Zora's downfall with military precision and I couldn't help but wonder how many other families would do the same to hasten their path to power.

A chorus of wailing started. Thousands of feet up on the edge of the summit I could see an enormous torch being lit to mark the start of the ceremony and the calling of families to order. The song, if you could call it that, lasted no more than two minutes and immediately afterwards an absolute silence descended. The members of the Council stood as one and starting at the outermost end of the spiral each man bowed to the centre of the circle. The effect was hypnotic and reminded me of toppling dominoes. At the end, they held up their individual torches and a young woman rose at the centre. This must be the current ruler, little more than a teenager but holding herself with tremendous dignity. She was dressed in midnight blue robes representing the end of her reign. Her family were the Polevoi, field spirits, who'd made it their mission to slow ecological deterioration in the human world and they were popular rulers for it. There followed a lengthy section of the ceremony where the Polevoi ruler went to each Council member, starting at the centre and moving outwards round the stones, extinguishing his torch and saying a few words to each man in turn. When she finally reached the outer edge of the spiral a cry went up from one group of watchers. I could just make out the similarity of their features to the outgoing ruler and realised that this was a mourning sound to mark the end of their reign.

I heard rustling in the bushes behind me and could feel the presence of one of the Vilya. Ellette, I thought, she's finally coming. I spun round to greet her, stopping myself calling her name out loud. It was lucky I did not; my own wishfulness had fooled me. It was one of Ellette's companions, Serenta.

'Still no news?' I asked. She shook her head and held a finger to her lips to caution me to be quieter.

'This is it,' she said. 'For the next few minutes whilst the Council are given new torches Manitu is without a ruler. Unless Zora appears for mother to present her to the Council the Perelesnyk will move to offer their Matriarch's first born.'

I held my breath. I had no reason to believe it and yet in my heart I was sure that James and Ellette would appear to put the balance right. A girl's voice rang out among the crowds.

'According to the tryst of peace sealed with the blood of every family I pass on my crown.' I realised that all the families were starting to stand. Word must have passed that Zora was missing and everyone was straining to see what would happen next. I took the opportunity to move through the trees and stand behind the Perelesnyk. I didn't have much time. I saw Perun crane his neck in my direction and was sure he could sense my presence. He looked disoriented but then seemed to shake it off. I enjoyed the irony that he'd convinced himself it was just his imagination playing tricks.

'Come forward, Anousk, matriarch of the Vilya, and give your first born to serve Manitu.' I watched Anousk rise to her feet. She was less steady than I had expected and her head was bowed low. A lump rose in my throat and I wished there was something I could do to help her but it was more important than ever that she had no idea what was about to happen. She stood alone before the Council and there was an uncertain pause. Whilst everyone knew what was supposed to happen next, it had never come to pass that the oldest child was absent. Anousk turned to the crowds and raised her head to speak.

'My daughter Zora is not here to take the crown. The Vilya will not be...'

'The Vilya will not be represented by Zora,' I cut in, years of speaking in court coming to the most unexpected use. 'I am Eve, first born daughter of the Vilya. Anousk is my mother.' I walked through the centre of the Perelesnyk family. 'Perun of the family Perelesnyk told me of my true heritage and showed me the way back to Manitu to take my proper place amongst you.' The crowd parted to allow me access to the spiral stones where the Council stood open mouthed. I stopped as far from my mother as I could to avoid any chance of touching her. 'Thank you, mother, for presenting me. You may step back.'

I wanted everyone to believe that Perun had brought me here so that the Perelesnyk would be unable to argue my ascension. If they did I would have no hesitation in accusing them of taking Zora, something that was too much of a risk for the rest of my family. I, on the other hand, had nothing to lose. I needed my mother's shock to be genuine and she really did look as if she'd been struck by a thunderbolt. The outgoing ruler recovered her composure before anyone else and held her hand out to me.

'Eve, daughter of the Vilya, you must approach each member of the Council to validate your ascension.' I walked forward and tried to ignore the gasps of shock running through the crowd. I was surprised I got as far as I did before Mandalina protested.

'The child Eve was sacrificed as a babe in arms by Anousk. She has lived a lifetime in the human world. She cannot be allowed to ascend to the throne here. She does not share the values of the families of Manitu. It is the right of the Perelesnyk to put forward my first born to rule.'

The first Council member on the edge of the spiral stood on his stone to be heard and seen more clearly.

'Do you deny, Mandalina, that you brought Eve of the Vilya back to us?' Mandalina paused for a split second too long to make a lie credible and she knew it.

'I do not deny it but surely we should debate what the right course is for every family's sake. I had no way of knowing that Zora would not be here to ascend. We brought Eve here to take her place within the Vilya, away from the poison of the human world. We did not foresee these events.'

'But she is the first daughter of the Vilya and I see no-one rising to claim that she is anything other than a full blood child. In truth, you would have had more reason to challenge Zora's ascension than you do Eve's. Present yourself to me, child.' I stood before the Councillor with a confidence I didn't feel. 'Do you accept servitude of the families gathered here to witness your ascension?'

'I accept,' I replied.

'Then light my torch, Eve of the Vilya, for I acknowledge you as ruler.' A flaming stake was thrust into my hand and I lit the Councillor's torch with it. He indicated for me to move round the circle and each councillor asked me the same question. I went around the circle until each man had acknowledged me and every torch was lit. By now the sky was streaked with light and the torches looked bright white in the coming dawn. I was taken to the plinth at the centre of the spiral where a necklace of different stones was placed around my neck. Each stone represented one family and the circle reflected the joining of them all in unity with their new ruler. Looking out at the faces of the Perelesnyk, and some of the other tribes around the circle, I wasn't entirely sure that unity was the right word for what they were feeling at the moment.

The innermost Councillor stood on his stone and raised his torch.

'A new reign begins,' he cried and threw his torch on the damp ground to burn out. The other Councillors rose together and did the same. With the torches out and the new dawn upon us, I was ruler of Manitu. Cries went up throughout the valley and I could hear the sound of wood knocking on wood and stamping. One by one the tribes began their own strange song, some sounding close to animal cries and others almost choral. One of the Councillors took me by the hand and kissed my cheek. I was welcomed home and embraced as ruler whilst the valley erupted into celebration. Ellette's companions came to my side as quickly as they could to guide me through the masses. The Vilya greeted me coldly and with suspicion. I had replaced their beloved Zora at the behest of the Perelesnyk, they thought, and for all they knew I was responsible for her disappearance. It hurt me to deceive them in this way but I wanted to avoid reprisals by the Perelesnyk against my people. If the Vilya were seen to have nothing to do with my presence it might just protect them.

Last of all I stood before my mother. She stared at me hard showing no sign of her earlier grief. She dismissed those around us but we could not create enough distance to stop prying ears, everyone wanting to hear our first exchange. She bowed formally.

'I am here to serve you, ruler.'

'You do not have to bow to me,' I said. 'That's not why I came.'

'I have no idea why you are here. Ellette told me you left Manitu the first time unwillingly. She did not think you would return.' Her coldness was like ice and the reunion I had played over and over in my mind seemed like a ridiculous fairy-tale now.

'I came because the Vilya should not lose their time to rule and because I believe that under your guidance all can be protected,' I reached my hand out to her then dropped it again quickly. 'I wish no harm to Zora.'

'I know that, child, but if you have come at the bidding of the Perelesnyk then harm will follow whether you want it or not.' She was upset and letting her guard down. Others had come closer to hear what she was saying and I had to stop her before anything could be construed as an accusation against the Perelesnyk. I was saved by one of the Councillors requesting my attention. There was a great feast planned for the first breaking of bread after the ascension and I was expected at the table. My mother made her excuses and I saw her disappear into the bushes. It was just as well, otherwise she would have been sat next to me at the table and avoiding physical contact with her would have been nigh on impossible. The last thing I wanted was to inadvertently expel Zora out of Manitu and into the human world, if that wasn't where she was already. I took my place at the table, smiled as genuinely as I could and asked endless questions about the traditions of the Council and the different families. I ached to be able to tell my mother the truth, to tell her that James was looking for Zora and that I wasn't here to take her place. For the next few hours the celebrations went on and there was no way I could disappear to find her. She needed to know that everything I'd done was for the good of the Vilya. I looked into the sea of strangers and felt my heart sink. I hadn't planned for the eventuality that James and Ellette wouldn't return.

Twenty-two

The revelries went on throughout the day. There was dancing, music, each family having its own traditions and members of the Council were given gifts by the Polevoi to thank them for their service. It was never ending and I wished I could have been there as a simple observer rather than the centre of the attention. I was able to rest in the early evening as part of a ritual where the first born of each family had their hands decorated laying on pelt beds. It was a preparation for the evening. As dark descended tiny lights appeared in the trees around the valley. Oil was burning in shells hung from the branches and the effect was mesmeric. Everything was illuminated and the colours of the shells were extraordinary. It was truly beautiful and for a minute I stopped obsessing about Ellette and James, until I wished they were here to share the moment with me. Even if they hadn't found Zora, I'd expected them to come back sooner than this. Ellette would have to hide James first but soon her absence was going to cause serious concern.

Slow dance music started as the darkness was complete and I felt a familiar hand take my arm. This was one moment I'd hoped to avoid. Perun pulled me to where people were gathering to dance. I agreed with all the pleasantness I could muster. There was an audience watching and it wasn't worth ruining the illusion I'd created. I let myself be swayed to the music in his arms.

'Well, that was unexpected,' he murmured. 'Do you have any idea what you've started?'

'I'm here because you came to find me. It's you who started this, not me. If you're not pleased with the consequences you only have yourself to blame,' I pulled my head far enough back far enough to see his eyes. 'Anyway, I thought this was what you wanted. You worked so hard to get my attention: Angela Smyth's rape, back in Krakow, that was all your doing, knowing I would get involved. It was a bit crude, really, but it worked.'

'A rape? It never fails to astonish me how human women delude themselves. She was begging me to violate her and when I finished she was on her knees wanting more. I left her sobbing at the depths of her own depravity and when she couldn't comprehend her own behaviour later she cried rape. The story is always the same.'

'I don't understand why you despise humans so much, when your race cannot procreate without them. You should be grateful. And anyway, everything you did brought me here in the end, so why the bitterness?'

'I did not bring you here this time. You did that all by yourself and after fighting it all that time. I just cannot understand the sudden change of direction.' His fingertips were pushing hard into my side and I forced myself not to flinch.

'Seeing Nate with that girl, the girl you sent, I felt nothing. I realised I had no reason to stay there any longer. Your little charade may not have got the reaction you expected but it achieved the same result. It just took me a while to figure out how to get here. I hadn't realised my appearance would deprive you of the chance to take power. I apologise.' He laughed, enjoying the pain he was inflicting with his nails, knowing that I wouldn't dare cause a scene.

'No, Eve, it is I who must apologise. I underestimated you so badly that it must have felt insulting. So let me be direct now. No more games. You have come here and taken power in circumstances which can only mean the Vilya will reject you. It must have been painful, seeing the loathing in your mother's eyes.' I flinched and he sneered. 'I tried to tell you that we were your true allies. If you had listened earlier, you could have been spared this.'

'You told me she was dying,' I bit back. 'You lied to me for your own purposes. Don't talk to me of alliances.'

'It was for your own good, you needed a reason to come. Manitu has no real leadership, no real government. The world we know is being slowly eroded, humans are damaging this place from the outside in and we are not permitted to act against them.

What our families need is a partnership, a union that will secure our future.' His grip had loosened and I felt him press his body against mine. 'You and I are equals, Eve. We know how to get what we want and how to use the gifts we have. Together we could shape a new world. You have the next five years to rule here and I shall have the five after that. Think what that could mean if we were bound together.'

I leaned my body into his and put my head into the fold of his neck, paused for a long time and then whispered to him.

'I would sooner die than bind myself to you. You lost, Perun. Now go take your malice out on someone who will gratify you with fear. I will not.' I stepped back as he pulled himself to his full height. In a heartbeat I picked up my skirt, did a passable curtsy before him and whirled round to take the arm of a passing Council member as I feigned tiredness. I left Perun still standing where we had stopped dancing, looking like an angry viper. It wasn't shaping up to be the best of nights.

I was surrounded by people for the next few hours. Some I had real difficulty communicating with and finally found myself rescued by Serenta who took my arm and walked with me, pointing out different tribes and explaining their traditions. She told me that the partying would continue until dawn when everyone would go back to their camps ready for my reign's first Council to convene after twenty-four hours of resting.

'Come, let me show you where you can wash and change your clothes,' she said, a little louder than was necessary, leading me into the trees where the Vilya had set up a smaller camp. We went into a dark tent and I collapsed gratefully onto the mossy floor. 'We have had news of a landslide, a substantial one, in the mountain range where Ellette was heading on the other side of the river.' I sat up again quickly.

'Was anyone hurt? How did you hear about it?'

'That is all we know,' she said. 'We haven't heard from Ellette and there is no word of Zora. A small group of Polevoi were travelling that way to join the celebrations late and were talking about it. We have no way of knowing if it has anything to do with us.'

I thought it did. It had everything to do with us. If Zora was lost then everything I'd done had been for nothing and I was stuck here alone and out of my depth.

'Does Anousk know?' I asked. Serenta looked down at her hands. 'Serenta, what is it? Tell me, please.'

'She has gone,' the girl said. 'She left as soon as you two finished speaking. No one knows where she has gone. It is unusual. The matriarch of the ruling party should not leave the ceremony. We do not know what we should do.' She was expecting me to have the answer and must have been disappointed. My own mother had run away because she thought I'd betrayed her and I was stranded in a foreign world with no idea what to do. Tears formed in my eyes and I forced them back so I didn't alarm Serenta.

'What am I supposed to be doing for the rest of the night?' I asked.

'You will be missed if you do not return to the Rock soon. Shortly there will be marriages for you to approve. Then everyone will be passed chimantra to drink and welcome the rising sun.'

'What's chimantra?' I said, more concerned about what the Vilya should be told about Anousk's disappearance.

'It's a drink,' she said. 'Very strong, I am told, although I have never tasted it. It is only drunk before everyone goes to rest and is supposed to send you visions of the spirit of nature. If you take too much it can be a little uncontrollable, I think.'

'Sounds like one to avoid, for me at least. Listen, I must get back before anyone starts asking questions. I want you to send a party out to locate mother. If any of the Vilya is missed I'll say I've sent you to prepare my tent. I don't care what else happens tonight, just find Anousk and bring her back safely. Tell her this, Serenta. It is not what she thinks. Alright?'

She nodded then disappeared along the pathway into the forest and I made my way back to join the celebrations. As I walked back into the clearing several Council members approached, keen to take me to a grassy river bank where couples were gathering for marriage ceremonies. Each pair was brought to meet me and I was expected to join hands in a circle with them and announce that Manitu would bless their marriage. It took about an hour to get through all the couples. Serenta had told me that whilst people could marry at any time, except on the winter solstice, it was considered especially lucky to marry at an ascension so there was plenty to do. After I had done my part the official marriages took place and then the merry making took a much more serious turn. Various young females from different families arrived with huge pitchers and ladles. Lines began to form with people holding whatever cup, shell or bowl they could find and into each was poured a single measure of the liquor chimantra. People sipped it slowly and I could smell the bitter spices in the air. You could tell those trying it for the first time by the unexpected grimaces on their faces. It took half an hour before I really noticed anything happening but after a while more and more people began staring in awe at the trees and stars, some transfixed by the river, others exploring the faces of their loved ones as if they were seeing for the first time. Some started dancing with complete abandon to music only they could hear, others ran off into the forest howling like wild animals and many fell straight to sleep on the ground. It was good natured but wild and fascinating to watch although I was glad I'd been warned not to try it.

'Will our new ruler not take a drink with her people, then?' Perun's voice shouted behind me. Everyone nearby turned to see what was happening.

'I shall not, but thank you for thinking of me, Perun.' I bowed my head to him and made to exit quietly before he could call more attention to us. It was clear from the glassiness of his eyes that he'd had more than his allocated single measure already and the effect was not making him any more pleasant. Faster than I could get away he was in front of me, blocking my way.

'Oh come now, Eve of the Vilya, at least taste the drink by which we mark your blessed reunion with our world.' He raised his glass and a chorus of cheers went up. There were calls for me to be given a cup and Perun didn't hesitate, placing his own in my hand. I had no idea what effect it might have on me and how vulnerable I would be. I stared at the greenish liquid in the cup and wondered how to get out of this. If Perun was so desperate for me to drink it then I was anxious not to, even though I knew my refusal wouldn't make me any more popular. I followed my first instinct.

'Perun, I cannot drink this. I am recently returned to Manitu and would prefer to remember every second of this extraordinary night with a clear head.' I watched him take another huge swig of chimantra and hoped that soon he would fall asleep. Instead he gained momentum, made braver by the hallucinogen. He stood on a boulder, raised his arms in the air and began shouting.

'The Vilya refuse to keep our traditions. They sacrifice their first born in trade with humans and in return bring those with tainted blood into our world. They will not drink with us or join us in dance. I invite you, Eve, to dance through the night in my arms. As you said, it was me who brought you here. Are you finished with me so quickly now you have achieved your purpose?' Perun had a grin on his face that made me feel nauseous. I looked around for an ally to bail me out but saw only curiosity and drunkenness. I had sent most of the Vilya off to find Anousk. I was on my own.

'Perun, enough. I will not drink or dance with you. I am most grateful to the Perelesnyk for bringing me here but now I am going to rest. I believe you would benefit from doing the same.' I span on my heel to walk off, a mixture of fear, repulsion and exhaustion making the shadows more menacing now than they had a few minutes ago. His grip on my arm took me by surprise and I stumbled, landing at Perun's feet.

'At last you have found your proper place, human. You were never fit to come here, I see it now. You reject the hospitality of your people but give yourself to human men without a thought. You may have been appointed ruler by the Council but your dirty blood will never be accepted by the families.' I looked up for something to pull myself up with but as I raised my face he spat at me. I could feel his saliva, slimy and stinking of the chimantra, across my eye and running down my cheek. I was raging and terrified at the same time. Before I could get to my feet I heard a slap ringing out across the shocked silence and saw Perun staggering backwards with onlookers stepping away to clear space around him.

As my vision cleared I saw Anousk standing in front of Perun and if she were not my own mother I would having been running terrified by what I saw in her face. Her eyes shone with a fury I have never witnessed and her lips were pulled back in a snarl. She looked like a lioness about to kill and I remained as still as I could. Perun recovered his balance in just a few seconds and walked up to put his face as close as he could to my mother's, a good head taller than her.

'It's a little late, Anousk, to be playing the good mother to this piece of filth, is it not? That said, at least now I understand why you were so anxious to throw out your waste.' Perun was enraged and the hatred between the two of them was palpable. 'You should never have been allowed to continue as matriarch to the Vilya after what you did. And for what? Your love of a human? You have covered yourself in the stench of their world and dared to propose one of them as our ruler.' He paused for her reaction and rather than allow herself to be intimidated she pushed her face even closer to his. I must have been the only person close enough to hear what she said next.

'It would please me to kill you for spitting on my daughter. The only reason I will not do so is so that you can witness the failure of all your plans. Do not defile my blood again.' His curiosity got the better of him and he stepped back to get a better look at her face to see what she was talking about. I watched her, ready to fight with her life for the insult done to me and when she met my eyes they were shining with love. Gasps and shouts behind me broke the spell and I turned to see what everyone was looking at.

Zora stood at the edge of the clearing, Ellette's arm around her. She looked tired and a little battered, but generally unharmed. When she saw me she let out a squeal and ran forward in greeting. She threw her arms round me and I looked to my mother, knowing that embracing her adopted child was the closest I would ever get to holding her. Zora clung to me like a child, unashamed of the public show of affection. I stroked her hair and told her everything would be better now as she rocked in my arms. Over her shoulder I could see Ellette and, with my eyes, asked the question I couldn't say out loud. She motioned with her head back into the cover of the trees and I breathed a sigh of relief. James was with them, safe.

'This changes nothing,' Perun shouted. 'The dawn has passed. What is it you hope to achieve by bringing that human here?'

'That is my daughter and she is a Vilya. You will stop this hatefulness right now or suffer the consequences.' My mother's voice rang out loud and clear.

Another figure joined the centre of the circle. 'And what consequences would those be?' Mandalina was very still and spoke quietly but there was no mistaking the menace in her. Anousk stared at her, unmoved. 'My son is not alone in his opinions Anousk. You are blinded by misguided love. You have made a mockery of our traditions and our laws.' She turned to the crowd and threw her head back. 'Anousk willingly caused a child of Manitu to be sacrificed. Now that child is back amongst us, as our ruler no less. Manitu demands the scales be balanced. Zora must be returned to the human world. Anousk, embrace your true daughter and complete the circle. You cannot have them both.' There was silence and I thought Mandalina must have been out of her mind. Then came the first cry of agreement from the back of the circle of watchers, riled and thirsty for excitement. Suddenly there came another and another. We had underestimated the Perelesnyk's power fuelled by the effect of the chimantra. I knew I had to do something fast, before all reason was lost.

I ran back to the centre of the spiral of stones and stood on the plinth as I had earlier, yelling above the noise of the growing rabble.

'I will have quiet!' A thousand or so heads turned towards the sound of my voice and there was silence. 'Zora will not be made your ruler. The Vilya know the laws, the dawn has passed and with it the chance to present her, as would have been her right, to the Council of Families. I am your ruler and you will listen to me. I recall the Councillors forward as my witnesses.' One by one they reappeared, some taking their time to be summoned from tents and camps. When they were all present again I motioned for Zora to come to me at the centre of the spiral and she did so, Ellette at her side, ever protective. I kissed them both and as the Council seated themselves I asked Ellette where they had found her.

'She had been left to wander the mountain passages, a maze that runs for miles. Only those who know their way can navigate them safely. James tracked her and we saw that the entrance to the passages had been loaded with a trap, a landslide. We found her and released the trap to make them think they had stopped us.'

'So you're sure it was the Perelesnyk. You have no doubt?' Ellette shook her head. Seeing Zora's smiling, beautiful face, the light within her undiminished by the scare she'd had, I knew I'd done the right thing in coming here.

'Eve,' Zora whispered and I bent my head to hear her. 'I knew you were coming for me. I saw you in my dreams. It made me brave. James carried me through the mountain. You look pretty in that dress.' I held her face in both my hands and didn't try to hide the tears flowing down my cheeks. As I addressed the crowd I could look nowhere but into my mother's eyes. I couldn't have felt more a part of this family if I had spent every minute of my life here and I was sure that her pain on giving me away had been greater than mine ever was. I only wished I could have been given the time to ask why. But not now. Now I had to finish what I'd come here for.

'Members of the Council. I have to be absent from Manitu for a time. I have accepted the rulership and I cannot pass it to another. According to your rules though, in my absence I can appoint one of my family to exercise power in my place. I appoint Zora as my ambassador whilst I am gone with the delegation of all my authority. She will command in my name fairly and with only love and goodness in her heart.' I took the necklace of stones from round my own neck and put it on Zora. She took it without question, smiling serenely. In her eyes I saw more wisdom than anyone credited to her. She was, to all extents and purposes, restored to her proper place. Justice had been done.

'Our traditions have been abused,' Mandalina's voice rang out. 'I will not accept the human as our ruler. She has neither the right nor the capacity. I demand that the Council refuses to allow this.'

The Councillor at the edge of the circle stood. 'Zora is not ruler, she will be acting in place of our ruler and our laws allow that. You cannot challenge this; it is within the creed that every family agreed centuries ago.'

'Then the Perelesnyk will not recognise the authority of the Council or the laws it follows. We have been played, all of us. This was what they had planned all along, depriving us of the right to object to the human taking the throne at the proper time.'

'Played?' I choked. 'Do you want me to tell the Council how Zora came to be found wandering the mountain passages on the far side of the river? A river which she could not have swum or crossed by herself?'

Mandalina stretched back her shoulders and narrowed her eyes. 'Do you accuse me? I am a matriarch of one of the oldest families. Say whatever you will but understand this, child. There will be repercussions from such an accusation and you will not be here to protect your family. I suspect the child you leave wielding your authority might find herself out of her depth in dealing with the trouble you are stirring, don't you?'

As I was steeling myself to reply a smaller voice intervened. 'Please don't fight, I'm not hurt. You were all happy before, I heard the dancing and singing from all the way across the valley. Please Eve, let's not argue.' I looked down at Zora, as eager to please as ever, and saw not a child but a woman who had just done her best to dampen a heightening argument. There were murmurs of agreement from the Council members, keen not to lose the opportunity to return to peace.

'Of course, Zora, you're right. It's a night for celebration and we have so little time left before dawn,' I bent down and hugged her again. 'You'll be an inspirational leader for Manitu.'

'The Perelesnyk will be bloody corpses before she will hold authority over our people,' came a voice and there was no mistaking the battle cry that followed it. The Council members leapt to their feet as the first rock landed. I grabbed Zora's hand and pulled her to the ground shielding her body with my own. More rocks followed as Ellette shoved us out of the spiral of stones towards the base of the Rock of Ages. Behind us chaos was descending. The light was gloomy but I could make out bodies charging towards us through the crowds and the Vilya crossing the clearing to intervene. People were picking up makeshift weapons from all around them, branches, stones, some had spears already in their belts. Lamps were being knocked from the trees in the melee and you could see small groups lit from below as the flames hit on the ground. The ferocity of the fighting was sickening and it seemed that the word demon was closer to the truth than I'd wanted to believe. When the first body fell in front of us I stooped to see if I could help then saw the stake that had cracked the Polevoi's ribcage in two. The violence was beyond anything I was prepared for. A dark figure on all fours was rushing towards Ellette and I saw her unsheathe a dagger from her belt and slit the creature's throat without missing a step. All around us blood was starting to flow and the chimantra had given the fighting a frenzy that was chilling. In the distance behind us I could see a group of Vilya surrounded by Perelesnyk.

'Ellette, I have to go back to help mother.' I started back towards the entangled bodies.

'No!' she shouted. 'She is a warrior, she needs no help. You are in much more danger than her. Stay with me. James will know where to find us.' We found the mountain trail and I put out my hand to hold the rock face as we climbed. We had no torches and boulders slowed our progress every few steps. We finally paused at a small recess and I could hear the escalation of the battle below. Amidst the screams of pain and bloodlust I could make out spears flying through the air. I guessed from the reactions to Zora earlier that as many people supported the Perelesnyk as would stand with the Vilya against them.

'Stay here,' said Ellette and she dashed out of our hiding place to check what lay ahead. The second she was out of sight two creatures looking like cavemen appeared, grabbing Zora and me with a strength it was pointless to fight. As hard as I struggled it achieved nothing and Zora just allowed herself to be held, showing no sign of distress. I started to speak and a fist lashed out, backhanding me across the face. My head whipped round, not expecting the blow and I tasted blood in my mouth. Pain exploded through my skull and I thought that if a broken nose was my only injury today I would be very lucky indeed.

The men began to trek back down the mountain trail but even given their extraordinary strength it was difficult to carry us over the fallen rocks. Eventually the one holding me had to release the hand across my mouth and I screamed like a banshee. With no warning at all, feet were landing all around us from the ledge above. I heard a furious screech from Ellette who had returned with more Vilya to assist. I watched her fight and marvelled at her tenacity, never holding back or concerned for her own welfare. She and the Vilya were fierce warriors and I was embarrassed by my own weakness. I stayed with my back pressed into the cliff, holding Zora tight. They set about the men who had taken us but even so it took all of them to restrain the two Neanderthals. Finally both men were on the ground with Ellette kneeling over the one who had taken Zora and only then did she speak.

'Are you unharmed, sisters? I am so sorry, I should never have left you alone.' As she said the last word I heard her splutter and her body went into spasms. She swayed where she was, looking confused and rasping for breath. I heard him laugh then, a horrible throaty gurgle and the world went into slow motion as the other Vilya and I dived towards her flailing body. Three of the Vilya threw themselves on top of her attacker and wrestled the hidden weapon from his hand. He'd been wearing what looked like elongated crocodile teeth on his knuckles, sharpened to deathly points. He had chosen not to use them during the fight, waiting for a perfect moment to inflict maximum damage when least expected. We rolled Ellette onto her front and pulled the teeth from where they had been shoved, deep into her spine. She was losing consciousness fast. I was babbling about doctors and hospitals, making no sense to the people around me. One of the Vilya held Ellette's head in his hands and I could see blood coming from her mouth and nose.

'They put poison on the end of the teeth. There is nothing we can do.' He looked at me and I scrambled to the ground lying next to her to hold her close.

'Can't I heal her? I've done it before, I just need a little time.'

'It won't work here; you are not in the human world now. It is her time. We do not fight nature.'

'This isn't nature, it's those murderous bastards.' I was shouting but it ended as a sob. I knew he was right. Comforting her was the only pathetic, useless thing I could do but I held her for the awful minutes that passed until she was beyond the grip of pain. She bled from her eyes and her ears, convulsing and groaning, while I told her that she would make it, that it would pass. When her body was almost done she whispered to me.

'It was all worth it, Eve. I am so proud to have known you. Protect Zora for me.' She started to choke on the blood and I turned her head to one side so that it would drain but she couldn't get enough oxygen and I knew I would never forget the horrible guilty relief when it was over. I lay on the ground and sobbed into her hair. After a short time they pulled me up as I stepped back to let Zora say goodbye to her sister. She was calm. Crying, I could see, but serene.

'Sleep well, Ellette.' She kissed her sister on the lips, the eyes and the forehead then smoothed her hair. 'I'll see you soon.' I wasn't sure if she really understood what had happened until she came and hugged me. 'Don't worry about Ellette, she's still with us.' I sobbed with the pain of losing a sister and this half-woman, who so many people believed could scarcely function in the world without help, gave me the strength to carry on. We hid Ellette's body where it would be safe until we could return for it, bound the two attackers and knocked them unconscious then carried on up the slope of the rock to higher ground. I could see fires raging on the valley floor and a freezing terror was seeping through my veins. If this didn't stop, too many lives would be lost either from battle wounds or a forest fire that would soon be uncontrollable. As hard as I tried to control myself all I could see was Ellette's face, bloodied and gasping. We reached a point about half way up the cliff and I could bear it no more, collapsing to my knees. I growled with a viciousness that was feral and thrashed my fists against the rock. No-one tried to stop me and I was grateful. Eventually I put my head to the rock. I could smell blood, sulphur and ash making bile rise in my throat. I had no idea how to express the savagery of my emotions, rolling onto my back and screaming into the sky.

I wanted to find the family responsible for this and rip them limb from limb. I imagined myself biting them, throttling them, drowning them and I relished every second of the vision. When I felt the dried blood washing down my face, I realised it had begun to rain and it brought me back to reality. With Ellette gone I had to protect Zora now and if I let my emotions get the better of me I'd go straight back through to the mortal world where

I would be useless to her. I could see Zora bathed in the blossoming light of dawn and gazing up at the sky, a half smile on her face. As I got control enough to stand, there was enough sun for me to see all the way down into the valley. My nails were cutting into the soft flesh of my palms where my fists were rolled so tight and I tried to make out where our enemies were. What I saw was the river rising swiftly below. I felt the wind grow in strength, the trees bending hard in its path.

I was shaking with adrenalin and barely aware of the others pulling me down off the cliff face into a shallow cave to shelter from the storm. From our position we could see everything. There is no glory in bloodshed, all dead bodies are grotesque when limbs are severed and blood has coloured everything crimson but the whites of the eyes. It doesn't matter what side you're on, it's all just chaos and waste. The flames that were eating steadily into the forest were cutting off pockets of fighters, making victory a false cause. The wind whipped around us and down the mountainside tearing branches from the trees below, beating the fire along faster and faster through the undergrowth. At last I caught sight of the Vilya near my resting tent, Anousk amongst them, still battling with the Perelesnyk and the cavemen demons who had murdered Ellette. I stared at the river, focussing my temper successfully for the first time and watched as the current swelled and chopped then burst the banks. The swirling wind was lifting a trail of dirt and debris off the valley floor and when it crossed the path of the rising water a funnel began to form. The river waters were gushing now, spreading like a plague across the clearing. In seconds the spiral of stones was underwater.

'Mother!' I whispered, but Zora's hand was on mine, warm and firm.

'She will be safe,' she said. 'I can feel the strength flowing through her.' I stared at her in surprise. She may have been born human but she was something more than that now. She motioned back down towards the valley with her head. The wind funnel, now a full water spout, had crossed the flooded land and entered the woods. As it travelled, it extinguished the worst of the fires and the rain ensured that the remaining trees were too damp to burn. The ferocity of the storm had made the last fighters flee, unable to continue in such a harsh environment and scared of getting caught in the flooding. There were bodies littered across the ground but perhaps not as many as I'd feared. It was enough, though: Enough for me to question if I'd been right to come here. Was all this my fault? I closed my eyes and resigned myself to never knowing the answer to that.

When I opened them again James's face was appearing over the cliff ledge outside the caves. In spite of the battering winds he'd found us. I held my arms out to him and when he reached me I felt the hatred that was consuming me subside. I buried my face in his chest and tried to find a moment of peace.

'They took Ellette from us. She died saving Zora and me.'

'I'm sorry, Eve, I'm so sorry,' he said. I was dimly aware that he had reached out to hold Zora's hand. She was grinning at the two of us as if she hadn't a care in the world.

As James calmed me so the storm began to die down. The rain eased off and we went back to the cliff edge to assess the damage.

'I have to go and find mother,' said Zora. I nodded and readied myself to go with her. She shook her head at me. 'You're going home now, aren't you?' I started to protest but James had made the decision for me.

'Yes, we're going home now. Will you be safe?'

'Of course I will, silly. You saved me. This was how it had to happen. Mother told me the value of peace is measured against the horror of war.' Zora stood on her toes and kissed James on the mouth shyly. 'Thank you. It's not forever, you know.' She took the hand of one of the Vilya who began to guide her down the cliff. 'Come back soon, Eve, mother will miss you,' she called over her shoulder.

James put an arm around me again.

'Was it all worth it?' he asked. I thought about it for a moment.

'Yes, but only just.' Above us the sun was starting to show its face and I lifted mine to get some warmth from it.

'Any idea how we're going to get out of here?'

'I'm burnt out,' I said. 'I can't feel anything.'

He sat down dangling his legs over the cliff ledge and motioned for me to sit next to him. I let my head fall onto his shoulder and felt the strength of his body revive me. He stroked my hair, my face and my neck while my pulse slowed and I embraced the stillness. I opened my eyes and studied him. Each tiny wrinkle that started spread out from the corners of his eyes; the frown line in the centre of his forehead when he was concentrating; the lips that were the first feature to show his anger; the almost invisible scarring on his cheek from a long forgotten accident. All the things that made him human and individual were the things that made him beautiful and irreplaceable. He ran a finger over my lips and spoke softly to me.

'Let's try this,' he said. 'This is all we need to lose ourselves together.' Then he kissed me. He started by just brushing his lips against mine and then grazed my bottom lip softly between his teeth so that I opened my mouth enough for him fill it with his tongue. I let my body go limp in his arms and thought of nothing but him, his passion and his grief. I met his tongue with my own, together in every breath, every movement. I could feel the heat of his rushing blood and his kiss was like wine in my mouth. I felt every part of him reach out for me and I gently took his tongue between my teeth and pulled him into me further. A rainbow of colours was appearing before my eyes and I felt as if I were tasting sunshine. There was a cool breeze around us and I knew we were starting to pass over, just as James had believed would happen. I opened my eyes to see him in the moment we passed over so that I would never forget the way he looked right then and there.

I caught the rushing movement as I opened my eyes and Perun had grabbed us both before I could pull my mouth from James's to scream. In a blur of flying scree we were propelled off the ledge. Perun went with us, so great was his determination to finish what he'd started that he'd lost his footing when he shoved us so hard. For the first few seconds we all fell as one. I reached my hand out to find something to anchor us but there was nothing, only air above and below. As I looked up I saw Perun's face disappear above me, then we hit the wall of rock and every bit of air thumped out of my chest. James and I were rolling together over and over. I was conscious that James hadn't let go of me, one hand pulling my head into his chest and this other wrapped around my back, protecting me from the vicious blows battering our entwined bodies. The rock face wasn't a sheer drop but it was long and unforgiving.

When we finally landed in a heap at the base, I lifted my head to ask James how badly hurt he was. His arms fell away rather than releasing me and I knew something was wrong as I heard the thud of his hands hitting the ground. It took me a few seconds to recover my blurred vision but when I did I saw a puddle of red spreading out beneath the back of his skull. I picked up the bitter coppery smell of blood and heard a woman start to scream in the distance. Footsteps around us gained momentum and there were voices calling from all directions. I reached out to hold James's head but hands took hold of me and surrounded him and I saw hikers' boots. The world went into slow motion, muffled as if the sound had been turned down. I was struggling to make sense of what they were saying. Animated faces were shouting into mobile phones and then someone said they couldn't find a pulse. My world stopped.

I looked at the limp body on the ground. Someone was trying to put a coat around my shoulders and wipe blood off my face. I summoned every bit of will I had left and pushed away the arms around me to stand up. I strode forward and fell to my knees at James's side, bending over and pulling him into my arms. I could hear people telling me not to move him, that I would make his injuries worse. I didn't think that was possible and I knew every second I wasted was a second too late. I thought of Naomi in her bathroom being sick, of Xander on the beach with his foot bleeding and I begged for my strength to flow into him. I would have given every bit of life in my body to save him but he was slipping away and I couldn't bear any more loss. I put my mouth over his as I had on the mountain ledge when I'd realised that this was the only man in the world I had ever loved. I kissed him as if it were the last thing I would ever do and pleaded with whatever spirits could hear me to save him.

I felt the earth trembling with the oncoming wind from the helicopter before I heard it. Air rescue was above us, unable to land but sending down a stretcher. When the medic hit the ground I had no choice but to let go of James and leave his fate to others. I had the chilling sensation that I was about to lose him and I wasn't ready to let go. The medic strapped him into the sling and they lifted him away in a matter of minutes. I watched him being winched high above me into a bright blue sky and allowed myself to be led away by the park rangers to safety. The next hours were a blur.

I was given medical attention at the ranger's station in Yosemite Valley and was able to remember Sabina's details. I was told that James had been taken to the trauma unit at the Doctors Medical Center of Modesto but I had no way of knowing if he were dead or alive. One of the rangers found James' car and we began the long drive back to the ranch. I closed my eyes and feigned sleep for the journey. Sabina was not there when I arrived and a housekeeper told me she'd gone directly to the hospital. Finally the news I'd been waiting for came.

James had been alive when he'd arrived at Modesto, although barely. They were amazed that he had any life left in him and he was in surgery, having lost a huge amount of blood and sustained a blow to his skull that he wasn't expected to survive. I was escorted back to my house, people talking in hushed tones around me. I told them I wanted to be alone and my tone must have been enough to dissuade them from argument. I sat down in a chair in my lounge, pulled a blanket over me, put the phone on my lap and began the dreadful process of waiting.

Twenty-three

It was nearly nine hours later when the phone rang. Sabina sounded exhausted.

'He's alive but he hasn't regained consciousness,' she said. 'It's a miracle he survived at all. All we can do is wait and hope he comes out of the coma but they have no way of knowing how long that will take.'

'Is there any brain damage?' I asked, unable to bear the thought that this man, who spent every second outdoors, on horseback, on the beach, walking through the mountains, could be confined to life within four walls.

'They won't know until he wakes up. This is the best place for him Eve, the care here is excellent. Get some rest. I'm coming home. I'll come over to see you when I get back.' I thanked her and hung up. At last, still wearing the white robes of the Vilya I'd worn all day and all night, James's blood mixed with my own encrusted upon my hands and body, I slept.

Sabina's knocking woke me. She was using her walking sticks and looked as if she hadn't slept for a week. She walked forward and put one arm around my shoulders letting her stick fall to the floor. James was still in a coma. She'd sat with him, held his hand and talked to him gently about the horses and the ranch. There was no sign that he could hear or understand. I busied myself making tea for her.

'Sabina, I don't know how to carry on,' I said. 'There's nothing to hold on to, nothing feels real.'

'You carry on the way we all do,' she answered. 'You set a routine and use it to get through each day. So here's what you'll do. You'll carry on with the play. You'll come to rehearsals and learn your lines and let Xander make a fuss of you. You'll drive to see James whenever you have the energy and tell him every tiny detail about your day. You'll come home and have dinner with me and tell me wonderful tales about your life in England. You will keep busy and not let yourself stop and think.'

I gazed at her. She hadn't even asked me what had happened yet. She wasn't surprised at the state I was in. I opened my mouth to ask why and paused, unsure how to put it. She'd seen my hesitation and it made her smile.

'You don't need to explain anything to me,' she said. 'I lived with Adela long enough to learn that whatever questions I asked would never really be answered. She would disappear sometimes. It might be for hours or it might be days. I learned to accept it and not press her for an explanation. I worried about her terribly and when she came back she always seemed, well, different. After a while she would be back to her normal self. It was something we never spoke of,' I couldn't meet her eyes and walked to the window instead.

'You may not be related to Adela, Eve, but you are the closest thing I have to her. I want you to stay. It feels as if you belong here.' I nodded, knowing tears would choke me if I tried to speak. 'Good,' she said. 'Take today to rest but you dine with me tonight. Tomorrow we rehearse; opening night is closer than you will believe. Tomorrow afternoon I will have my driver take you to James.' She left, very quietly. She was an extraordinary woman who had never let herself be beaten. I put my shoulders back and took courage from her example. I showered and tidied, washed clothes and read my script. In the evening I went to Sabina's to eat and by tacit agreement we talked trivia until I was tired enough to go straight to bed. When Perun's face entered my dreams I thought of my mother and the love in her eyes and was grateful that at last I'd found her. When I could feel Ellette's body shaking to death in my arms I thought of the goodness of Zora and told myself that the sacrifice was worth it.

I did as Sabina had told me. Each day I went to the theatre. Xander was as good a friend as he could have been. I emailed Naomi and kept her up to date with what was happening. We agreed to avoid the subject of Nate, talking about weddings and the play and her cases. I spent my late afternoons holding James's hand, rehearsing my lines and telling him the gossip from the theatre. Within days I didn't need Sabina's driver any more and was back on my bike. I enjoyed the long periods of driving to and from Modesto, about two hours from Carmel. I did my best to pretend that the world was as simple and normal as I had imagined it to be before that fateful trip to Krakow. I carried on.

About a week before opening night I was at James's bedside, reading the newspaper when I felt his hand pulling at mine. I leaned forward with my heart in my mouth not daring to hope that this could be the moment I'd been dreaming of. Then he opened his eyes. It should sound more dramatic than that but it wasn't. It was calm and peaceful. He looked at me and smiled. I just sat there grinning back at him. I didn't cry or shout or jump up and call for doctors. I just wanted it to last forever, that little piece of quiet and the wonder of seeing him watching me, holding my hand in his.

'You have to go,' he said.

I looked at his hand in mine and bent my head to kiss it. I didn't want to meet his eyes. I already knew the determination I would see there.

'You've seen what the Perelesnyk can do. We've been through too much to doubt it. I'm cursed Eve. Every minute I spend with you I fall deeper and deeper...' I sobbed and covered my mouth.

'What will you do?' I said.

'Travel, I think. Maybe I'll go to Europe, I always wanted to. Say you understand.' I did but that didn't make it any more bearable.

'Will I see you again?' I was clutching his hand so hard it was turning white.

'I don't know. But not while I still feel like this. Losing you would be...' he stopped speaking and I leaned over to hug him one last time so that he didn't need to find the words. Then I did the only thing I could for the man I'd fallen so completely in love with. I tucked my newspaper under my arm and slipped on my jacket.

'Probably just as well,' I said. 'I always found you infuriating. And I'm busy with the play, you know what a task master Sabina can be.' He smiled and the sight was so wonderful that it made my heart twist with agony. 'At least I won't have to worry about you spying on me when I'm standing at my window naked any more.' He laughed out loud at that and I walked to the door before I lost my resolve. 'If this is it, if this is all we can ever have, then it was still worth it. Goodbye James.' I grasped the handle of the door, steeled myself and left. I didn't pause once although every step felt as if I had been ripped in two. I climbed on the bike and drove. I concentrated on each road sign, every speed limit and all the other vehicles until I got myself home. I knew better than to go to my house and be alone so I walked straight to Sabina. I was pleased to see that Daniel was visiting again and the two of them seemed perfectly happy in each other's company. If nothing else then my coming here has brought two lonely souls together, I thought, even if it's taken them a lifetime. It made me long for a future with James, with the prospect of growing old together.

'James is awake,' I said. 'He's going to be fine. He doesn't need me anymore so I can stop visiting the hospital now.' She put down her tea cup and stared at my face.

'We were just about to walk down to the horses. Will you join us?' Daniel offered her his arm and we stepped outside. 'Is Naomi going to make it over for the opening night? I have some more recipes for her, I've been going through the boxes I've had in the attic for years. And Daniel hasn't met her yet, have you darling? I think they'll get on terribly well.'

She talked endlessly as we walked to the paddocks. I nodded in all the right places and kept my face interested as she and Daniel entertained me for the next hour. When I finally made my way along the path to my house I stood at the base of the tree where I'd seen James looking up at my window. I cried for a future I had lost before I got a chance to find out if it was even real. I wept for the sister I had been given so little time with; a mother I hadn't been able to hold in my arms and a man whose pain I couldn't take away. I wept, as sorry for myself as it was possible for a person to be, and then swore that those would be the last tears I would cry. I'd had enough pain to last a lifetime.

When opening night came it was the first time I'd felt any emotion other than sadness in a long time. Nerves caught in my throat every time I tried to speak and Xander looked more terrified every time he saw me.

'It's good to feel nervous,' he said, more for his own sake than mine. 'You'll be fine, you'll be amazing actually. Please tell me you can speak.' I couldn't so I just nodded at him. 'God help us,' he muttered under his breath. The auditorium was packed. It was a balmy, clear night and everyone who was anyone was there. Naomi had come over with her fiancé Tim although I suspected that was just adding to my nervousness. Sabina had been keeping herself out of the way so we could all focus on the job in hand but with ten minutes to go she appeared.

'You were made for this,' she said. 'You just have first night nerves. The instant you get out there you'll be fine. I believe in you.' She paused a moment. 'I have a present to give you,' she said. 'I was going to wait until later but you need something to take your mind off all the people out there.' She put a heavy cardboard box into my arms. I opened it and could just make out piles of different sizes and colours of notebooks and old diaries. I put the box down on the dressing table.

'What is this?' I asked.

'They are Adela's journals,' she said. 'As long as I can remember she kept a diary. I found the box when I was going through the attic for the recipes for Naomi. I would have given it to you before but, forgive me for this, I didn't want you distracted or disappearing again before the play opened. I hope that whatever you find brings you some peace. Break a leg my darling.' She disappeared out of the door and I stared at the box, not daring to touch it. Jake poked his head round my door to announce five minutes to curtain up. I ran my hand over the dusty cardboard and my nerves dissipated.

When I walked onto the stage I was struck by how silent it was. For a second I thought I wouldn't be able to do it, project my voice and become Katharina and let the audience lose themselves in the play. Then I caught sight of a face in the front row, only partly visible because of the brightness of the lights, but I could make out the eyes and that was all I needed. He leaned forward just enough so that I could see his smile and as I said my first line I felt his warmth give me the courage to go on.

James' farewell appearance was like a blessing. I kept my promise to myself and didn't weep again. I'd had one more chance to see him and it was a gift not to be spoiled by tears. The play had gone as well as I could have imagined. Sabina was called on to the stage by the audience who stood in appreciation of her talents. At the end Xander hugged me, kissed me and spun me round until I begged him to stop.

I didn't try to find James afterwards; it would have been futile anyway but more than that it would have ruined the moment. It felt like a split second, the duration of that opening night, knowing James was there watching me, willing me to succeed. When we went to take our curtain call I was able to look him right in the eye. It was enough to make everything perfect for that night.

And now? Well, I have Adela's diaries to read. I have this extraordinary theatre to come to for the next three months and after that who knows? I have a lifetime to wait and see if the man I love can find a way back to me. Some time, when I can bear it, there is Manitu and my mother waiting. I don't know if I can go there without James by my side but I know that there are people waiting who might still need me.

I picked up Sabina's box and put it into the back of the limousine that had come to collect us. As much as I wanted to race home and start reading, I had a party to go to and I felt as if I'd earned some celebrating. There had been enough sacrifices made. I took Sabina's hand and together we beamed into the flashing cameras as the press shouted our names. For the first time in a very long time I did nothing but enjoy the moment. Tomorrow could wait.

Printed in Great Britain
by Amazon